A Chance Encounter

'Perhaps you should actually see Strawberry Hill before you agree to a visit there. I believe one should be prepared for any eventualities.'

Felicia knew the strangest reaction to his clasp of her hand. He'd not let it free and now he drew closer to her. Surely he dared not kiss her while standing in the entry of his house? It seemed he did.

It was a mere whisper of a kiss, over before she had a chance to react, to register its effect.

He looked down at her hand, then back to meet her gaze. 'Forgive me,' he begged softly. 'I'd not meant to do that.'

Felicia pulled her hand from his light clasp and wordlessly rushed up the stairs, pausing at the top to look back to where he still stood, watching her. She had intended to ask him if he had learned anything of import regarding the will and now she dared not seek him out to inquire. It wasn't that she didn't trust him. She didn't trust herself!

A Chance Encounter

Emily Johnson

ROBERT HALE · LONDON

ISBN 978-0-7090-8413-6

Robert Hale Limited
Clerkenwell House
Clerkenwell Green
London EC1R 0HT

www.halebooks.com

2 4 6 8 10 9 7 5 3 1

Typeset in 11½/14½pt Erhardt
by Derek Doyle & Associates, Shaw Heath
Printed and bound in Great Britain
by the MPG Books Group

Chapter One

'**Y**ou have been cheated, my dear Felicia,' Edward, Lord Brook said in a faint, raspy voice before closing his eyes for a final time and going aloft.

At his bedside, the Honorable Felicia Brook stared at her now-departed uncle, her gray eyes perplexed. What was this all about? Why did he wait until the last moments of his life to inform her that she had been cheated? And cheated of what?

'Cheated?' queried a voice from behind Felicia, echoing her thoughts. 'How so? And of what, I might wonder,' the gentleman concluded.

She turned to face her unwilling host, the lordly gentleman who had given Felicia and her uncle shelter following an accident that had killed Felicia's disagreeable aunt and now deprived her of her only uncle. William Chessyre, Lord Chessyre, had been frigidly polite, unfailing in civilized behavior, but obviously suspicious toward Felicia – quite as though she had managed the accident just so she might meet him, the odious creature! The carriage had overturned not far from the gates to Chessyre Court, and his lordship had taken charge of matters with a chilling aloofness. His cool blond hair and icy gray eyes fit his personality to a tee, never mind that he had broad shoulders and was a fine figure of a man, as her father used to say. She moved away from him.

'I fear I am as much in the dark as you, my lord. Unless. . . .'

Felicia knew a spurt of hope that swiftly died. What she wished was most unlikely.

She drew the sheet up over her uncle, then turned from the bed, unable to shed tears for the man who had been a party to her humiliation and grief with never an objection. There was a slight touch of Lord Chessyre's hand on her elbow, guiding her from the room.

'Come, perhaps we can reach a conclusion downstairs in the library.' He opened the door for her, ever the courteous gentleman.

Felicia wanted to rage at him. Her world had just fallen completely apart, and he was so very, very polite. Manners, she had once read, are what vex or soothe. He was both vexing and condescending. She decided that he would *not* know her inward fears.

He walked sedately down the stairs, at her side, guiding her over the vast entry to reach the door of the library. Here he ushered her inside, seating her in a comfortable leather chair. 'Something to settle you, I believe.' He crossed to a table on the far side of the book-lined room, poured a small quantity of some amber liquid into a glass, then returned to her side. 'Drink this, it will help you.'

Felicia was too numb to argue with him and obeyed, gasping after the fiery brandy had slid down her throat. Her bravado was all well and good, but she must find a place to go, a refuge. *Where!*

'Good,' was the only comment offered by her host, as he took the glass from her trembling fingers. 'Now, where do things stand as of this moment?'

His question was not unexpected, but she would have rather put it off until she'd had time to consider matters. She had no clue as to a sanctuary, and she knew she needed such.

Squaring her shoulders, Felicia folded her hands neatly in her lap and spoke slowly, gathering the words as she did.

'I have lived with my aunt and uncle since my father's death some four years ago. I was sixteen – with nowhere else to go' she explained.

'And now?' he prompted with chilling courtesy.

'My cousin Basil inherits the estate. I expect Cousin Willa will live with him for the nonce, until she weds. I must find a position.' Not for anything would she be dependent upon her odious cousins. She couldn't explain to this stranger that she feared Basil and his quest-ing lips, searching hands. Nor was it likely she could convince this man that the charming Willa was a vixen who would make Felicia's life a misery. No, Felicia would beg charity before returning to her ancestral home, Brook Hall.

'You prefer a position to your home?' Lord Chessyre asked, amaze-ment clear in his voice at this most peculiar female. Obviously, young ladies of quality did not, in his estimation, seek paid positions when there was a respectable alternative.

'It is no longer my home,' Felicia reminded. 'It now belongs to my cousins. I will not impose on them. It was one thing to be obligated to my aunt and uncle. It is quite another to be a poor relation to my cousins.' She snapped her mouth shut; she'd said too much already.

Surprisingly, he nodded with what she would have said was sympa-thy in anyone else. However, she doubted if Lord Chessyre was famil-iar with that emotion.

'You received an inheritance from your father, I imagine. Was it invested on your behalf?' he queried, retreating to the leather chair behind his magnificent mahogany desk. He studied a paper on his desk, so missed her look of pain at his question.

'There was no inheritance; I was quite cut off.' Her bewilderment at this event was evident in her confused expression as well as in her voice.

He stared at her as though he didn't believe her. 'Surely not?' he gently questioned.

'I do not blame you for doubting my word, but there it is. The will was declared valid, and I had not a pence to my name.' Felicia tilted her chin, daring him to doubt her words.

'Perhaps your father expected you to be wed before he died?' his lordship mused, his eyes studying Felicia as though searching for some redeeming factor.

She almost laughed. What a picture she must make in the drab navy dress deemed appropriate for a companion by her late aunt. Even if it was her sole winter pelisse, Felicia was glad that in the acci-dent that dreary garment had been torn and was tattered beyond use.

Lord Chessyre had seen her garbed in the better of her clothes, this navy dress, and for evenings, a dull black silk made over from a gown her aunt had disliked. She'd owned pretty dresses at sixteen, but one had a tendency to grow. What sane man would take to wife so unprepossessing a creature who had no dowry to offer him in compensation?

'I do not know. Perhaps he intended to provide for me and never remembered to do so. He was not an old man when he died; he may have postponed the matter.' At least that is what Felicia had convinced herself was the case.

William studied the girl seated so defiantly before him. She was brave, he had to admit that of her. And with proper dressing, she might show to advantage, for she was not a homely woman. Rather, she was too thin – her large gray eyes dominating her face. Navy was too harsh a color for her, as was black. She ought to be wearing lavenders, pale blues, and violets in chiffons and laces. In spite of the severity of her dress, she was quite feminine with a quiet voice and pretty manners. She'd been most gentle with her uncle in his last days, caring for him with efficient tenderness. He'd seen that for himself.

Then he shook himself inwardly for his nonsensical thoughts. Women could be very deceptive. He'd also seen that. He didn't believe in chance encounters.

'With the way things stand, I can see nothing for myself but to find a position as governess or companion. What else is there for one of my birth?' Felicia asked, hoping he might think of another path she could take.

'I quite agree,' he said. 'My aunt may know of someone.'

The library door to the hall had been left open, and when the knocker of the main door was vigorously pounded on solid oak, both looked up, listening. From her vantage point near the library door Felicia turned her head. She watched as Jeffers, the dignified butler, shortly ushered in a couple Felicia knew all too well. She rose to her feet without thought, just wishing she might hide until they went away.

William was surprised at Miss Brook's dismayed reaction to the newcomers. Obviously, she knew who they were, and with equal transparency, she wished she were elsewhere. She composed herself, and with an apologetic glance at him, stepped forward to greet them in the entry.

He was around the desk and at her side before he considered his actions or how they might be construed by others. He eyed his new guests with disfavor. 'The cousins?' he rightly guessed.

'Indeed,' Miss Brook replied softly.

The pair stood in the entry, a maid and valet tending to the cases behind them. The young woman was not so unattractive if one overlooked a pointed nose. The young man emulated the dandy, his cravat overblown and his waistcoat a disaster. The contrast between the quality of their garb and that of their cousin was cruel.

'Good day,' William said to the couple, who stared at him with wary expressions. 'I'm Chessyre.'

Felicia hastily made her cousins known to her host.

Basil turned to Felicia at once and blustered, 'Now see here, Felicia, what is all this nonsense about an accident? We were having a marvelous time at the Tinsleys. Could you not deal with the problem?'

'Indeed, Felicia, it is too bad of you to bother us so,' Willa added with a coy glance at Lord Chessyre, one he was all too familiar with to ignore.

William narrowed his gaze into what he'd been told was an intimidating stare. 'Obviously, you have not heard what has transpired. I regret to inform you that your mother was killed in the accident, and your father passed on not an hour ago, succumbing to internal injuries.' He might have been more gentle to imparting this information had it not been for their disgraceful attack on the hapless Miss Brook. William might be wary of the slender girl; he would not tolerate such rudeness to anyone while in his home, however.

What Basil and Willa might have said or done following this bald announcement was not to be known, for a rustle of silk preceded the arrival of Lady Emma.

'William, dearest, did I hear the door?' she queried in a fluting voice from the landing. The lady who drifted down in a flurry of lavender sarcenet and lace with a delicate lace cap on her pale blond hair reached the bottom of the staircase with seemingly no effort at all. 'Guests!' she exclaimed with interest.

'May I present my cousins, Wilhelmina and Basil Brook, Lady Emma?' Felicia asked hesitantly, stepping forward as if she might prevent them from taking advantage of the charming older woman who had been all kindness to Felicia in the past few days.

Introductions completed, the dear lady sympathized with Basil and Willa on the loss of their parents.

If Felicia was correct, Basil was calculating on what his estate was worth and how he'd spend all that lovely money. Willa was no doubt considering how best to cozen her brother into increasing her dowry. Surely he'd want her off his hands as soon as possible!

'You are welcome to spend the night here, but I imagine you are anxious to remove your parents to your home church for burial, not to mention consult with your family solicitors regarding the transfer of the estate into your hands,' Lord Chessyre said with a courteous bow in Basil's direction. Willa, he ignored, to Felicia's secret amusement.

'Indeed, you have been most kind, my lord,' Basil said with a sagacious nod. 'We are greatly in your debt.' Now that Basil knew the identity of the gentleman who had housed his cousin and father, a man of the highest *ton* and invited to all the best places, he made himself toadishly agreeable. He would have waxed eloquent on the matter of his fortune, when Lady Emma placed a hand on Willa's arm, drawing her to the stairs.

'I declare,' she said in her pretty fluting voice, 'you must be settled in rooms before making any decisions. And tea!' she cried. 'Tea always makes things better.'

Willa meekly followed, but Basil paused as though to argue, or perhaps ask a question.

'Come, come,' Lady Emma said impatiently. 'Discussion later. At tea,' she insisted, then led the pair up the stairs and along the hall.

Felicia watched until she saw the last of them, then turned to face her host. 'I am sorry about that. I fear they do not always think before they speak.'

'What would have happened had I not been here?' Lord Chessyre wondered aloud. He guided Felicia back to the security of the library, where a fire beckoned them to its comforting warmth.

'Well,' Felicia temporized, 'perhaps they would have been more agreeable in time.' Nothing was said about the orphaned pair's lack of grief at the loss of their parents. Oh, Willa had managed a tear to be wiped away with a scrap of cambric, and Basil had looked suitably sad for a moment until he realized that all that money was now his.

'I begin to see why you insist upon being independent,' his lordship said while nudging a log with the toe of his boot, thus avoiding Felicia's clear gaze.

'It is not because I am an independent person by nature, you must know,' Felicia said, wanting this gentleman to understand she did only what was necessary for her survival. 'I should wish nothing more than a little place to call my own and peace and quiet to go with it.'

'And a cat?' he said with a smile, at last looking up to meet her candid gray eyes.

Really, his lordship was dangerously attractive when he smiled. She recalled his earlier chilling formality and backed away, on her guard once again. 'As you say, and a cat. I'm exceedingly fond of the beasts. Excuse me, my lord. I shall go to my room to change for dinner.'

William nodded his dismissal and watched as Miss Brook left the library to run lightly up the stairs, disappearing from view almost at once. He pitied the girl, poor thing; to be left in such a shabby state was unthinkable for a gently bred young woman.

He turned his back to the fire, staring off into space as he considered what must be done. He would have to make arrangements for the uncle and aunt, of course. Perhaps the lately departed pair would be conveyed to their home churchyard for burial with little difficulty, tomorrow if possible. The cousins could go as well; he had no intention of housing those two longer than absolutely necessary. It might be a breach of the country hospitality for which he was known, but the new Lord Brook and his guileful sister were not welcome. Brook was a trifle too unctuous; William never trusted chaps like that.

He contemplated the other member of the family and wondered what miracle Miss Brooks might conjure to make her drab black gown more suitable this evening. It seemed beyond hope to him. He reckoned without his aunt.

A little time later, Felicia heard a gentle rap on her door. She quickly crossed to answer, only to discover Lady Emma standing without, a bundle of lavender wool in her arms.

The lady bustled into the room softly, exclaiming as she did, 'Poor dear, to be encumbered with *such* cousins. I ought not say so, but I scarcely believe they are related to you. You are not much alike,' she observed while studying Felicia by walking around her, examining the black gown with a polite expression that most likely concealed distaste.

Felicia couldn't blame her; she didn't like the dress, either. The makeover was not skillfully done, but it covered her – which was about the best one might say for it.

'Ma'am?' Felicia inquired, confused by the dear lady.

'Your Wilhelmina is quite a dasher, up to the minute with her styles. I suspect Basil is as well. You are not. Forgive me for saying so, but it is true. I wondered if there was anything we could do about that dress. You do not have another, I suppose?' Lady Emma looked with hope at the clothespress, as though expecting a fashionable gown to pop out for inspection.

'My aunt deemed this respectable, Lady Emma,' Felicia replied, quite unable to keep a wry note from her voice.

'It is, indeed, my dear. Most respectable. Alas, not very fashionable. Perhaps this shawl may help a bit?' Her ladyship draped a gossamer length of whisper-light wool around Felicia's shoulders, then stood back to see the effect. The lavender was kind to Felicia's pale cheeks and brought forth unexpected depths in her gray eyes. 'Indeed, it will do nicely until we can attend to the problem.'

Felicia dared not ask what that might involve. She had quickly learned that Lady Emma had her own notions as to how the world ought to be run. One queried at one's peril.

'Not a farthing?' Lady Emma asked out of the blue. 'Forgive me, dear, but I overheard what you said to William while in the library. I cannot believe a father would be so cruel.'

'Nor can I,' admitted Felicia while wondering how Lady Emma seemed to be everywhere at once.

'Leave it to William. He is very clever, you know. I believe that were it to occur to him, he might well take a notion to look into that peculiar and unnatural will. Basil inherits all, you say? Surely your uncle must have provided something for you?'

'I sincerely doubt it, my lady,' Felicia said, not wanting to say anything unkind about her uncle or cousin, yet knowing she must tell the truth of the matter. 'I was hoping that you might know of a situation that might suit me?' Felicia asked, wondering if this constituted begging.

'Allow me to think on it. I am certain something will occur to me. It always does. Or dearest William comes up with something terribly intelligent. Did I mention that William is very clever? He is, you know.' Lady Emma tilted her head to one side, frowning at Felicia's hair.

'Indeed, Lady Emma, I feel sure he is,' Felicia said with great tact. She adjusted the lovely shawl about her shoulders a trifle, then took a step toward the door.

'Your hair, dear girl. I believe you forgot to brush it . . . or something,' Lady Emma said vaguely. 'Please allow Trotter to style your hair. She has a dab hand at hair, my dear girl.' The abigail appeared in the doorway, as though summoned.

Deciding that Trotter could do not worse than she had, Felicia hastily perched on a small chair before the dressing table. The reflection in the looking glass was not very satisfactory. Her hair looked dreadful, all screwed up in an untidy bun. But then, she'd not had time to concentrate on herself as of late what with spending most hours at her uncle's bedside.

Trotter swiftly pulled out the pins and in a trice had the mass of nut brown hair brushed into a shining fall that came well below Felicia's shoulders.

'A French pleat,' the maid murmured, and before Felicia knew it, her hair was draped back into a rather becoming twist. A wisp of curl was allowed to dangle at either side of her face to soften the somewhat severe style.

'Better,' her ladyship said with a pleased air as she surveyed the results.

Felicia offered gracious thanks for a job only a superior lady's maid could have accomplished.

The surprised look from Lord Chessyre when she entered the drawing room made her glad she had accepted Lady Emma's kind help. His words surprised her even more.

'I thought lavender would do well on you.'

Felicia could see at once that he'd not intended to make such a personal remark, and so pretended that she'd not heard him for he had not spoken very loudly.

Basil entered with his typical swagger. 'There you are, cousin. I suppose you have made arrangements for us to take the parents home.' There was a hint of command in his voice. True, he was accustomed to having Felicia run the house at Brook Hall; servants had always obeyed her better. But now he was master, and he would never let anyone forget it for a moment.

Giving him a cold look, Felicia shook her head. 'You can make whatever arrangements you please. I shan't be returning with you.'

Basil gasped at her as though he hadn't heard right. Then he looked at Lord Chessyre, a speculative look in his eyes. Any charge he might have made died on his lips at the frosty stare coming his way from the elegant lord. Even the usually dense Basil could see he'd get nowhere making wild accusations against this man.

Willa entered the drawing room at that moment, preventing Basil from making any further demands. Instead, Basil turned to his sister to report, 'Felicia says she isn't coming home with us.'

'Not coming home? Who will take care of things, I should like to know?' Willa demanded, her voice sounding a trifle petulant, reminding Felicia forcibly of the late, unlamented Lady Brook.

'You must come,' Basil demanded.

'I insist,' Willa declared. 'Who else will run the house? Goodness knows I cannot be bothered with such mundane things.'

Before Felicia could inquire just who Willa thought she was to demand that Felicia turn into an unpaid housekeeper – for that was likely what the spoiled darling had in mind – Lord Chessyre spoke.

'Miss Brook has kindly agreed to be a companion for my aunt while she goes to London. Is that not right, Aunt Emma?'

'Yes, indeed,' Lady Emma replied, not the least ruffled that she was telling a lie. Turning to Felicia, she softly added, 'I knew he would think of something, and he did. Such a clever boy,' she concluded fondly.

The 'boy' as Lady Emma called him was in his early thirties or at best late twenties, tall and well-formed, with gorgeous blond curls and nice gray eyes – when they weren't frosty. Anyone less a 'boy' Felicia couldn't imagine. Of course it was merely a ruse to help her escape from her cousins, and for that she was most grateful.

'It is true,' Felicia said with her customary polite manner. 'Lady Emma is all that is gracious, and I look forward to spending time with her in London.'

'London?' Willa snapped, knowing full well that Felicia had been denied her come-out two years ago and that Willa had gone instead, taunting Felicia with all the fashionable doings. Willa had not taken, however. She'd three Seasons on her plate, and finding a husband was becoming less likely with each passing year. Time was not kind to her.

Jeffers appeared in the doorway to signal that dinner was ready so that Felicia was spared a reply to Willa's lone comment.

Basil was not silent, however. 'I think it is the height of ingratitude that you would consider going to a stranger instead of your cousins who need you.'

Felicia gave him a knowledgeable look, then said, 'Why should I come home when I can be paid for doing less elsewhere?' There were moments when direct speech could not be avoided to spare one's blushes, and this was one of them.

He blustered a bit, but fell silent when Lord Chessyre escorted Felicia into the dining room, seating her at his side with proper manners. Basil walked with Lady Emma, leaving Willa to follow behind, grumpy and out of sorts.

Under the cover of the general conversation and the noise of the servants handing around the excellent dishes of food, Lord Chessyre leaned toward Felicia and said, 'I trust my idea appeals to you. I do not like to see my aunt go to London alone, and she has her heart set on it. There is someone in the city she wishes to see.' He thought a few moments, then continued, 'It would ease my mind greatly if you could see your way to doing this kindness.' Then he mentioned what that kindness would pay, and Felicia nearly fainted again as she had when she'd climbed from the carriage after the accident.

How could she refuse? Even if it didn't work out, one or two months would ease her way and she could look for another position. Lady Emma was a dear, if a bit featherheaded. 'Of course I will,' Felicia promptly replied and was rewarded with a thawing of the ice in those gray eyes.

The evening was strained and concluded at an early hour. William gravely assured all that he was certain Lord Brook and Miss Willa wished to retire early and give vent to the grief they had been so nobly holding within all these hours. There was nothing more to be said to that other than a good night.

Felicia retired to her room, propping a chair against the door in case Basil renewed his amatory ideas.

The following morning William was disturbed at his desk in the library by a hesitant rap on the door. When he bid whoever it was to enter, he was surprised to see a neat and exceedingly plain young woman, the maid who came with Miss Brook if he remembered rightly.

'I be Primrose, maid to Miss Willa. If I might have a word with you, milord?' the maid begged hesitantly.

'Go on,' William urged, curious as to what this creature had to say.

'Miss Felicia is getting short shrift from Miss Willa. I been maiding her these past years, an' I know that Miss Willa helped herself to the pearls that was rightfully Miss Felicia's. Old Lady Brook insisted that those pearls were a part of the inheritance, but they were a gift from Miss Felicia's papa. I hoped you might help Miss Felicia, for she'd not stand a chance on her own against Miss Willa. I'm quitting,' the maid added. 'Without Miss Felicia to keep peace, Brook Hill won't be fit for living.'

William stared in amazement at what obviously was a long speech for one accustomed to remaining silent and in the background.

'I want to see justice done, if you please, milord. I'll see to it Miss Willa wears 'em down,' the maid concluded while backing toward the door.

'And you believe I may be of help?' William gently queried.

'Lord love a duck, iffen you can't scare her into returning the pearls, no one could,' the maid replied before slipping around the door and disappearing.

When the group gathered for a light noon meal with the thought that Brook, his sister, their late parents, and the rest of the entourage would depart directly after, William watched Willa with a sharp gaze. The maid had succeeded in placing the pearls around the neck of her mistress.

'Those are lovely pearls, Miss Willa. Your father gave them to you, no doubt?'

Startled at his comment on something she had no claim to wearing, Willa darted an annoyed glance at Felicia before calmly saying, 'Indeed.'

Basil gave a rude snort of laughter.

'You disagree, Lord Brook?' William asked with care.

Willa glared at Felicia. 'She told you a lie if she said they are hers. They are mine. Mama said so.'

'Indeed?' William inquired with raised brows.

Basil, still basking in the pleasure of being called by his newly acquired title, looked scornfully at his sister. 'Those pearls are Felicia's, and you know it. Mama was too pinch-penny to buy you a string of your own.'

'Surely you will restore them to their rightful owner before you leave,' William said with all his powers of persuasion brought to the fore.

Lady Emma murmured, 'Very bad *ton* to keep pearls that belong to another.'

Hoping to provoke her cousin into rash behavior, Felicia said, 'Well, Willa? Basil is right, and you know it.'

Looking about the table and finding not one smile or sympathetic expression, Willa angrily reached up and removed the offending pearls, tossing them at Felicia. 'You will replace them, dear brother,' she threatened.

Her brother merely grinned, finished his meal, and made his farewells to his host with more manners than Felicia had thought he possessed.

When the departing Brooks – both living and deceased – had passed through the gates, Felicia turned to thank her host for all he had done on her behalf. 'I'd not thought to have my necklace again, for Aunt was adamant that they were no longer mine. Thank you.' She frowned, then continued, 'I hope your aunt may suggest a position for me.'

'I really mean for you to go with her to London; it was not a ruse to foil your cousins. And' – he turned to espy the plain maid who had lurked in the shadows – 'I believe you have acquired an additional member for the London household.'

'Primrose?' Felicia cried with surprise.

'I refused to go with Miss Willa. Iffen you won't hire me, could I travel with you to London? I'll maid you better than I did Miss Willa, and once in the city work would be easier to find.'

'Oh, mercy,' Felicia whispered.

'Do agree, dear girl. Tupper cannot do for two, and I would have you looking up to snuff once in London,' Lady Emma cried as she drifted down the stairs in a cloud of lavender sarcenet.

Felicia exchanged a look with Lord Chessyre, surprised to find amusement in those gray eyes.

'Do I have any choice in the matter?'

'None whatsoever,' Lord Chessyre replied.

Chapter Two

There was a whirlwind of activity the remainder of that day and the days that followed. Lady Emma began her preparation for the removal to London, and it appeared that she felt a great many things were necessary lest they be deprived of something important.

'Dear Lady Emma, I do believe there are a vast number of shops in the city where all manner of goods may be purchased,' Felicia pointed out while Lady Emma debated as to which set of china she ought to bring along. 'I have heard that the Wedgwood showroom is most excellent.'

'But I prefer my own dishes and linen,' her ladyship softly argued. 'I do not wish to waste my time bothering with things like linen and china when there are more interesting fields to explore.'

Regarding these fields, nothing was said, and Felicia was reluctant to ask. It could be that Lady Emma desired to visit the British Museum or perhaps the Tower of London. Maybe she fancied paintings. Shopping crossed Felicia's mind to be instantly dismissed. Lady Emma possessed a charming wardrobe, mostly lavender or misty blue, and quite up to date if the fashion plates were any guide. That Felicia would love to spend a bit of her earnings on a new dress was firmly nudged aside. She must save that money to tide her over until she found another position. Lady Emma certainly didn't intend to be in London forever, and she scarcely needed a companion once she returned to Chessyre Court.

Of Lord Chessyre, Felicia saw little or nothing. At breakfast she learned he had been down and gone. He rarely made an appearance during the day. Come evening, he joined them at dinner, dressed with his customary good taste and looking far too splendid for Felicia's peace of mind.

However, the food was excellent, and she refused to permit him to disturb her enjoyment of her meals. How lovely it was to eat all she wished without receiving a summons to fetch a shawl from the other end of the house. True, if she kept on eating at this rate, she'd need to let out her one decent gown.

After dinner Lord Chessyre usually chatted politely and distantly with her and Lady Emma, then retired to read or check over papers in his library. He seemed to have an inordinate amount of correspondence, she thought, and said as much to Lady Emma.

'Yes, well, as of late it does seem as though he is much occupied,' her ladyship admitted with a frown. Then her brow cleared. 'I fear he is shy of pretty ladies,' she declared with a confiding air and a quick smile.

Felicia raised her brows in surprise. 'Lord Chessyre? Shy? I can scarce believe that. He seems much the polished gentlemen to my poor mind.' And if Lady Emma included Felicia in the pretty lady category, she was far and wide off the mark.

'The dear boy was disappointed in love. So tragic. His best friend married the girl William had selected for his own.' Lady Emma sighed and gave Felicia a wistful look. 'I would so like to see him settled with a wife and family. I have plans of my own, you see, and it would help me greatly were he to marry so I would be free.'

Felicia tried to imagine what those plans might be and utterly failed in her efforts. Then she attempted to conjure an image of a woman who could possibly prefer another man to Lord Chessyre and failed there as well. He might be a touch frosty and more than a little reserved, but with the woman he loved, surely he would thaw? She had seen those eyes warm and suspected there was a heart lurking somewhere in that solid chest that could be warmed as well.

It was surprising how her pearls dressed up that dowdy black silk. Going down to dinner garbed in the detested dress with the lustrous pearls around her neck and the pretty shawl loaned by Lady Emma draped about her shoulders, Felicia felt almost like her former self – the pampered daughter of the wealthy Baron Brook.

That Lord Chessyre was remotely polite made little difference in her self-esteem. She had decided that Lady Emma was wrong. He was not shy; he was merely uninterested. No man with his virile good looks could be backward in his interest of the opposite sex. Besides, she had caught a gleam in his eyes more than once, and even with her quite limited experience, she recognized it for what it was. For some reason – no doubt her lack of wealth or personal beauty – Lord Chessyre was deliberately keeping his distance. It was agreeable, she assured herself. She didn't like him anyway. She had other questions to plague her.

In the back of Felicia's mind lurked the possibility of locating the solicitor who had handled her late father's estate and probably composed the will. His office was in London. While sipping her morning tea, she mulled over the best way to approach the man. Surely he could tell her if the will approved by the judge was the actual will her father had wanted. It had been very hard to accept that he would cut her off without a competence or dowry – especially as wealthy as he had been. He had seemed to dote on her – so why would he cut her and give all to his brother? she wondered – not for the first time.

She'd inscribed the solicitor's name in her journal, now carefully packed in her small case. She'd liked to ask his lordship's opinion on the matter, but with him being so remote, she dared not request his time.

'Dear girl,' Lady Emma intruded on Felicia's mental reflections while consuming a quantity of toast, 'you must send to Brook Hall for your things. I presume you have other clothes you would need in London?' Her look was gentle, but Felicia had learned that Lady Emma in pursuit of information was like a dog after a juicy bone. She did not cease in her quest.

The query was embarrassing, for Felicia had left behind very little, mostly the things she hated or had outgrown. 'Not that I miss, I fear.

I could send Primrose with a list – if she is willing to go. I'd not wish her to be compelled to remain there against her will. However, she does know where things are located and what to do.'

Primrose was sent for and readily agreed to fetch the precious mementos Felicia cherished and the few items of clothing that might be useful.

'Iffen you don't mind my saying, your clothespress don't hold much of interest,' Primrose stated flatly. 'And don't worry about me none, for it'll be an icy day in hell when that madam can make me stay at Brook Hall again.' Ready and willing to go at a moment's notice, the maid bustled off to hastily prepare a small valise.

Lady Emma ordered a carriage readied and sent Primrose off with instructions to bring back all that was on the list and anything else she knew her new mistress would want. 'And hurry, Primrose,' Lady Emma softly demanded. 'I find I am eager to reach London even if winter is coming and the Season is far off. I have plans to make.'

'Yes, ma'am,' the plain little maid replied while wrapping herself in a stout cloak of frieze, the heavy woolen fabric guaranteed to keep her warm against the chill.

Felicia marveled at the speed with which Lady Emma could act when she so chose. Otherwise, it seemed she deliberated with maddening consideration over what to take. She frequently consulted Felicia, but even more often she sought out her nephew.

At last the day arrived when Lady Emma decreed that they could make the journey to London. Primrose had returned with all of the nightclothes, undergarments, and the keepsakes on the short list. She had also brought the miniatures of Felicia's father and mother, plus a collection of books that had been in Felicia's room.

'I didn't say nothing to Miss Willa nor his new lordship that be. I just found old Risford and explained to him what was wanted and he let me set to on my own. I fancy those cousins of yours didn't even know I was in the house.' Primrose exchanged a knowing look with Felicia. Both of them knew full well that Willa paid no attention to the servants, other than to issue orders. Basil did notice the girls, but they avoided him as much as possible.

Two carriages awaited the ladies when they left the comfort of Chessyre Court. The first was an elegant, well-sprung traveling coach intended for Lady Emma and Felicia. The second was slightly less pretentious, and in this coach rode Primrose and Tupper along with the little dog Lady Emma had decided to take along for company. It was a King Charles spaniel, which Felicia surveyed with distrust.

'What? No cat?' Lord Chessyre murmured to Felicia while his aunt was supervising the loading of the cart that hooked on behind the second carriage. It would take the china and the piles of linen as well as all the other items she decided to take with her. The cart was not large, but well-built and ought to deliver the goods to London in good shape.

'I was informed that Cleo couldn't be left behind. Her vanity is such that it would break her heart.' Felicia exchanged a look with his lordship, revealing her amusement at that notion.

'The dog usually remains in my aunt's quarters, for she knows how I feel about that dratted animal. I cannot count the slippers I have had chewed to bits by the precious Cleo. Beware, Miss Brook, guard your slippers and anything else you value. Never leave anything near the floor or it will be reduced to rags in no time.'

'I promise, sir. No slippers on the floor by my bed.' Her gaze met his, and she found her cheeks warming at the expression that had flashed into his eyes. Lord Chessyre might have kept his distance from her, but she'd wager a goodly sum that he was not cut out to be a monk.

Finally, Felicia tore her gaze from the intriguing light in his eyes and studied the ground at her feet. 'I have a number of things I hope to accomplish while in London, but I also promise that I shall do my best to be a good companion to your aunt. I have seen how very fond you are of her. I think that a most admirable thing, my lord.'

'Do you, indeed?' He thought a moment, then said, 'It may be necessary for me to come to London this winter. There is little I can do here, and it would be nice to spend Christmas with my aunt. She's all I have now, you see.'

Felicia merely nodded. Who knew what the circumstances would be by Christmas?

'I will see you then?'

Puzzled as to why he would wish to pin her down on that, Felicia nodded once again, then joined Lady Emma as she poised to enter the traveling coach.

'Good-bye, dearest William. Join us for Christmas. I vow we shall be merry even in the city. The change will do you good,' the lady insisted.

Felicia turned her head in time to discover the earl was studying her, and again she felt her cheeks warming. Gracious, if this was to be her reaction every time he looked at her, she had truly best find another position before Christmas.

'Have a splendid journey, Aunt. Miss Brook. I shall see you at Christmas.' With that he waved them off, and Felicia felt as though she might draw a comfortable breath again.

'Such a dear boy. I expected he would come for Christmas. Who knows, he might join us before then. It depends on how bored he becomes here all by himself. You see, I hope that if he comes to Town, he may find himself a wife. He certainly will never find one at Chessyre Court!'

Felicia nodded, unable to speak, for the idea of the golden-haired Lord Chessyre with his fine physique and lovely gray eyes finding a wife could not please. Of course, she reminded herself, she was not interested in the man, yet she hoped he could not merely *find* a wife, but someone he could love. His tender regard and care for his aunt revealed that within that cool exterior was a warm heart. He deserved better than a marriage of convenience with a proper member of Society, she thought.

The trip went well. They were cushioned in a fine coach and had ample money to pave their way. They stopped at the best inns, ate of the finest food, and in general found the journey far less tiring than might be expected. Primrose and Tupper pampered the ladies with devoted care.

Felicia soon decided that she could quite easily come to favor this style of life. It was so vastly different from the one she had known the past four years.

The London house possessed a fine address and was most pleasing to the eye in the late autumn sun.

'We are next door to the Marquess of Bute, not that you may expect to see much of him,' Lady Emma said upon disembarking from the traveling coach. She glanced at the imposing house on their right, then turned her attention to the house before which they had stopped. It had four well-proportioned floors with a fine brick exterior and large windows to allow the sun to warm the rooms within. To either side of the front door were large stone urns containing geraniums and ivy, both in the best of health.

'Come, come, dear Felicia. I am famished and weary to the bone. We must have a cup of tea, then rest. After that I will begin my final plans. I have such high hopes, you see.' With that vague remark, Lady Emma sailed forth into the house, greeting the man who opened the door with the ease of one who has known him a long time. The man ignored Cleo, who proceeded to dance about his black slippers with yips of delight.

'Alford, this is Miss Brook, who is a dear friend and my companion. I trust you will look after her as well as you do me.'

Felicia found herself being appraised with knowledgeable eyes and flushed when the butler bowed ever so slightly to her, a mark, she felt certain, of his approval.

Primrose bustled in with Tupper, and the two abigails – for Primrose had given herself a raise in title – hurried to tend to their mistresses.

Felicia allowed the others to go ahead. She wandered slowly through the rooms that were to be her milieu for the coming months. The furnishings were of the highest quality and artistically arranged against pale straw-colored walls. It was nice to see rooms not overly crowded with furniture. Draperies were elegant, but not overdone. The carpets Felicia paused to admire, for even she could guess they were the finest Turkey carpets to be had. Over all she acquired the impression of quality and refinement, restraint and taste. The colors were nice, with dull greens, soft blues, and an odd shade of wine used. There was not one thing she'd have removed. It was all quite, quite perfect.

After strolling up the stairs to the first floor, she decided which was her room by the sound of Primrose's voice scolding some hapless soul. Pausing at the door to the most elegant bedroom she'd ever had the privilege to enter, she at first thought there must be a mistake. But Primrose never made mistakes.

'Lovely, ain't it, Miss Felicia?' Primrose said, beaming a smile. She shooed the little maid from the room, and the girl scuttled as though afraid Felicia would trounce her.

'Now, Primrose, it is not seemly to act so,' Felicia said while turning about to absorb the glory of the room. The walls were the palest lavender, and the Turkey carpet a rich collection of soft blues and dull reds, accented with black and white. The magnificent bed had a tester draped beautifully at each post with fabric that matched the bed cover, all a delicate lavender damask. Surely his lordship had nothing to do with her having this room. He might have remarked she looked well in lavender, but it was silly to fancy that he would request such a thing.

'I do hope you like it?' Lady Emma said from the doorway, Cleo firmly in her arms. 'William thought you might.'

'I am overwhelmed,' Felicia answered truthfully. So he had thought to house her in this room. Perhaps he merely liked to picture people in a particular setting? But that would mean he thought of her at all, and that was preposterous.

William paced about the confines of his library, wondering why word had not arrived to let him know his aunt and Miss Brook had reached the London house without mishap.

It was a good thing they had left, although he'd begun to think his aunt delayed merely to tease him. Try as he might, it had become more and more difficult to remain aloof from the charming Miss Brook. It would never do for him to become enamored of a woman like her. It simply would not do at all.

True, she had admittedly coped with the deaths of her uncle and aunt. She certainly had known how to handle those odious cousins. However, caution urged him to beware the girl who was no more than twenty, if a day. That accident had been just too pat, happening right outside his gates. Granted, they likely hadn't anticipated the extent of the injuries – people often miscalculated. If she had but known the number of carriage accidents that occurred at that location, she would have blushed even more than when he had studied her while trying to take her measure.

Oh, she had to be a clever one, even if his heart told him otherwise. He'd learned not to trust his instincts when it came to women. After all, he'd thought Sophie his, and she had ended up marrying Jonathan, his best friend.

He felt his aunt was safe enough. Although, perhaps he ought to travel to London to keep an eye on her. He'd think it over for a bit. Not too much could occur in a few weeks, not if he knew his aunt. First would be her calls on her mantuamaker. He wondered just how many garments would be pressed on Miss Brook and grinned. That young lady was in for a surprise, unless he missed his guess.

It was difficult to apply himself to estate business when he'd prefer to consider Felicia Brook in the lavender bedroom, particularly the bed.

On the third morning following their arrival in London, when Felicia had hoped to venture forth to the heart of the city in search of the solicitor, Lady Emma attacked.

'I desire you to come with me today. I wish to see my mantua-maker. I am tired of pale blue and lavender. I think I should like something in pale rose, perhaps a dusty jade green. And slippers. I go through slippers at a shocking rate, and I am nearly down to my stockings. And that reminds me, I require those as well, and some new reticules, of course a bonnet or two. Handkerchiefs. Underpinnings. Oh, and a new robe. Cleo chewed the hem of my present one, and although it is a favorite, I fear it must be replaced.'

'You mean to do this in one day?' Felicia said, utterly bewildered at the list offered.

'Well, we shall do what we can today, and what we can't shall be done tomorrow.' Lady Emma rose from the breakfast table and drifted from the room. Cleo peeked over her shoulder and panted happily at Felicia.

'Mercy,' Felicia murmured. Her quest must be postponed.

The day was a haze of discussions with the mantua-maker over colors and fabrics, what sort of bonnet to buy, and if one required matching gloves or should they be contrasting. When Madame Clotilde suggested the gloves match the slippers, Lady Emma cried with delight that it was the very thing and didn't Felicia agree.

Which brought Madame's attention to her. A glance darted to Lady Emma, who nodded slightly, brought forth a considering study from Madame Clotilde.

Puzzled as to quite what was going on, Felicia anxiously looked from one woman to the other. Mercy, she didn't have the money for one gown from this establishment, let alone the number of garments ordered by Lady Emma.

'Indeed. I agree that lavender is an excellent choice. However, she has nut brown hair, and she will look well in the same colors you enjoy. Shall we?'

Lady Emma rose and took Felicia's arm in a firm clasp that brooked no argument. They went to a little room in the rear of the establishment, and in short order Felicia found herself measured, pinned, and unpinned in fabric after fabric. Madame used her scissors like a weapon, bent on reducing as many bolts of fabric as possible.

Felicia tried to call a halt and discovered anew, when Lady Emma had made up her mind regarding something, it was utterly useless to oppose her.

That evening Felicia sat opposite her ladyship at the dinner table and wondered how best to scold her. Or, did a companion scold one of her rank?

'You ought not have ordered so many gowns for me, your ladyship. I admit I needed one or two dresses, but day dresses, carriage dresses, an evening gown – as though I would be attending parties – and a new pelisse! Well, my lady!'

'Admit that you cannot wear that old pelisse of yours again, no matter how cleverly Primrose tried to repair it,' Lady Emma demanded, pointing a fork at Felicia in an accusing manner. 'Tomorrow we do bonnets and slippers. I declare that I have missed shopping exceedingly while at the Court.'

Felicia accepted that there was nothing she might do to stop her ladyship in her chosen path. She was like a stone being pushed from the top of a hill – once it began rolling there was no stopping it. At least, Felicia consoled herself, she didn't have to endure Lord Chessyre's knowing gaze. *That* would have been insupportable.

It was far too easy to wear the pretty lavender pelisse when it arrived a week later along with a charming bonnet possessing deep lavender ribbons. Dark gray gloves and slippers, half boots of excellent black leather, and finally a modest ermine muff to guard against the winter cold arrived within days of ordering. But it was the dainty white nightgown embroidered with tiny rosebuds that had a pretty white wool robe, also with rosebuds on it, that caused the explosion.

'Now I ask you, my lady! This is not done!'

They argued, and as Felicia might have known, she lost. She went off to her room to calculate the expenses on her behalf and was horrified at the total. If she worked for years, she could not begin to repay the cost.

It meant, of course, that she could not look for another position.

She also found, for one reason or another, that it proved impossible to make her way into the city to hunt for the solicitor. That she might have summoned him to Lady Emma's home on South Audley and that the gentleman would have scurried to the door never occurred to Felicia.

It was nearly two months after their arrival that his lordship arrived. Christmas was nearly upon them. Felicia had almost forgotten that they were threatened with his arrival close to that time. She was in the drawing room, hunting for a deliberately elusive Cleo, when the door opened.

'I believe she is back in the corner, my lady. Not to fear, I shall have her in a trice,' Felicia muttered, presenting a delightful view of her posterior as she crawled on hands and knees to snabble the disobedient dog.

William studied the picture presented with the eye of a connoisseur. He'd viewed many female forms, and it appeared that Miss Brook had fulfilled the promise in hers. She was no longer too thin. He leaned patiently against the wall, waiting.

There was a high-pitched yap, followed by soft muttering and a rather loud, 'Ouch, you little beast.' At last Miss Brook retreated, Cleo in hand. She rose, shook out her skirt, and patted her curls – most modishly arranged after a call from Mr Tremont, the fashionable hairdresser. The soft frill at her neck framed a flushed face, one that assumed a horrified expression at the sight of him.

'Lord Chessyre! You are here! Oh, dear. What you must think of me, crawling about on the floor. It was Cleo, you see. She refused to take her walk, and your aunt insisted she must, so I said I'd persuade the dratted little beast, that is, I mean, the dear little dog. . . .' Miss Brook gave him a despairing look, then concentrated on the cause of it all.

William wanted to laugh as he hadn't since Miss Brook had departed for London. 'Do not give it a thought. I just now arrived from the Court. Is my aunt to home?'

Miss Brook gave a sigh of relief. 'Indeed, sir, she is in the dining room, enjoying a cup of tea. She did not wish to see Cleo captured.'

William turned to leave the room, then paused, looking again at the lovely woman he had found so attractive when she was at Chessyre Court. With proper clothes and a very pretty hair style she was even more attractive. Christmas was going to be far better than he'd expected. 'Miss Brook, as I said before, lavender becomes you.'

Felicia looked anywhere but at the handsome lord who blocked her retreat from the drawing room. 'Thank you, my lord. You must give all credit to your aunt, who stubbornly insisted I must have so many dresses.' Felicia looked up to face the person who ultimately must be her benefactor, for she suspected that he paid the bills. 'I shall not expect to be paid a wage, sir. These clothes were not inexpensive and I'd not feel right about taking any payment.'

William stared at her. Not take any payment when he knew she must be at his aunt's beck and call from morning to nightfall?

'I mean it,' she added when he remained silent too long.

'Nonsense. I suspect you earn every penny of that small stipend you receive. And if my dear aunt wishes you to be appropriately garbed for your position, I'll not gainsay her. Is that understood?' he concluded gently, not at all like the frosty manner he'd used while at the Court.

Felicia might have been impervious to his words had he spoken them in his previous cold way. But, when he smiled at her and said the words with such understanding of her position, she just melted and blushed and wished she were a million miles away.

Chapter Three

What a dreadful development this was! Felicia thought as Lord Chessyre left the room in search of his aunt. Cleo wiggled and gave an annoyed yap before Felicia recalled her duties. She fixed on the leash, slipped on her new pelisse, and left the house before anyone could learn her intentions.

A bracing walk was precisely what she needed. What a silly girl she was to think that his lordship would so much as look at her. She was his aunt's companion, for pity's sake. That was it. His smile was a part of him and was certainly not directed toward her. Not that it meant she would find it any easier to be around him.

That was the solution. She would take care to avoid the dratted man. Surely that would put any foolish notions far and away from her head. Besides, had she not decided she did not like the earl?

Her steps took her to the park, where there were few people out and about in the chilly, damp weather. Freed from her leash, Cleo dashed madly first in one direction, then another. Felicia watched the little dog while her mind was on other matters, like taking a hackney across town to find that solicitor. She surely had a day coming to her; she'd not had a moment to herself since they arrived in London for there had been so much to do. As well, she felt so guilty about Lady Emma bestowing all those clothes on her that she could not abide asking for time away. But things changed as of today. Now her quest became imperative.

She had just reattached Cleo's leash and was standing up when she caught sight of her cousin. There was no mistaking Basil. He had nut brown hair, swept into a careful Brutus that didn't quite conceal the thinning hair on top of his head when he removed his hat. And the folds of his cravat couldn't conceal his jowls – the result of eating his share of the meals and likely Felicia's as well. In addition, there was the way he held his head. No mistake.

Felicia searched the area for someplace to hide and was dismayed to find that the trees were too spindly and Cleo *would* bark, the dratted pup.

He saw her and approached. What was he doing in London? Perhaps he'd decided to pay his £9 fee due on the introduction of a peer in the House of Lords. It would, to him, be an investment.

'What a surprise, Cousin,' Basil said in that unctuous manner he'd adopted. 'And what do you do here?' He had a faint sneer in his voice and Felicia longed to tell him that she was merely strolling for her health. But with no maid in attendance that was unlikely. Besides, she was a truthful girl – most of the time.

'I am walking a dog,' Felicia stated with perfect candor, even if it was not what her cousin really wanted to know.

'You came to London with Lady Emma Chessyre, then?'

'I did.' Felicia had learned long ago that brief answers made Basil furious. 'And what brings you to the city?' She had also learned early on that Basil liked to brag about himself and his doings. If she could persuade him to launch forth on his own business, she might edge her way out of the park and along to the house on South Audley Street before he realized what she was about.

'I wished to take my seat in the House – and see to my investments, my dear girl. I am on the way to making my fortune.'

Felicia gave him a puzzled look. He was the last person she'd have thought to be interested in commercial enterprise. 'A fortune? How lovely. Willa will like that. And how is my cousin? She is with you, of course.'

'Wilhelmina is at Brook Hall, where she ought to be. She turned down a most advantageous match and can stay there until she reconsiders.'

Felicia looked at her cousin's hard, cold face and shivered. He was so like his parsimonious mother at that moment it was uncanny. How thankful she was that she had left Brook Hall. Better to be walking dogs and relatively free than under Basil's control. And who would he have paired her with? That is, if he hadn't wanted her to remain as his unpaid housekeeper? Not to mention warming his bed upon occasion. Most likely he would have found the richest man in the land regardless of his age and found some way to force him to wed Felicia. That was probably what he'd done to Willa.

'Poor Willa,' Felicia murmured as she edged to the park gate.

'I have an appointment with Rothschild this afternoon. At present I am looking about for a respectable address at which I might reside while in the city.' Basil looked down his nose at Felicia, then added, 'Where does Lady Emma live?'

Knowing that he could find out easily enough, Felicia replied, 'South Audley Street, next door to the Marquess of Bute. It is a lovely home. Most of the homes in this area are likely rather dear. Why do you not reside in Brook House? It is still part of the estate, I believe?'

' 'Tis rented for the coming Season, and I do not know how long I shall be here. I might still have need of the house when the tenants come.'

'Rented! Are you in financial difficulties?' Felicia dared to ask.

Basil gave her a smug look. 'Not I. I shall make my holdings the finest in Britain. The sum left by your father will be most useful to assist me in my goal.'

'I should have liked to inspect that will,' Felicia said, then scolded herself for admitting to her curiosity.

Basil took a threatening step toward her, an arm outstretched in what was definitely an angry gesture. 'It is none of your affair, dear girl. Women ought not bother their little heads over financial matters. 'Tis proven they do not have near enough brains.'

If Felicia had not thoroughly disliked Basil before, she would have now. She had managed her father's household for several years before he died and done well at it.

'Well, well, what have we here?' Lord Chessyre asked with a narrow look at Basil and a suspicious one at Felicia as he joined them, having entered the park unseen by her.

'I was walking Cleo when I chanced upon my cousin. Basil is look-ing about for suitable housing in this area.'

'A land agent is what you want,' his lordship said with a frozen demeanor firmly in place as he glared at the mushroom peer.

'They charge a fee,' Basil said curtly. 'A lot of rubbish, that. I can do as well on my own. Perhaps Felicia will assist me?' He stepped forward as though to grasp Felicia's arm, but she withdrew, afraid of her cousin in this more belligerent attitude.

'Come, Felicia,' Basil ordered contemptuously. 'You can well manage time to help your cousin.'

Then she felt Lord Chessyre's arm at her back. He was scarcely touching her, but it gave her the feeling of being protected, of a safe haven from Basil's anger.

'No, Basil. I am not under your control. I am beyond the age of a guardian or trustee – not that I have a farthing to bless myself with.' Felicia stared at Basil with all the loathing she felt revealed on her face.

It was difficult to describe the look he gave Felicia then. She might have said it was victorious; it certainly was smug. And, had he but known it, Basil had just stirred two people to a strong urge to inspect that infamous will for themselves.

'Excuse me, Cousin. Lady Emma desired my company this after-noon. Calling, you know,' Felicia added in what she hoped to be a maddeningly gracious manner.

Cleo barked and tugged his leash from Felicia's loose grip to attack Basil, nipping at his heels and taking a firm hold on a hem of his black – and somewhat dusty – pantaloons.

'Call off your beast, Chessyre,' Basil said nastily, while trying to kick Cleo.

Not about to allow her dratted relative to harm the dog, no matter how provoked, Felicia darted forward and rescued the dog, getting a bruise on her arm from Basil's shoe in the process. Too angry to say a word, Felicia clutched the dog close to her and stalked along the walks until she was safely before the Chessyre home.

'I do apologize, my lord,' Felicia began as they entered the house. She handed Cleo to Alford, then unbuttoned her pelisse before turning to face the man who ultimately was her employer. 'My cousin is wanting in manners.' She removed her pelisse, absently allowing Alford to take this as well.

'He seems quite fond of money, however,' Lord Chessyre said, placing a hand firmly under Felicia's elbow and forcefully guiding her up to the drawing room. 'Did you never see a copy of your father's will? Not a glimpse?'

'Not a glimpse. As Basil said just now, women are deemed to have little in the way of brains, so what would I do if I did see the dratted thing?' she demanded. Memories of all she'd once had and lost returned, causing her eyes to be suspiciously bright with unshed tears.

They entered the drawing room and halted in the center, where Lord Chessyre stood a moment in abstracted thought before turning to Felicia, who was recovering from her momentary lapse.

'With your permission I should like to look into this on your behalf. Your unsavory cousin does have a point in that solicitors are more willing to discuss financial matters with a man. Whether you like it or no, that is the fact of the matter.' He gave Felicia a level look from an impassive face that concealed any emotion that might have lurked there.

'My father employed Aloysius Smithers as his solicitor. I intended to seek him out upon my arrival, but I scarce. . . .' Felicia hesitated in her speech. She was reluctant to tell him that she'd not had a day to herself for months; that smacked of tale-bearing and complaining. Lady Emma was such a dear, and what Felicia did could scarcely be labeled work.

'If I know my aunt, I could say that you have not had a day off to yourself since you arrived in London. Am I correct?' he queried with that reserved look firmly in place on his face again.

'Yes, sir,' Felicia said, studying the stitching on her new gloves with an intensity they did not merit.

'First of all, allow me to call on the solicitor. Secondly, choose the day you would wish to take off, and I shall see you have it.' His lord-ship walked across the room to lean against the fireplace mantel, turn-ing to observe Felicia standing uncertainly where he had left her.

'I would prefer to handle my affairs on my own.' Felicia gave him a respectful look when she would have much preferred glaring at the dratted man. 'The will has nothing to do with you.'

'Did I hear the name Rothschild drift to my ears?' Chessyre inquired, ignoring Felicia's rebellion completely.

Giving up for the moment, she replied, 'Yes. Basil claims to have an appointment with a Rothschild this afternoon.'

'I have met the gentleman on occasion. I believe I shall renew my acquaintance with him.'

Felicia raised her eyebrows in inquiry, but said nothing. After all, her brains could scarcely be expected to understand the workings of a gentleman's mind. She'd noticed Lord Chessyre hadn't refuted that bit of Basil's nonsense.

'Still want the house and the cat?'

Surprised he had remembered her remark, Felicia nodded. 'I think most single women would like such an arrangement. It is far better than being dependent upon relatives!'

'There you are, Felicia,' Lady Emma cried as she whirled into the room in a drift of pale green sarcenet and lace, a scarf wafting behind her like the tail of a kite.

'I was delayed in my walk. Cleo was exceedingly good.'

'Yes,' his lordship added in a wry manner, 'she tried to bite Miss Brook's deplorable cousin. I fear she succeeded in tearing the fabric of the man's pantaloons and earning Miss Brook a bruise when she rescued Cleo from Basil's pointed toe.'

Nothing would do but Lady Emma had to have Tupper tend the bruise, which was turning a splendid shade of purple by now. Lord Chessyre kept his distance, presumably content to allow the abigail to deal with the matter.

'Aunt Emma, has Miss Brook had any time to herself? It is custom-ary, you know, for a companion to have one day a week to do as she pleases. Does Tuesday please you, Miss Brook?'

Having no preference – for indeed, she did not know what she would do with her day off – Felicia nodded her agreement.

'What shall you do with your day?' Lady Emma queried with a frown. 'You mentioned the British Museum and the Tower of London. Surely you cannot be serious in wanting to see them?'

'Actually, I thought to go up to St Paul's. The view is said to be splendid from the top,' Felicia admitted.

'Best not go alone. That part of the city is a bit unsavory,' his lordship said, pushing himself away from the mantel and crossing to the door. 'Let me know when you intend to go, and I shall see you are safe.'

There was nothing that Felicia would have liked better, but she was not about to permit this high-and-mighty lord to attend to her as though she were a mere child.

'Thank you, my lord.' She neither said she would tell him when she wanted to go, nor did she deny she wanted his company. Which she did, of course. But not on his terms.

Come Tuesday, Felicia took off by herself after assuring Primrose that it was perfectly proper for the maid to take the day off. Felicia was certain that she was the only companion in London to have a maid.

Primrose had made no effort at finding a new position. Perhaps she was as frozen in her little niche as was Felicia?

The hackney Felicia found was not the tidiest, and it smelled of moldy straw. The jarvey gave her a knowing look when she gave him her destination.

The bumpy ride across London left her shaken, but not quite as shaken as the sight that met her eyes when she exited the carnage. Three lads in tattered clothes were beating a cat. It was a pathetic creature – a thin gray cat with not the slightest pretense to a pedigree, but that made no matter to Felicia. Wielding her parasol like a sword, she charged up the steps until she reached the cruel tormentors.

'Leave be,' she cried, striking one lad over the shoulder. 'How dare you beat an innocent cat! Fancy picking on a poor creature like that. Bullies, that is what you are. I demand you leave at once.'

The boys whistled, and several more lads quickly appeared on the scene – considerably larger and far more menacing. Felicia made a grab for the moth-eaten cat, wrapping it in her scarf. Then she began a strategic retreat down the steps, clutching the cat tightly against her. She ignored the faint mews in her concentration on escaping from the menace she sensed about her.

'She hit me, she did,' the lad who had been beating the cat whined.

'Hurt our Ben, did ye?' the largest of the lot asked in an ominous tone.

Belatedly, Felicia realized they felt she was fair game. How stupid she was, to venture forth without a maid or companion. Naturally these louts thought her no better than some poor maid, never mind that her clothes were good. With the cast-off clothing given them, many maids were as finely dressed as their mistresses.

'He was beating this animal,' Felicia said, hoping she'd reach the bottom of the steps soon and that a hackney would be handy for a quick escape.

'And what's it ter you? Cat fur brings a fair price,' another of the big boys said, taking several steps toward Felicia with a sly grin on his face. 'Gorm, wouldn't ol' Molly take to this one, lads? She'd fetch us a pretty price, she would.'

Growing close to panic, Felicia froze as a voice came from behind her. That faintly bored tone with edges of frost to it was, for once, most welcome.

'Ah, lads, and what is this I see?' Lord Chessyre inquired in that intimidating way he had. 'You would never be thinking of placing a hand on this lovely lady, now would you?' He placed a firm hand under her arm, then continued, 'Sorry I'm late, my dear girl. The press of carriages was dreadful. Do you still wish to see St Paul's, or would you prefer another day?'

'Another day,' Felicia managed to say with amazing calm, considering how her knees were trembling.

She found herself ushered into a lovely carriage at once, the sort of carriage only the very wealthy could afford. 'Thank you, my lord,' she whispered as she sank back against the squabs.

'Indeed. I can understand why your detested cousin refused to allow you to see that will if this is an example of your common sense. Did I not tell you to permit me to see you arrived here in safety?'

Felicia sat perfectly still, wondering if she should just faint as she longed to do, or try to argue with the man seated across from her. The cat meowed more forcefully, and that settled the matter. Avoiding any sort of reply, Felicia gently examined the thin gray creature sitting so pathetically in her lap.

'You now have a cat. Perhaps not quite the one I'd have selected for you, but it is yours, nonetheless, is it not?' he asked with the tone of one who already knows the answer.

'Of course I shall take care of it – that is, if your aunt will allow it?' Felicia said with a quizzical look at the earl.

'You need not fear that. She is as soft in the head as you are.' His expression was inscrutable as usual, but there seemed to be a gleam in his eyes that she had noted before.

In spite of his remark, Felicia felt she had not truly displeased him by her rescue of the cat.

'I must apologize, my lord. You obviously were on your way to an appointment, and I have upset your plans.'

'True, you have upset my plans, but I fear it cannot be helped at this point. I have been to see Rothschild and had a most interesting conversation. It seems your cousin, the mushroom, has a substantial sum of money he wishes to invest at the best possible rates. I believe Rothschild found him contemptible even as he viewed the money with considerable interest. It may be that the odious Basil will end up an exceedingly wealthy man since he has no scruples as to how he earns his money.'

'Poor Willa,' Felicia said, recalling what Basil had said, and even more, implied. 'I suspect he intends to offer her to the highest bidder – whoever that might be.'

'Some elderly merchant with a fat purse and a desire to marry a baron's daughter. You escaped this fate.' It was more of a statement than a question.

'I suspect I'd have been in the same position had I remained. Basil becomes more like his mother as time passes – and that is not a compliment.' Felicia recalled the tiresome frugality found in Lady Brook's domain and shuddered at the memory.

'I gather she was not well liked.'

Felicia thought it better not to reply to this leading remark. Instead, she considered what she'd learned regarding Basil. 'I do not recall Basil was so occupied with making money or the multiplying of it,' she mused.

'That is undoubtedly better than gambling it away, but the acquisition of money can become as much of an obsession as gaming. Tell me, did he begrudge giving charity, or was he reluctant to pay his share of an expense?'

'Neither he nor his mother parted with a crown if half a crown might do.'

'I attempted to meet with your late father's solicitor and found he is out of the city. At least, that is what the sprout in the office told me. I'd not give a farthing for his veracity.'

'My, we seem to be surrounded by cads and liars and cheats,' Felicia said, thinking back to the frightening experience with those bullies at St Paul's. 'Those boys mentioned a Molly who would pay well for me. Is she what I think she is?' Felicia asked hesitantly, not wishing to ask, yet knowing he would be the one with an answer.

'That she is an abbess, or what some call a madam?' he replied grimly. 'Do you realize now how foolish you were? Please – spare my nerves and never do anything like that again. I vow I lost a year's growth when I saw you on those steps with those bully boys coming at you.'

Felicia's eyes widened at his words. She'd not expected to hear anything like that from his lordship. 'Indeed,' she answered meekly. Her stubbornness had given her trouble again, and she had best learn to judge the difference between interference and sensible warnings. 'I shall take care to have Primrose go with me when next I venture forth.'

'See that you do,' came the curt reply. Lord Chessyre leaned back against the squabs and looked out at the passing buildings.

Felicia bent her head to check on the cat, who looked to be most confused.

'Have a name?' came the laconic query from the other side of the carriage.

'Merlin? He needed a bit of magic back there, did he not?' Felicia said with a shy smile.

The frost thawed considerably when her gaze met his. How lovely it was when they weren't at odds with one another.

Lady Emma was as the earl had predicted. When he told her the horrifying tale of Felicia's rescue of the cat and his deliverance of Felicia, her ladyship clutched her bosom and sank onto the nearest chair with a dramatic sigh.

It was then they learned there was a guest in the drawing room.

'Done like a true Chessyre, right, Pelham?' her ladyship cried.

Felicia turned to discover a distinguished older gentleman sitting on the far side of the room close to the fireplace. He rose at these words and moved forward to greet Felicia and Lord Chessyre.

'Lord Pelham, an old friend of mine.' Lady Emma cast a wistful look at the man who approached, and Felicia suddenly knew why Lady Emma had wanted to come to London. She'd learn the particulars later, that was certain. Lady Emma had a difficult time keeping anything secret for long.

'Back from your travels, eh, Pelham? Where were you this trip?' the earl queried jovially. To Felicia he added as an aside, 'Pelham is a traveler *extraordinaire*. There are few places on this globe he has not investigated.'

'Lapland. Fascinating place. Remind me sometime to regale you with a few of the episodes not suitable for feminine ears.'

'Lord Pelham, indeed, you are a rascal. When will you ever settle down to manage your estate?' Lady Emma inquired with a very casual attitude. Politeness, nothing more.

'Actually, I am giving up the travels. Injured my leg this trip. Too old to be jauntering about the world anymore. Decided I'll settle down and write a book. That's what all the old gaffers do, is it not?'

he concluded with a dry laugh.

'Really?' Lady Emma said, darting a glance at her nephew. 'You must come to dine with us this very week. I would hear all about the latest journey.'

'Dear Lady Emma, you are my best listener, I vow. Well, if you have the same cook, I'll never say no. Many a time I have recalled the fine meals at your table while dining on some strange food in the wilds.'

'The country of the Laplander,' Lady Emma said quietly. 'That must have been cold. And with a hurt leg? You poor man, what trials you have endured.'

Felicia watched another moment while Lady Emma and Lord Pelham walked over to the window and continued to chat. Then a faint meow reminded her that she had a duty to perform, and Lady Emma was beyond needing a chaperone.

'You join me, my lord?' Felicia queried softly before she left the room. He paused at her side, glanced back at the pair by the window, then nodded, but on the floor below left her to go to his library while she went on to the kitchen.

The cat didn't take kindly to a bath. It was the only way Felicia could stand to have the animal in the house – what with fleas and all. Her own clothes would need treating, she was certain of that.

'Poor thing is starved. Pierre, is there a scrap or two for Merlin?' Felicia begged. 'Oh, by the way, Lord Pelham is abovestairs. He was most complimentary on your cooking. Said while he was off in some wild country he thought longingly of the meals he had here.'

The pleased cook deigned to offer Merlin a handsome collection of scraps, which Felicia removed to a far corner where the cat would be out of the way.

The earl entered the kitchen at that point and everything became restrained. 'Cat all better?' he asked, then after a look at Felicia added, 'Miss Brook, may I suggest that you consider a change of clothing? You are wet and disheveled.'

His observation was such not to endear him to a girl, Felicia thought. 'Indeed, I was about to go to my room as soon as Merlin finished eating. I'd not have it encounter Cleo just yet.'

'Wise move.' He stood back to allow Felicia and the cat to leave the kitchen and watched her hurry up the stairs to her room on the first floor.

Felicia found Primrose waiting for her. One look and the abigail whisked the offending dress from Felicia with muttered scolding all the while. 'Finally, get you some decent clothes, and you are bent on ruination. All fer some dratted cat.'

Merlin stretched out on the bed, curled up, and commenced a most ragged purr.

'He's not had an easy life,' Felicia said by way of excuse. 'Who has, I'd like to know?' the maid demanded.

Felicia quickly donned another of her pretty new gowns, then sent Primrose with the one she'd removed to clean it and rid it of any fleas.

About an hour later, Lady Emma knocked hesitantly on Felicia's door, entering quickly when bade.

'What did you think of Lord Pelham, my dear?' she inquired after a bit of conversation.

'He seems an interesting gentleman. I fancy you could listen to his tales for hours,' Felicia said, sympathetic to her dear employer.

'I have waited for that man for twenty-three years. I intend to wait no longer. We will be married, and before long, if I have my say,' the delicate lady said firmly, most out of character. 'I'd appreciate your help – if you think of anything to the point,' her ladyship said meekly to Felicia, lapsing back into her more usual preoccupied ways. She walked to the window, absently toying with her chiffon scarf.

'I do not see how he can resist someone who has a memorable cook, a sympathetic ear, and a charming smile,' Felicia said fondly. 'He will be yours before you know it.'

'Indeed! I have waited quite long enough.'

Chapter Four

Merlin demanded Felicia's attention, and Lady Emma moved to leave her room, but not before adding, 'I shall quite depend upon your support, dear girl. I suspect I am out of touch with how to bring a gentleman up to scratch. There are most likely new stratagems not considered when I was a girl.'

'Lady Emma,' Felicia said as that lady paused at the open door, 'I truly haven't a clue how to go about the matter. I have not had any success to date,' she ended, reminding her ladyship that she was twenty and still unmarried, not that she'd had a chance to so much as look for a husband. At the few rural assemblies Felicia had attended, the local gentlemen had been well aware of her impecunious status and turned elsewhere, although not to Willa, much to Lady Brook's fury.

'But then, you were not in London, were you?' Lady Emma replied before drifting off along the hall.

Felicia looked to the cat, who was admittedly still bedraggled, but at least now clean. 'I do not know what that has to say to anything. It is not as though I were a staggering beauty, or moved in the upper strata of society. Now if I had a decent portion or were an heiress – well, that might be another thing altogether.'

Merlin merely meowed and looked pitiful. Feeling sorry for the poor thing, Felicia cuddled the cat into an old scarf that she ought to have thrown out but hadn't. She thought long and hard before tossing out a garment. If it might be turned or taken apart and made into something else, it remained in her wardrobe.

Primrose bustled into the room, carrying an off-white gown Felicia didn't recognize. 'This just come a bit ago from Madame Clotilde, so the box says. I saw her ladyship, and she says to tell you this is to wear to the opera come Saturday night.'

'But I have a presentable gown for that evening,' Felicia objected, while admiring the delectable fabric that reminded her of a soft cloud. 'Really, this is too much.'

'Perhaps 'tis a bit like a livery, miss? She has her footman in blue and silver and puts you in white?' Primrose offered with a tilt of her head.

Felicia made a wry face at her maid. 'Put like that, I can scarcely refuse to wear it, can I?' She took the gown from her maid and held it against her. Her reflection in the looking glass was charming, perhaps too charming for a companion? But then, she was hardly the usual sort of companion, was she? In her understanding, companions did not have a maid, nor an elegant bedroom like this one.

She placed the gown in Primrose's care and left to seek out Lady Emma, whether to scold or to merely thank, she was not certain.

Thinking she might find her ladyship in the little breakfast room she favored, Felicia hurried down the stairs, rushing around the corner at the bottom to run full tilt into Lord Chessyre. 'Oh! Forgive me, sir. I was, ah, looking for your aunt.' Felicia knew she blushed and backed away into a more dimly lit portion of the hall until her face could return to a more normal hue.

He turned from wherever he intended to go to walk at her side to the breakfast room, much to her discomfiture.

'Aunt informs me we are to attend the opera Saturday evening. I trust you will have recovered from your disastrous outing to St Paul's by then. You enjoy music?' he asked with the cool civility she'd heard in his voice before.

'Indeed,' she replied more warmly than she might otherwise have said, desiring an opportunity to see a glittering production of which she had heard much and not expected to view. 'I find it most pleasant, although I have attended only small concerts in the country before this. I look forward to the experience.'

'Do you play the pianoforte?' he queried before ushering her into the breakfast room, where Lady Emma sat at her needlework.

'I do, sir, but very poorly. I should practice more, but never seem to find the time,' she confessed.

'Good,' Lady Emma said from her chair by the window, looking up to the pair entering. 'You can play while I entertain. I have always wanted to have someone who could play while I serve tea.'

Felicia glanced at his lordship, uncertain what to say. 'About the dress,' she ventured to Lady Emma when she thought his attention had been caught by the newspaper on the table. 'You really ought not, you know,' she said in a near whisper.

'Ought not what?' his lordship asked quick as a wink.

'I saw the prettiest fabric at Madame Clotilde's that quite reminded me of Miss Brook, and so I had it made up in a simple enough style. I believe she intends to scold me,' Lady Emma pouted, recalling to mind a thwarted child.

'Quibbling again?' he queried Felicia with that remote expression that she was coming to dislike very much.

'No, that is, I am sure no other companion in all of London has such a lovely wardrobe as mine. You are too kind, Lady Emma. I scarce know what to say,' Felicia cried, trying to be composed and sure that she failed.

'Wear them in good health and help me,' her ladyship said with a sharp glance at Felicia that immediately turned vague when her nephew looked at her. 'Besides, it is the grand opening of the opera for the winter season. All who are in town at present will be there. I would have you make a good impression. I believe Lord Pelham is to join us,' she concluded with a meaningful look at Felicia.

Felicia interpreted that sharp gaze and the plea for help as having a connection with her ladyship's plan to marry Lord Pelham. Felicia was happy to do what she could, but failed to think what it might be.

Lord Chessyre studied his aunt a few moments, then turned to Felicia. 'You were deprived of your day out yesterday. Since you say you are quite recovered, I propose to guide you to several places of interest tomorrow, if that is agreeable.'

'I came to no harm, sir.' Then Felicia frowned at his lordship, adding, 'However, it is not in the least necessary for you to guide me about London. I shall take Primrose with me next Tuesday, and we shall do very well.'

'It would be far better for you to have William as your escort, my dear,' Lady Emma inserted. 'He knows everything of interest in and about London.'

'I am certain he does, but I am equally certain that he has far more important things to do with his time than to guide your companion about London!' Felicia said with as much civility as she could muster. For some unexplained reason, she wanted to avoid his lordship as much as possible.

'I should like you to be acquainted with the city,' her ladyship reflected. 'It would not do at all were you to be uninformed and one of my guests wished to speak on some exhibition or whatever,' she concluded obscurely.

Felicia was definitely at sea. In her limited experience, companions were to be seen and not heard. However, if Lady Emma desired her to chat with callers and entertain them in some manner – when she wasn't playing the pianoforte – she had best go along with her wishes for now.

Accordingly, the next afternoon at one of the clock Felicia presented herself in the small salon on the ground floor, dressed in her new pelisse with the dainty ermine muff in a gloved hand and a modest velvet bonnet on her head.

'The carriage is waiting. Shall we go?' Lord Chessyre inquired from the hall.

She was most fortunate to have him as escort, but she wondered just where he would take her. Felicia obediently walked from the small salon out to where a splendid shiny black curricule with wheels picked out in yellow and drawn by a fine roan awaited them.

It was a nippy day, but with a lovely warm fur robe arranged over her lap and her hands tucked into her new muff, Felicia decided she didn't mind in the least.

'I believe it best to acquire an overview of the city before settling on any one particular sight to inspect more closely. You may discover some of the touted attractions not to your liking in the least. Do you still have an interest in viewing St Paul's? Or would you prefer prowling about Bailey's glass shop in St Paul's churchyard? There is also Wedgwood in St James's Square. Are you attracted to viewing paintings or seeing what is on display at Bullock's Egyptian Hall on Piccadilly?' he asked with a hint of amusement. 'Perhaps Somerset House is to your liking?'

'You must know very well that I do not have the slightest notion of what is best to be seen. However, I stopped at Hatchard's yesterday while on an errand for your aunt and purchased a small guide, the *Picture of London* for this past year. A perusal of this leaves me to believe that if I were to spend every one of my days off, I could not begin to see all of interest in two years!'

He laughed at that bit of nonsense, and suddenly the day appeared brighter and the air a trifle milder. They traveled along the various streets of the metropolis with Lord Chessyre offering instruction on anything of import as they went. She discovered that the places of interest that most appealed to her were within easy reach.

He instructed her regarding the use of hackneys, reminding her to always take note of the hackney's number before venturing inside. 'This way,' he advised, 'should there be any difficulties, you will have the number and can complain about that particular jarvey.'

'I doubt I would do such a thing, but I appreciate your suggestion. I have discovered Primrose does very well at handling matters I find difficult.'

He glanced at her, then turned his attention to the traffic surrounding them. It seemed to Felicia that there was an incredible press of vehicles. She sat quietly while her guide negotiated the throng of carriages, looking idly at the people they passed. Then she sat up straighter, for there was her cousin stepping along the street and looking more smug than usual.

'I see Basil is settling into London very well. At least he does not appear the least unhappy,' she commented to Lord Chessyre.

'He walks? I should have thought he would have sprung for a carriage.'

'I expect that my cousin prefers the simpler life,' Felicia replied tactfully, suspecting Basil did not want to spend the money required to set up a stable in the city. 'He has seen us. Must we stop?'

Lord Chessyre nodded, then expertly guided his horse and carriage to the curbing. 'Good day, Brook.'

Looking most gratified at receiving notice from one of the premier gentlemen of London, Basil bowed most correctly, then cast a bland look at Felicia. 'Keeping busy, Cousin?'

'Lady Emma desires that I become acquainted with the city so that I may intelligently converse with her guests,' Felicia said while wondering what Basil was doing in this particular area. 'You have found a residence?'

'A tolerable place not too far from here,' he replied with a superior smile. 'I have rooms on the second floor for only five guineas a week. You may be certain I was very particular about what is to be furnished with the rooms.'

'How nice,' Felicia said faintly. 'I fear we must be going. I would not keep Lord Chessyre's horse standing in this weather.' Why was it that when she spoke with her cousin, the air grew colder and the sun disappeared behind clouds?

'I will see you soon, Cousin,' he said. To Felicia his words had an ominous sound.

'I think it rather strange that my cousin lets Brook House and rents rooms elsewhere while he is in the city,' Felicia said softly, although it was all of a piece with his not keeping a carriage. He might have rented equipage, however, and not have been compelled to walk.

Lord Chessyre was silent for a few moments, then said, 'He is able to rent rooms on the second floor of a private home for far less than it would take to open Brook House for himself. In addition, he may desire the income from the rental. A house in the better part of the city can bring in close to a thousand pounds for the Season.'

'A thousand pounds! Never say so,' Felicia whispered. She could easily see why Basil preferred to rent and expected he would be content. It seemed to her that he now placed more interest in making money than enjoying comfort.

When at last they returned to Lady Emma's house, Felicia had rosy cheeks and was somewhat chilled. Yet she'd not have forgone the experience of dashing about London with such a knowledgeable gentleman for all the toasty warmth to be had. The only contrary aspect was that the drive had made Lord Chessyre far too appealing. In spite of his reserved manner, she had seen a sensible and charming side of him, one that attracted her. And she had too much common sense to allow that to happen. Something would have to be done before she permitted that attraction to grow out of hand.

There were several people in the drawing room when Felicia entered by herself, Lord Chessyre having gone off to attend to some business of his own. Lord Pelham sat in the chair closest to the fireplace, seeming to like the warmth. Felicia crossed the room to join him.

'Good afternoon, Lord Pelham. I trust you do not find this cold too hard to endure?'

'Warmer than up near the North Pole, you know,' he said gruffly.

'I expect that no one goes near there in the winter,' she replied sedately.

Attired in a new gown of misty rose crepe with tiers of delicate embroidery, Lady Emma looked like a confection. She signaled to Felicia to join her.

'Will you play now? Something romantic, I believe,' Lady Emma said, darting a glance to where Lord Pelham nursed his leg by the fireside.

Romantic music? What in the world was *romantic* music? Slipping across to the pianoforte, Felicia hoped her poor skills were up to the task. She began with a fine rendition of 'Für Elise,' then softly played several simple French pieces she knew by heart. Fortunately, there was a pile of music on the floor next to the instrument. After a hasty perusal, within minutes she was again playing simple pieces well up to her skill. She continued to play quietly, thinking that they might wish to talk, not listen to her.

When Alford entered the room with the silver tray containing the pots of tea and hot water along with various plates of biscuits and cakes, Felicia was beginning to believe that she would definitely earn her wages were this to be required often.

Once Lord Pelham had finished most of the biscuits and cakes and several cups of bohea tea, he rose to leave. Felicia thought he did so reluctantly. He paused at the pianoforte and murmured, 'You must be a great comfort to Lady Emma, child. She is fortunate to have such a companion.' Then he left.

Within minutes the remainder of the callers in the drawing room had also gone.

'Those dreadful tabbies,' Lady Emma declared when the door had closed on the last of the women. 'They all hope to entrap Lord Pelham. Word has spread that he intends to make his home in England with no more roaming the world. There are widows aplenty who would like very much to be Lady Pelham.'

'You are the prettiest, I vow. And,' Felicia added with a twinkle in her eyes, 'you have the additional advantage of having a chef much to Lord Pelham's liking. I observed that he ate his biscuits and cakes with great relish.'

'Someone once said that the way to a man's heart is through his stomach. Perhaps that is true,' Lady Emma said, her eyes large with speculation. Then she turned to Felicia and nodded, 'I think you did very well with the pianoforte. It is not necessary to astound listeners, I believe. It is well enough to play pleasant pieces.'

'Were they sufficiently romantic, my lady?' Felicia dared to ask.

'Indeed, I think they were. We shall explore that stack of music tomorrow and see what else might lurk there. I believe I shall enjoy the pursuit of Lord Pelham very much.'

Felicia reflected that if she had Lady Emma's fortune, position in society, and a nephew who would indulge her every whim, she might enjoy such a thing as well.

Come Saturday evening following a splendid dinner at which Lord Pelham revealed the full extent of his pleasure in excellent food, they left for the opera.

In Felicia's modest estimation her new gown was a success. At any rate, Lord Chessyre had looked at her with something approximating admiration, and Lady Emma had declared herself most pleased with her companion. Felicia thought the luminescent beauty of her pearls most satisfying when worn with the new gown. How nice that they were hers again.

Their box was situated so that the stage was in excellent view – as were the other boxes and the pit. Felicia settled onto her chair, cautiously looking about with a curious gaze. She had never imagined anything quite so magnificent as the interior of the opera house.

The fronts of the boxes were painted silver with small gold frames, and each tier varied in decoration with wreaths, festoons, and cherubs in abundance. Looking up, she was delighted to see the dome painted to represent a sky.

'You like our opera house?' Lord Chessyre said quietly so as not to disturb her aunt who was in animated conversation with Lord Pelham.

'The whole effect is rich and quite magnificent,' Felicia said, taking another look at the closest cherub.

'It is within two feet of the size of the opera house in Milan,' he offered.

'Impressive, indeed,' Felicia replied, repressing a smile. As though she would ever see the Milan edifice to make a comparison.

'The boxes hold nearly nine hundred persons, and I would hazard a guess that all will be filled this evening. Catalani always draws a crowd.' He most casually placed his arm across the back of Felicia's chair in order to lean closer so he might point out various personages in attendance. There were women in gorgeous gowns and elegant gentlemen in great numbers. Enough jewelry to stock a shop bedecked the ladies, Felicia was certain.

She glanced to Lady Emma to see how she fared. If Felicia was to assist in her ladyship's plan to lure Lord Pelham, surely Felicia ought to be doing something?

'Christmas is coming before long. I have made arrangements so we may attend the concert of the Cecilian Society. They present but three grand concerts a year – St Cecilia's Day and Christmas Eve as well as one other they choose. Since you enjoy music, I think you will like it.'

Christmas. Would she still be with Lady Emma? She wondered precisely how long it would be before she must depart for one reason or another. Were she a wise woman, she would be searching for a possible position elsewhere.

At the intermission, Felicia sat quietly, reflecting on the glorious music that had enticed her ears. Had she ever expected to hear such magnificent sound?

'I gather, from the rapt expression on your face, that you enjoyed the music,' Lord Chessyre commented at her side.

'Very much, indeed,' Felicia replied, coming down from her cloud. 'It would have been better had those tiresome people in the audience remained silent. Why do they come to the opera if they do not wish to listen?' she complained.

Her companion laughed. 'They come to gossip, to see and be seen, and above all to show off the latest in gowns and evening hats. One does not have to like music to attend the opera.'

Felicia thought she liked the sound of his laughter very much. It was a rich sound of pure enjoyment with no malice in it. She recalled his aunt's words to the effect that Lord Chessyre had been disappointed in his plans to marry and did not believe in love. That was a tragedy. Not that Felicia was in love with him; she didn't particularly like him. However, she did feel sorry for one who professed not to believe in love. Still, he was a considerate man, kind to his aunt, and civil to his employees. And she was greatly indebted to him for this treat.

The curtains behind them parted, and a woman of charming appearance entered, followed by a dashing gentleman. Rather than look to Lord Chessyre, as might have been expected, the lady made her bow to Lady Emma and greeted Lord Pelham with grace. She introduced her companion, then turned to the man she sought.

'When shall I persuade you to sit for me, sir?' she asked Lord

Pelham with a hint of roguishness in her manner.

'Miss Brook, allow me to present Mrs Damer, the noted sculptress. I believe she would like to immortalize the lion of the moment, for Lord Pelham is quite famous for his travels, you know,' Lady Emma said, all politeness.

Felicia sensed that Lady Emma felt Mrs Damer to be a threat to her ladyship's future hopes.

'I cannot believe that my old phiz would be of interest to anyone,' Lord Pelham inserted, looking far too pleased at the notion for even Felicia's peace of mind.

'But sir, even the Duke of Wellington was taken with his likeness. I feel certain you might be as well. Come, say you will agree,' Mrs Damer begged prettily.

'You are most persuasive, ma'am,' Lord Pelham replied with a fine bow – in spite of that injured leg. Felicia observed that Lady Emma had also taken note of this and looked rather worried.

'I have always wished to watch a sculptor at work,' Felicia declared suddenly. 'Do you ever permit one to view your work in progress?' She noted that Lord Chessyre stiffened at her words. Perhaps he considered such behavior improper. Pity. She thought that perhaps she might manage to watch while Lord Pelham was having his like- ness taken, thus preventing anything truly improper from occurring and protecting Lady Emma's interests at the same time.

Mrs Damer gave Felicia an amused look. 'You wish to observe Lord Pelham during his sitting?' she rightly guessed.

'If his lordship would not take it amiss,' Felicia said modestly, cast- ing a hopeful look at Lady Emma.

That lady suddenly smiled and nodded. 'I think it would be a very fine thing for you, Felicia. I do hope you will permit her viewing, Mrs Damer. Miss Brook is in London to observe and learn. This will be an enlightening experience for her.'

Mrs Damer glanced from one woman to the other and smiled briefly. 'Once Lord Pelham agrees to a time for his sitting I shall notify you, Miss Brook. I assure you that you will find it a most, er, enlightening experience. Good evening.' She nodded to Lord

Chessyre and swept from the box, her escort following.

'You desire enlightening experiences?' Lord Chessyre queried with an odd expression in his eyes.

'It was the first thing I could think of, bearing in mind your aunt and her wishes,' Felicia explained.

'My aunt?' the earl questioned, casting glances first at his relative, then her escort.

'You must know that she desires a closer connection with his lordship,' Felicia whispered.

The fleeting grin that crossed the earl's face made Felicia long to bring laughter and delight to him more often. He was undoubtedly a handsome man, but far too serious. He needed amusement.

The remainder of the opera was lost to her in her reflections that it would be a good thing for her to hunt for some other position as soon as may be. She was coming to like the earl, and that was not good. He showed little interest in her – indeed, why should he? As well – an attraction to the aloof gentleman at her side could only bring disaster and heartache.

Once at the Chessyre home they were served a late supper, which Lord Pelham found much to his liking. He complimented Lady Emma on the selection of dishes and her chef, jesting that were she not careful he would steal the chap away.

It was very tempting to inquire why Lord Pelham simply did not marry Lady Emma and acquire the best of both worlds. Felicia heroically refrained from such improper words, true though they might be.

A clue to his thinking came when Lord Chessyre was asking his aunt about something or other and Lord Pelham turned to Emma.

'Lady Emma has little need for company with you and her nephew at her side, I think. It is agreeable to have young people around.' He looked wistful, Felicia thought, as though he rather missed younger people in his house.

'Lady Emma is not all that old, sir. She cannot be but in her early forties, being the youngest of his lordship's aunts. I have an aunt who gave birth at three and forty. What a pity her ladyship has never married. I wonder why?' Felicia asked daringly.

'She is a charming lady,' he mused.

'Surely she must have had numerous offers over the years.' Felicia knew she overstepped the bounds of what was proper, but she so wished to help the woman who had been so kind to her.

'True, true,' he reflected with a perusal of her ladyship.

Lady Emma was in fine looks this evening, wearing a becoming rose gown that reflected pretty color into her cheeks. Her animated conversation with her nephew brought a sparkle to her eyes, and when she laughed, it could be readily seen that her ladyship yet possessed all her teeth – something a good many women could not claim.

Lord Pelham said no more on the matter, and Felicia dared not pursue the topic. She had gone beyond what was permissible as it was, speaking of such personal matters to a gentleman she scarcely knew.

'You will sit for Anne Damer, will you not, Pelham? If only to please Miss Brook, who intends to watch the process with great attention,' Lord Chessyre joked.

'You will find Mrs Damer's home most curious,' Lady Emma added. 'She was bequeathed Strawberry Hill by Mr Horace Walpole, and if you have read nothing about the place, you are in for a surprise.'

'I fear that was not a part of my education,' Felicia replied with lively interest.

'The house is a Gothic monstrosity,' Lord Chessyre said with a wry look. 'There are enough pointed Gothic arches to satisfy the most exalted of bishops. The furniture looks as though it came from some ancient monastery.'

'There is reputed to be a copy of a Renaissance pergola taken from the Borghese villa at Frascati. I should like to see if it approximates the original, which I saw a few years ago,' Lord Pelham added enthusiastically.

'He began with a small home and kept expanding and adding Gothic elements and decor – every room is stuffed with objects. He was deliberately outrageous, I believe,' Lord Chessyre said, again with the wry note in his voice. 'I understand Mrs Damer offers amateur theatrical productions in the large drawing room – Gothic dramas, most likely. The house is well suited to the mood.'

'I cannot wait to see it,' Felicia said, an idea taking root in her mind. This might well be the solution to her dilemma, if she could play her cards correctly.

Chapter Five

'**M**y dear Lady Emma, do you not see? It would seem that Lord Pelham believes you to be in an excellent state with a nephew to dote on you and me for a companion. I suspect that he thinks you quite well off without a gentleman at your side. If you truly wish him to propose marriage, it may be that he must come to feel that you need *him*.'

'I always knew that Reginald, that is, Lord Pelham, was a nodcock, but this proves it,' Lady Emma declared. She rose from the slipper chair by the fireplace in Felicia's room to pace back and forth, deep in thought. 'How could he not think that I need a spouse? When William marries, I will be alone!'

'I had not realized that Lord Chessyre was to be married. Is the event to take place soon?' Felicia inquired carefully. Odd, that restriction in her chest. It must be something she had at breakfast.

'Heavens, no,' her ladyship said with frustration in her voice. 'I do not know if he has found a suitable woman as yet. He merely asked me if I would mind living here on my own. The only reason for that is if he was to marry. Not that I would begrudge the dear boy. I would that he be happy. I never felt that Sophie was the girl for him. I am pleased she married Viscount Lowell instead. They were cousins, you see, but they married anyway.'

'Close cousins?' Felicia inquired, curious about the woman Lord Chessyre had sought to wed.

'No,' Lady Emma said after some thought. 'Perhaps third or fourth once removed or something of the sort.'

'But Lord Chessyre withdrew from Society or was obviously unhappy following the wedding?' Felicia asked, pursuing the topic of poor Lord Chessyre. She could imagine those gray eyes stricken with grief or longing.

'Now that I think on it, he did not seem desolated, merely quiet. Perhaps it just gave him pause.'

'Or perhaps he resolved to find a woman he could love, if indeed the Lowell marriage was a love match,' Felicia concluded slowly.

'I suppose that is possible. However, our speculation does not solve the problem of dear Reginald. I turned down other proposals, you know – a good many of them.'

'He wondered if you had,' Felicia remarked.

'Did he, now?' Lady Emma cried with great interest. 'And what else did he have to say, pray tell?'

So Felicia revealed as best she could of her conversation with Lord Pelham following the supper after the opera.

'Which brings me to the matter at hand. If I were to become attached to Mrs Damer's household in some manner, you would be left alone and quite vulnerable. Correct? And perhaps *then* he would feel you need a protector.'

'I need more than a protector, girl. I need a husband,' Lady Emma said dryly, for once the vagueness utterly gone from her speech. 'Cleo is a poor substitute.'

'Do not all single women?' Felicia muttered to Merlin curled on her lap in unaccustomed luxury. His looks had improved a bit what with all the tidbits he received from the chef and various members of the household.

'Well, we will have to do what we can. First of all, you must attend the sculpting sessions when Reginald goes to that house. She promised to let you know, but I shall inquire of Reginald as well. I do not trust that woman, the way she looked at Reginald. It is not proper to stare at a man so much.'

At that moment Cleo came dashing into Felicia's room, yapping and dancing about as she did when wanting a walk. Felicia tucked Merlin aside and rose to find her pelisse.

'I shall take Cleo for a walk and think on the matter. You consider it as well. Two heads and all that,' Felicia said before leaving her room to find Cleo's leash.

Some distance away in the heart of the city, Lord Chessyre sat in the musty office belonging to Aloysius Smithers. William marveled that anyone as astute as the late Baron Brook was reputed to have been could have employed this beetle-headed old fool.

'You must have a copy of the will in your files,' William insisted, using his most intimidating stare on the man.

Smithers was flustered, and William would have sworn that he was hiding something from him, but how to know?

'Files?' the man repeated in a stupid fuddle. 'Oh, yes, I expect I do have a copy somewhere. I recently fired my clerk for incompetence, my lord. I fear that my records are in somewhat of a muddle. I could not guess how long it might take to find the document.'

William wanted to add that the man's brains were in like disorder, but refrained. He rubbed his chin while considering his options.

'There is a copy in the court records, I trust?' William asked sternly. 'The will had to be approved as written?'

'The last will *and* testament of George, Lord Brook, was duly entered in court records. Of course you are aware that a testament and a will are not the same. A will is limited to land and a testament to chattels, the latter requiring executors. Every testament is a will, but every will is not a testament.' The solicitor pointed out this rather basic information to William as though revealing a hidden secret of great importance.

William nodded patiently, thinking that if he allowed the chap to drone on long enough he might say something of worth.

'Who were the witnesses?' William thought to inquire.

'The steward and the housekeeper, neither of whom were to gain much by the will.' The solicitor smirked, William would have sworn he did, although his expression sobered immediately.

'And they are now where?' Lord Chessyre asked, leaning forward with the hope he might actually learn something of value. It was surprising that the solicitor, who was so vague about all else, could recall the names of witnesses to a will he wasn't sure he could locate.

'The steward was unfortunately killed in a carriage accident recently, and the housekeeper died of natural causes – a heart ailment, I believe.' Smithers drummed his fingers on his desk, most likely wishing William to perdition, but not daring to order a peer of the realm from his office.

William leaned back once again, rubbing his chin while contemplating the chances of both witnesses to a will dying within four years after that occasion. 'Lord Brook signed the will in their presence?'

'Ah, er, no, that is, his seal was affixed to the document. I believe he was too ill to sign his name.'

'So there was no more than his X mark?' There was definitely an odor in the air, and not a good one.

'That is correct.' Smithers shifted in his chair, uneasily, William thought. 'The judge decided that a mark is sufficient, even in the case where the testator was able to write. The seal was affixed because property was involved. In Warneford versus Warneford, Raymond, the chief justice, ruled that sealing a will is signing with the statute.'

William thought this entire business stunk worse than Billingsgate fish market. Odd that the chap had all this information regarding a four-year-old will on the tip of his tongue, yet was unable to produce same.

'When was the will written?'

'Shortly before his death,' the answer snapped back.

'You did not think to question the omission of his only child from this will? Is that not a bit strange, sir?'

'Not at all, happens all the time. It was not my place to query the contents of the will, merely to see that it conformed to the legalities.'

It was quite obvious that William wasn't going to learn anything more from this character. The chap was cleverly evasive, even if he looked stupid. There must be a loophole in this affair somewhere. William rose and left the musty office before he did or said something he might regret later.

At his own solicitor's office William was dismayed to learn that the sealed, unsigned will had been perfectly legal.

Edmond Harding, eminent solicitor whose practice included some of the highest names in the land, exclaimed, 'It is legal, but is it sufficient? It would be very easy for one person to forge any man's will by this method. Anyone may put on a seal; no particular evidence arises from that seal. Just because Lord Brook's seal is affixed does not mean he put it there; no certainty or guard therefore arises from this seal. In other words, some character who stood to gain from the forged will could have done the deed and legally!'

'Two witnesses are dead,' William explained. 'The solicitor still lives, and I believe he continues to handle the Brook estate matters. Even the man who directly inherited died. It is his son who is the present Lord Brook and a more disgusting piece of goods you cannot imagine. Does this not smack of something unethical?'

'It does indeed. It is difficult to prove fraud without a witness to testify as to the conditions of the affixing of the seal. With the disappearance of two witnesses it will be difficult – but not impossible. Who was the third witness? Every will must have three.'

'Smithers failed to mention him.' William rose from his chair, feeling there ought to be something he could do for Felicia Brook, but wondering what it might be.

'What prompted your interest?' Mr Harding asked.

'Miss Felicia Brook was completely disinherited by her father's will and testament. Tell me, how often does a doting father make a testament without some provision for his only child?' William turned from the window to stare at the man who had so faithfully served him over the years.

'Not so much as a farthing? Never, in my experience. Let me look into this matter to see what may be found. I have no liking for cheating frauds, nor in chaps who are able to murder and not be caught. For that is what is at the bottom of this all – murder.'

William stared at his solicitor, aghast at the implications.

'The heart ailment can be a cover for murder; I've seen poison administered in a number of cases. Nasty business, poison, but often difficult to detect. As well, a bit of skullduggery and a wheel goes, thereby causing the death of a decent man. Happens all too often. It would be satisfying to have one of these people served with his just deserts. The mystery is – who is that third witness?'

William left the office, deep in thought, wondering just how much he ought to reveal to Miss Brook. He supposed he should caution her to avoid her cousin. What could he offer as an explanation? At this point he could prove nothing!

True – there was no reason for Basil to be troubled about Miss Brook. He would think her resigned to her penniless fate. She had taken a position as companion as witness to that fact. All the way back to Chessyre House, William mulled over the problem of Miss Brook. He decided at last that it was best to say nothing for the moment.

And then he had to wonder why it was that he cared so much what happened to her. Something about her had drawn him when they first met at Chessyre Court, yet he had fought against this attraction. He no longer suspected her of plotting to meet him. She had employed none of the usual coy methods he'd observed over the past years. As well, she seemed to avoid him rather than seek him out, quite as though she did not like him!

The very idea that Miss Felicia Brook might not like him was sufficient to shake William to the core. He'd not worried so about Sophie, content with a marriage with no emotional ties. But now he was in a state over this too–slim, quiet girl with her large gray eyes, wide mouth, and soft nut brown curls that framed a delicate, sensitive face.

When he reached Chessyre House, he left his equipage with the groom and stalked inside, looking for Miss Brook. He wanted to see her, note his reaction when he touched her again.

She was not to home.

'She is walking the dog, milord,' Alford explained.

'In the park again?' William wondered.

'I expect so, milord. Leastwise, she went that direction. The dog likes to run a bit, she says.'

William nodded and left the house, headed for the park. He might be correct that she was safe from Basil, but he was not positive about the matter. What if that nasty piece of goods took it into his head to eliminate Felicia as well as the housekeeper and the steward? If a man was mad, he might do anything!

He caught sight of the King Charles spaniel dancing around the hem of Felicia's pelisse while she laughed at the dog's antics, and he sighed with relief. The sight of Felicia's rosy cheeks, the slim, attractive form in the rather nice blue outfit brought him to a momentary halt. What was this peculiar sensation within him?

'Lord Chessyre,' she called upon espying him not so far away, 'have you come to see Cleo do her tricks?'

Gathering his wits about him, William joined Miss Brook, offering his arm – which she declined with a complete lack of fluttering lashes or simpering smiles.

Leaning over, Miss Brook snapped her fingers and commanded the dog to roll over, which, amazingly enough, it did. Then the animal sat up to beg a biscuit from Miss Brook. She snapped it neatly with the sharp teeth that usually preferred William's bedroom slippers.

'Toss a stick. With any luck at all Cleo will fetch it.' Felicia glanced at William, her eyes alive with mischief.

Her laughter was infectious, and William found himself smiling back at her. He tossed a small stick, and when ordered to fetch by the charming girl at William's side, the spaniel trotted off to return it nicely, her little buggy eyes seeming to beam with pride.

'You have done marvels with Cleo.' William had never believed the stupid animal capable of learning anything. It kept chewing slippers without cease, no matter how often scolded. It was extraordinary what Miss Brook had accomplished in so short a time.

'Thank you. Pity I shan't likely have a chance to work longer with the dog.' She snapped on the leash and turned in the direction of Chessyre House.

'Why ever not?' William demanded, a cold knot forming in his stomach.

'I am going to try to work my way into Mrs Damer's household if possible. I hope to be gone soon.' She looked up at William, her gray eyes questioning his interest.

'You cannot mean that!' William declared. He offered his arm again. This time she placed her hand rather tentatively on the fine Bath cloth that covered that arm. Odd, how protective it made him feel toward her. He couldn't recall feeling like this before, either.

Felicia looked at the man glaring at her in such a thunderous manner. 'I must.' Should she tell him of the plan to keep an eye on Lord Pelham lest he take a notion to court Mrs Damer? The lady was most attractive, even if a bit eccentric. But if Felicia could move there, she could watch Lord Pelham and perhaps lead him to believe Lady Emma needed him.

'Why?' William covered her hand with his other, quite as though he feared she might run off. Considering that awesome frown, she might well think about doing just that.

'You may as well know, for she is your aunt, after all. Lady Emma is concerned that Lord Pelham will entertain silly notions while having Mrs Damer take his likeness. She is a pretty woman, you know,' Felicia added, in the event Lord Chessyre had not paid proper attention to Mrs Damer.

'I hadn't noticed. I do not think it necessary for you to move to Strawberry Hill merely to keep an eye on Pelham.'

'I fail to see why not,' Felicia argued. She chanced a glance at her escort and discovered a rather frustrated expression on his face. 'Besides, I wish Lord Pelham to see that Lady Emma needs him.'

William wondered what he ought to do. Should he relate his fears regarding Basil? Ought he tell Miss Brook that he preferred to have her safely beneath his roof, so that in the event Basil decided to do away with her, William could keep her from harm?

He needed time. Edmond Harding had promised to look into the matter of the will and the other witness, and that would not be done in a day or two. William knew that it could take a week or longer. In the meanwhile, Felicia Brook could be in danger!

'You promised to be a companion to my aunt. That was the reason you did not go with Basil and his sister, as I recall,' William said, evading the issue for the moment.

'But it is your aunt who desires me to do this,' Miss Brook argued. She attempted to draw away from him, but William clamped her hand firmly on his arm and walked even closer at her side.

'We shall see about that,' William bit out, thinking that never before in his life had he known such a peculiar mixture of emotions. He wanted Felicia Brook safe in his house, and he knew a strong urge to shake sense into this exasperating female. He also experienced a desire to see what it might be like to kiss the generous mouth that now had firmed into a mutinous line.

The remainder of the walk was accomplished in silence.

Alford took Cleo, disappearing to the rear of the house, no doubt to dry muddy paws. This left Felicia alone with Lord Chessyre, who stared at her in the most disconcerting manner imaginable.

'I did promise your aunt that I would help her with Lord Pelham, you know,' she said at last when he failed to say anything.

'Perhaps. . . . Perhaps you should actually see Strawberry Hill before you commit yourself. I believe one should be prepared for any eventualities.'

Felicia knew the strangest reaction to his clasp of her hand. He'd not let it free, and now he drew closer to her. Surely he dared not kiss her while standing in the entry of his house? It seemed he did.

It was a mere whisper of a kiss, over before she had a chance to react, to register its effect.

He looked down at her hand, then back to meet her gaze. 'Forgive me,' he begged softly. 'I'd not meant to do that.'

Felicia pulled her hand from his light clasp and wordlessly rushed up the stairs, pausing at the top to look back to where he still stood, watching her. She had intended to ask him if he had learned anything of import regarding the will, and now she dared not seek him out to inquire. It wasn't that she didn't trust him. She didn't trust herself!

William shook his head as though waking from a sleep. Miss Brook had disappeared from view, and he wandered down the hall into what passed for his library and office in the city. It was small for a book room, but adequate for his needs. Elegantly furnished in mahogany and cherry woods, best of all it had comfortable chairs.

What a stupid thing for him to do – to succumb to the desire that had been building within him. Now Miss Brook – Felicia – would have good reason to leave this house. Prior to this he had kept all interest at bay. He admitted that the true reason he'd wanted her away from Basil and with his aunt was that she intrigued him. Fine kettle of fish he had managed to put himself in now.

'William, dear boy, are you there?' his aunt called from the entry-way. The door slammed behind her, and he could hear parcels being dropped on the hall table.

'In here, Aunt Emma.' He rose from his chair to meet his aunt. He'd have no need to ask her what she wanted; she would open her budget without prompting.

'Have you spoken with Felicia regarding her removal to Strawberry Hill? I believe it can be managed if I plan the matter carefully. I intend to take no chances. I've waited twenty-three years for that man, and I have no intention of allowing some upstart to snabble him now!'

Astounded at his aunt's flurry of speech and what she revealed, William urged her to be seated. 'Do you not think Felicia ought to at least have a look at Strawberry Hill, to see what she might face? And how can you be so certain that Mrs Damer will invite Felicia to stay with her?' William queried with more patience than might be expected, given the nature of his aunt's intentions.

'I learned that Mrs Damer intends to put on an amateur theatrical around Christmas. She adores theatricals, you know. Christmas is very close, and surely she must need assistance.'

'I'll grant you it is possible. So what do you intend?' he prompted, wondering if he ought to let his aunt know about the possibly fraud-ulent will and Basil's likely action when he learned of its being stud-ied after all this time. William had no doubt that the scurrilous Aloysius Smithers would inform his client regarding William's ques-tioning. Could Felicia be safe at Strawberry Hill?

'I shall invite Mrs Damer for dinner as soon as may be. Have you not considered having your likeness done, dear boy?' Aunt Emma gave him an appealing smile that would melt any resistance he might have known. Since he had none, it made matters simple.

'Now that you mention it, I believe it would be an excellent idea. As well, it would give me a chance to be on the scene at Strawberry

Hill. I believe Felicia needs protection.' William leaned against his desk, watching his aunt for her reaction to his words.

'Oh, dear. The reprehensible Basil is up to something?' she queried, a worried frown settling on her brow. 'It has to be him. Not another soul in the world would wish dear Felicia ill.'

'How clever you are. Lord Pelham is as good as in your pocket, my dear.'

'How nice,' Lady Emma said happily. She rose and drifted from the room, a cloud of delicate lavender sarcenet that had floating panels of embroidery. She paused at the door to add, 'I trust you will take care of our dear Felicia. I quite dote on the girl.'

William crossed to stare out at the uninspiring view from his window, his thoughts concentrated on Felicia Brook.

'My dear girl,' Lady Emma cooed, 'William believes Pelham to be as good as mine. I have the most famous plan, you see.'

Felicia turned from the window where she had been staring sight-lessly at scudding clouds overhead to invite her ladyship to be seated by a nicely burning fire.

'And what is your famous plan, may I ask?'

'Well, I thought and thought and decided the best thing would be to invite Mrs Damer for dinner. While here, it can be revealed that dearest William desires to have his likeness taken as well as Pelham. That way we can learn of her plans for the Christmas theatrical production. And you may offer your assistance in doing something – perhaps costumes? You do sew, do you not?'

Felicia considered all the clothing she had cut up and made into something else. 'Indeed, my lady, I sew.'

'Excellent,' Lady Emma said with a happy bounce on the chair.

Merlin looked across at her ladyship from where he curled in a contented ball and yawned.

'What shall I do with the cat?' Felicia wanted to know. 'I can scarcely ask Mrs Damer if I might bring a ragged-looking cat with me. Although he is clean and a trifle more handsome, he has a distance to go before he is presentable.'

Her ladyship shrugged. 'Leave him here. He is no trouble. One of the maids will look after the cat whilst you are at Strawberry Hill. After all, it will not be forever.'

'But if we succeed and you become the affianced bride of Lord Pelham, there will be no reason for me to return to this house,' Felicia pointed out reasonably. The thought of never being here again, not to see Lord Chessyre, was hard to consider, and she tried to put it from her mind.

'The affianced bride,' Lady Emma echoed, sinking into an abstraction that Felicia could see might be of some duration.

Actually, the invitation for dinner went out to Mrs Damer that afternoon, and her gracious acceptance was returned with the footman, bringing a look of smug satisfaction to Lady Emma's charming face. She twitched her dainty lace cap into place and said, 'Felicia, dear girl, we have to dazzle. In fact, I believe it will be necessary for you to dazzle all the while you are at Strawberry Hill.'

When Felicia objected to this plan, she was hushed and told in no uncertain terms that if they were to succeed it was *necessary*.

Another visit to Madame Clotilde was deemed a requirement, and that lady offered quick solutions to their dilemma. Dazzling might take a few days, but it could be accomplished. Lady Emma could shine with a frosted rose crepe ornamented with dainty rosebuds and blond lace.

'And you, Miss Brook, you will dazzle with this.' The mantua-maker produced a shimmery silvery-white fabric against which Felicia's pearls would be perfect. 'Something simple but elegant.' With that description, Felicia had to be satisfied. She'd quickly learned to trust madame's judgment in the matter of design.

And so it was four evenings later that Mrs Damer came to dinner at Chessyre House. Lord Pelham and Chessyre were in attendance and with Chessyre's heir, cousin Stephen Chessyre, awaited the ladies in the drawing room. Stephen had the look of the Chessyres, with the same blond hair and gray eyes, but not as handsome in Felicia's estimation.

It was Stephen who spotted Lady Emma. 'I say, Aunt Emma, you look smashing.' Then he turned to Felicia, obvious in his admiration for the creature in the ethereal silver-white confection of a gown that seemed to shimmer with a life of its own. 'And this is your companion?' he inquired with patent disbelief ringing clear.

'The Honorable Felicia Brook, daughter of the late George, Lord Brook,' Lady Emma announced happily. She seemed quite delighted that her dear Stephen was so taken with Felicia.

They were murmuring trivialities when Mrs Damer arrived, promptly ushered into the drawing room by a respectful Alford.

The evening proceeded precisely as Lady Emma had hoped. Before dinner Lady Emma let drop Lord Chessyre's desire to have his likeness taken by Mrs Damer. The lady raised a brow, but merely nodded her agreement and offered to arrange a time to suit him.

During dinner Lady Emma adroitly queried Mrs Damer regarding her Christmas plans. When informed of the coming theatrical production, Lady Emma remarked – ever so cleverly – that her dearest Felicia was a positive wizard with sewing. That her ladyship had never seen one article – except for the dreadful dress Felicia had worn when she first came to Chessyre Court – made little difference. Mrs Damer, looking rather amused, asked Felicia if she had ever attempted to create costumes and would she like to assist with the coming production.

'Indeed, Miss Brook, you have something of the look of my Gothic heroine – willowy and ethereal. Why do you not plan to stay at Strawberry Hill for a bit? The atmosphere will help tremendously in creating just the right costume.'

Felicia glanced to Lord Chessyre, who nodded imperceptibly, then to Lady Emma, who did the same. There was nothing for it but to accept.

'You are too kind, Mrs Damer. I should enjoy spending time at Strawberry Hill. I have heard much about it.'

'No doubt you have,' the lady replied with a darted glance at Lady Emma. 'I trust you will find everything to your liking.'

Felicia wondered at the dry intonation of those words. No doubt she would learn more of the lady and all the odd circumstances in the days to come. At the moment she could only realize that this would be one of the last times she would be at the Chessyre dining table, seated near Lord Chessyre.

'Capital,' Stephen Chessyre said. 'I do enjoy Strawberry. As I have a part in the play, no doubt I shall see you and often.'

Lord Chessyre frowned. Lady Emma looked pleased. And Mrs Damer merely smiled.

Chapter Six

The ladies withdrew following dinner, settling near the fireplace with polite glances among them. Felicia was conscious of an air of suspicion on the part of Lady Emma and a reaction of amusement from Mrs Damer, her rouged cheeks glowing with color not from the fire's warmth.

'Have you been in London long, Miss Brook?' Mrs Damer wanted to know.

'No. I came to town with Lady Emma about a month or so ago.' Felicia gave no reasons for her employment, nor offered any other particulars.

'And do you stay long?' Mrs Damer queried with a glance at the door. The sound of male voices floated up the stairway, an indication that the women would not be alone for long.

'As long as needs be. Should Lady Emma marry, I will, of course, have to seek another position.' Felicia decided to toss that tidbit into the conversation in hopes it might warn Mrs Damer away from Lord Pelham.

'I see. Is this a recent development, my lady? Are we to wish you happy?' Male voices came closer.

Lady Emma looked as though she could have strangled Felicia, then smiled – a smile that did not reach her eyes. 'One never knows about these things. It has not been decided for certain.'

'And you, Miss Brook. Surely a girl with your charming looks must have numerous offers from which to select.' There was a hint of a question that Felicia decided to answer.

'Not so as one might notice. It has been borne in on me that if one should wish to marry, it is best to have a fortune to hand. I recently heard someone say that single women have a dreadful tendency to be poor, which is an excellent incentive for matrimony.'

'How true,' Mrs Damer replied as the men entered the room.

If the three men noticed any constraint, it wasn't obvious. Lord Pelham strolled over to sit near Lady Emma, complimenting her again on the fineness of the dinner.

Stephen beamed a smile at Felicia and took a seat close to where she perched. 'William tells me he is to have Mrs Damer take his likeness. She's very good, you know. Bound to be an excellent image.'

'Stephen, you are too kind,' Mrs Damer protested. 'He is, you know,' she said to the others. 'The dear boy thinks everything I do is splendid, although I occasionally have a failure.'

Felicia took note of the use of his first name and wondered if this was part and parcel of the eccentric lady's manners or lack of them.

'But not, I trust, with *our* heads,' Lord Chessyre broke in to say with that beguiling smile of his. Would that the sculptress could capture that smile.

Mrs Damer gave him a speculative look, then said, 'No, I doubt you will be a failure – not at anything.'

Was Anne Damer a clairvoyant, that she could predict a string of successes for his lordship? Felicia wondered. Or was it simply a ruse to convince a patron that he was wise in selecting her to do his head in whatever medium she used.

Felicia ventured to ask, 'Do you use marble or work in bronze?'

'Marble, I think. Gray, undoubtedly. I have a rather fine piece at the Hill that will do nicely for Lord Chessyre. Lord Pelham requires a warmer color, perhaps a red-tinted marble for him.'

Felicia wondered if the red of the marble matched the rather startling rouge that graced Anne Damer's cheeks. Perhaps it was a mistake, put on in poor light, and Mrs Damer did not realize precisely how bright it was.

The conversation became general then, comments on the latest theatrical production to hit London, information about the water-color showing to come, and remarks about the current styles of deco-ration.

Felicia rose from her chair to gather up Merlin, who had wandered into the drawing room, where he ought not be. Lord Chessyre followed her across the room from where he had been leaning against the mantelpiece.

'Cat behaving itself?' At her shy nod, he continued, 'That is more than I can say of that dratted spaniel. Lost another pair of slippers yesterday. If I didn't know better, I'd think the cobbler gave that animal to my aunt, trained to the purpose of destroying a pair of slip-pers a week.'

'If I were to remain, I would attempt to train it otherwise.' Felicia stroked the cat, finding comfort in the soft little body that nestled so close to her.

'You will have to return – if only to teach Cleo.' He fixed her with a curiously intent look that Felicia couldn't begin to understand. If only she was not so inexperienced at flirting and conversation with gentlemen.

'Speaking of gowns,' he said with a glance across the room, where the ladies were praising a tunic dress both had seen recently, 'I like the thing you are wearing this evening. Makes you look like a water nymph.'

'Thank you, kind sir,' Felicia said, cuddling Merlin against her bosom as a defense against wanting to throw herself in Lord Chessyre's arms to experience another kiss. She had a feeling that they improved upon repetition.

'You will be careful at Strawberry Hill, will you not?' he asked quietly and rather soberly as well, causing Felicia to wonder what was going on in the back of his mind.

'You believe I have need of care, my lord?' she asked with equal solemnity. 'Is there something I do not know? Something I ought to know?' A frown pleated her brow as she considered possibilities.

'I'll explain more tomorrow,' he replied with another glance at the other four in the room.

'I see,' Felicia replied, not seeing at all, handing Merlin to the maid who entered the room at that moment. 'Put the cat on my bed and shut the door. He is not to be in here when there is company.'

'The cat sleeps on your bed?' Lord Chessyre asked with an odd expression crossing his face.

'Usually. I may put him elsewhere, but he sneaks back as soon as may be.'

'Clever animal,' he murmured. At least, that was what Felicia thought he said.

At Lady Emma's request Felicia played the pianoforte – selecting pieces from the stack Lady Emma had approved as desirable – while Lord Chessyre turned pages for her. The others chatted for a time until Mrs Damer rose, announcing that it was all too delightful but that she had best return to Strawberry Hill before it grew too late.

Lord Pelham's offer to escort her was overruled by Stephen. 'I know the way well, and there is no need for you to disturb yourself when I know you will enjoy the late supper Aunt has planned. I shall see you soon, Miss Brook.' He bowed before Felicia, then ushered Mrs Damer from the room with exquisite courtesy.

'I must say, William, Stephen certainly has very nice manners,' Lady Emma said with a smile – one that reached her eyes, lighting her face with charm.

'So often one hears that an heir is an obnoxious bore or a gambling idiot. He appears to be neither,' Felicia said with a questioning look at Lord Chessyre.

'No, he is a good chap, except for his fascination with amateur theatricals. Had he the money, I expect he would build his own theater at his country home and produce them himself.' He smiled at Felicia, so she knew that whatever the problem was, it didn't involve Stephen.

'He acts as well?' Felicia wanted to know.

'Not as well as producing, I fancy. But then, Mrs Damer is a bit uneven in her performances, or so I've been told.'

'What a pity,' Lady Emma murmured before rising to signal Alford to bring up the repast she had planned to entice Lord Pelham.

'I shall eagerly anticipate this amateur theatrical. I wonder what sort of costumes are required?' Felicia questioned as Alford brought in a large tray. He was followed by two footmen, each carrying trays of utterly delectable dishes. Lord Pelham was clearly in alt when he viewed the selection.

'I believe your aunt has conquered a certain someone with her dinners and late suppers. I shouldn't wonder if he would like to move in here,' Felicia murmured to Lord Chessyre as Pelham hovered over the contents of the trays, sampling this and taking hearty helpings of that until he had a plate heaped with delicacies.

'No, I believe *she* would far rather move, if you take my meaning. However, I no doubt would lose my chef, and finding another is a chance thing. I suspect Aunt would take him with her to keep Pelham happy,' Lord Chessyre said while Felicia perched on a chair near the fireplace and far from the trays of food where Lord Pelham hovered.

'I can well imagine.' Obtaining a decent cook for a country house hadn't been easy, either. Once found, one treated her with respect if one was wise. A fine chef would likely require even better treatment.

Once the food had been duly tasted by the others and praised by Lord Pelham, it was not long before that gentleman departed.

Lady Emma stood at the top of the stairs, waving good night to her guest.

Felicia placed her plate on the tray, then paused before going to her room. 'What I cannot understand is how Lord Pelham clearly enjoys eating yet stays so thin.'

'He leads an active life,' Lord Chessyre replied. 'I shall see you in the morning. Should I finish breakfast before you do, find me in my library.'

Felicia nodded, thinking that his words had not been a statement but rather an order. She had an unsettled night, waking to wonder what it might be that she needed to know.

Come morning, Felicia dressed with care in a simple blue morning dress with a white frill at the neck, then made her way to the break-fast room. It was empty. She sipped a cup of tea, nibbled on toast and buttered eggs, then at last gave up her efforts to eat. Uncertainty gnawed at her. Was his lordship to inform her that he was to be married and she was not to return to this house, even if Lady Emma stayed on? She left the table and hurried to the library.

'Enter, Miss Brook.'

'I would know what it is – immediately,' Felicia said, plunging into speech as soon as she had the door open.

'Be seated, please. I have been debating as to whether I should inform you of what I learned or not. I finally decided that with Stephen running tame at Strawberry Hill, you might as well know.'

'Something about Stephen?' she asked, utterly bewildered.

'Not in the least. He does not enter into the matter directly.' Chessyre returned to his chair after making sure Felicia was comfort-able in hers. 'I called on Smithers not long ago. I learned that your father's will and testament was quite legal, but had never been signed, merely had his seal affixed to it. Thinking this odd, I consulted my own solicitor. He assured me that the will is indeed legal, but that particular sort of *sealed* will is very open to fraud.'

Felicia gasped, her hand going to her throat in shock.

Lord Chessyre nodded at her reaction, then continued. 'It is particularly odd that two witnesses died within a short period after your father supposedly affixed his seal to the will. Apparently the will also had an X as a signature, which again is legal, but also easily conducive to fraud. We have yet to learn who the third witness is.'

Felicia shook her head, trying to sort out her thoughts. 'My late aunt would be the most likely suspect to attempt deceit. She was very ambitious, and more of a tyrant I cannot imagine. I believe she could persuade my uncle to do anything she wished. Do you think that his dying words about my being cheated might have something to do with this possibly fraudulent will?'

'I do. And there is another person to consider, one very much alive.' Chessyre fiddled with the pen on his desk, studying Felicia Brook's face as he spoke.

'Basil!' She licked dry lips and settled more firmly on her chair. 'He would not harm me, surely?'

'How well do you know your cousin?'

'Too well,' she grimaced, thinking about past injuries suffered at the hands of her disagreeable cousin. 'The steward and the house-keeper – I knew them. Both are gone? How?'

'I was told the steward had a carriage accident; the house-keeper died from a heart attack.'

'I see,' Felicia said, wrinkling her brow in thought.

'When you go to Strawberry Hill, you must be on your guard. I will try to be there when I am able to do so without it looking odd. Stephen wanders in and out at will. We both will make your safety the object of our concern. But there is no telling what your cousin may do when Smithers informs him that I have been to see him and asked uncomfortable questions.'

'Then what is to happen next?' Felicia asked, wondering how she was to sleep these following nights.

'My own man, Harding, is going to look into the will, examine it for defects, and see if there is possibly any clue to fraudulence. Mind you, it is extremely difficult to prove fraud once the judge has ruled – particularly with two witnesses dead.'

'How very convenient for Basil,' Felicia said, guessing that her odious cousin had something to do with the false will. In her heart she knew the testament had to be wrong; her father would never have left her without a farthing to her name.

Her thoughts were echoed by Lord Chessyre's next words. 'I believe the one point in your favor, as it were, is that whoever contrived the will omitted you. That greed might be his or her undo-ing. A judge may well consider it unlikely that a doting father would deny his only child a farthing to call her own. Very strange. It would have been better had the perpetrator given you a modest sum – suffi-cient for you to manage on your own. Far less suspicious that way.'

'My aunt would have been loath to part with a guinea, my lord. I suspect Basil is much like her, as we have had proof from his own speech.'

'If Basil believes that a judge might well do him out of a few guineas, there is no telling his reaction. The best thing is to be on your guard.' Lord Chessyre rose from his chair, coming around to stand by Felicia, offering his hand to her. 'I decided you had best know what is being done on your behalf. Should your cousin seek you out, be extremely careful. Avoid being alone, certainly never alone with him.'

Felicia rose from the comfort of the chair to give his lordship an uncertain look.

'You will find Strawberry Hill a most interesting place in which to live,' he continued. 'It is one of the most famous houses in Europe, I should think. You have read *The Castle of Otranto*, of course?' he queried as he guided Felicia to the hall.

'I confess I have never had access to the book,' Felicia replied with a dry look. 'My aunt did not believe in reading as a pastime. She felt my hours were more agreeably occupied with mending linen and doing needlework.'

'What? Not read *Otranto*? Allow me to lend you my copy. You can read it in an evening or two, for it is quite short.'

Felicia stood by the door while Lord Chessyre crossed the room to hunt for the book, then pull it from the shelf. She studied his handsome profile, thinking she would miss the gentleman once she left this house for Strawberry Hill.

'Here you are,' he said, smiling down at her. 'Read it, but not without excellent light and someone about you, for it is rather ghostly, and there is a bit of murder to stir the plot.'

'Perhaps I ought to read it while in the park?'

'If you do, take your maid and the dog for company,' he urged.

A footman came with a missive in hand, and Felicia left his lordship to read in privacy.

She had crossed to the stairs and was about to go up to her room when she heard her name. Turning, she discovered Lord Chessyre walking toward her in some haste, his footsteps echoing on the marble tiles.

'Miss Brook, this is a message from Mrs Damer. She requests that you join her as soon as it is feasible. Apparently, she has decided to perform a production of *The Castle of Otranto* this year in honor of her benefactor and wishes you to begin work on the costumes immediately. You will be pleased to note that since she inherited the place, she ordered all the spiders that had spun webs in the various rooms to be removed. Your room will be free of them, at any rate.'

'And what might I expect, sir?' Felicia inquired, placing one foot tentatively on the first of the steps.

'I do not know,' he admitted, far too serious for Felicia's liking. 'Promise me that you will be careful and send me a message if anything strikes you as peculiar.'

'I promise,' she said, again confused as to why this gentleman should be so concerned with her fate. 'Although I daresay this is all a great fuss for nothing. How could my cousin find me while I am at Strawberry Hill?' She bestowed a wry smile on Chessyre, then resumed her way up the stairs. At the top she paused and, seeing that he had remained at the bottom, asked, 'May I borrow the book for a time? It would seem that I shall not have a moment in which to read it here.'

'By all means, take it with you.'

Once Felicia Brook had disappeared from view, William retraced his steps to the library. He shook his head. There was something about this entire business of Strawberry Hill he could not like. Perhaps it was because Felicia would not be where he might keep a close watch on her. And why, a little voice mocked, is it so important to keep an eye on the girl? She is without portion. But, William argued with himself, she is a lovely girl of good ancestry, gently reared, and possessing not only excellent manners but a most agreeable disposition as well. And, he added as he spotted Cleo sneaking around a corner of the room with yet another slipper clamped in her jaws, she could make that dratted dog mind her.

'Cleo,' he called, 'drop the slipper!' The dog whisked up the stairs and around a corner, slipper in mouth, before William could reach the bottom of the stairs. If dogs could laugh, that animal would be chortling with glee.

'Felicia,' William murmured on his way to the breakfast room and a restoring cup of whatever was there at this hour, 'stay here. I need you.' This remark cast him into deep reflection.

Up in her room, Felicia sought and found her small case. She began removing her things from the wardrobe when Primrose entered the room. The exceedingly plain girl placed her fists on her hips and stared.

'Going somewhere? Without me?'

'Oh, I am to go to Strawberry Hill sooner than I expected. Help me to pack my things. And you know you are to come with me.'

Perhaps the distracted note in Felicia's voice cautioned the maid not to say more, for she shut her mouth and began to neatly fold each garment, placing it into the case with care. 'You'll need another of these cases,' she said, holding up the lovely white gown Felicia had worn the evening before. 'Unless you mean to leave some of these things here?'

Felicia sank onto the edge of the bed, frowning deeply. She must face the inevitability that she would not be returning to this house – in any capacity, no matter how much she yearned otherwise. Sighing, she rose and walked to the door. 'I shall see Lady Emma about obtaining another case immediately. Carry on.'

She found Lady Emma in the breakfast room, sitting by the window with a piece of needlework. On the far side of the room Lord Chessyre sat with a newspaper, a cup of coffee in one hand. He raised his head when she entered the room, and she was very conscious of his gaze upon her while she spoke with Lady Emma.

'I think it quite wonderful that you are to assist with costumes for Mrs Damer. Do keep an eye on the doings at that house, dearest girl. I shall wish a full report from you when next I see you. I have wondered about the goings-on in that place ever since Anne Damer inherited it. Sculpturing and theatricals, indeed! Sounds havey-cavey to me. Someone pointed out it is very improper for a female to stare at a man for hours on end. Most indelicate!'

Lady Emma crossed to the bellpull, then informed Alford to have someone bring Miss Brook another case for her things. 'There must be stacks of cases in the box room and attic. You will know what she needs.'

The butler bowed and left to do as bid. Felicia could hear soft-voice commands being issued and footsteps fading as a maid hurried on the errand.

'You intend to visit me at Strawberry Hill?' Felicia asked, unable to imagine the grand Lady Emma coming to call on the girl who assisted with costumes.

'I will. And Stephen will be there most every day, I imagine. Besides, you will return here from time to time. Surely you do not think Mrs Damer means to keep you a prisoner at the Hill! You shall have days off, and I mean to remind her in the event she forgets.'

At this point Lord Chessyre joined them, newspaper in hand. 'And you are not to take a hackney. Let Stephen know when you are free, and we will send a carriage to fetch you.'

Felicia felt a strange prickling of tears in the back of her eyes. These people were no relation to her and took more concern with her affairs than her own relatives had ever done. Why had her uncle not provided even a subsistence for her?

'You are too kind, my lady, sir. Excuse me, I shall see if Primrose has completed the packing.' Felicia hastily crossed to the door, only to pause when Lord Chessyre called her name. 'Remember, our carriage will take you to Strawberry Hill whenever you are ready.'

'Indeed, sir, I am most grateful. And I promise to take note of anything of interest, Lady Emma.'

'And keep an eye on Pelham,' her ladyship reminded with a defiant glance at her nephew as Felicia disappeared from view.

'I know all about the plan, dear Aunt. Poor Pelham has no chance of escaping.' He smiled at her expression of chagrin.

'I shall take Pierre with me, and Pelham will count himself the luckiest man in London, if not all of England, for he enjoys good food.' Lady Emma folded her hands meekly before her, staring at her nephew with determination.

'But then, he will also have you, dear Aunt. He would be a fool, indeed, not to treasure one of the nicest ladies I have ever known. Does he not, and I will settle with him.'

'Dear William, you ever surprise me. Now, you had best see to Felicia. If you were to go with her, you might discover what sort of welcome she receives at Strawberry,' Lady Emma said slyly. 'I would know which bedroom is given her. Pray it is not that Gothic horror Walpole called the Holbein Chamber. I vow the room looks more like a tomb than a place in which to sleep!'

'Sensible idea, Aunt. I shall go with Felicia to Strawberry Hill. Perhaps if I am there, they will know that the prestige of the Earl of Chessyre is behind her.'

'Just remember that she is *not* an actress, dear boy. She's a respectable young lady from a good family come on hard times. It is a situation that could happen to any one of us. And pray that her cousin does not learn where she is until you can do something about that will.'

'I agree.' He tossed the newspaper on the table and strode from the room, intent on ordering the carriage. He was determined to see that Felicia remain safe.

In the end Merlin went with Felicia to Strawberry Hill, for she couldn't bear to be parted from the little gray scrap of a cat. And, she reasoned, if she wasn't to return to this house, what would become of him?

Lord Chessyre seemed most understanding, she thought, murmuring something about his aunt taking Cleo with her should she change her residence. 'You wouldn't believe my annual bill for slippers.'

'The dog should have been trained to leave them alone.'

'Yes, well, of course it ought to have been trained, but by the time the animal took up at Chessyre Court, it was beyond hope, or so I thought. I hadn't met you then.'

'Poor Lord Chessyre, to be so burdened with strangers at his gate.

You had to arrange for coffins and carriages to convey them. Fortunate for me that no one questioned why I did not return for the funeral.'

'They would have tried to compel you to remain at Brook Hall – as an unpaid housekeeper, no doubt, since the previous one had met with a heart attack.'

Felicia raised her brows, agreeing with all he had said. 'I daresay you are right.'

They left London on the Bath Road, entering Twickenham sooner than Felicia would have expected. It was a pretty scene, with charming views, especially when they crossed the Thames.

The entrance to Strawberry Hill was quite ordinary – for a castle that entertained notions of being very ancient. Her first glimpse of the house was of battlements, Tudor chimneys, and quatrefoil windows blended into a huge Gothic castle of impressive scale.

They drew up to the front of the building with a flourish, and as Felicia was handed from the carriage by Lord Chessyre's groom, the door to the house opened and a butler of majestic proportions came down to greet them.

'Lord Chessyre, welcome to Strawberry Hill.' The butler's sharp eyes had quickly taken note of the crest painted on the door panel of the carriage and knew immediately it belonged to the earl.

Felicia and the earl were ushered into the grand entry hall with all due ceremony. Looking about her, she noted the Gothic style was even more pronounced inside the building. There were pointed arches enough to satisfy an archbishop, with colored glass windows such as found in cathedrals. To one side an ebony table and four chairs looked to have come from a Tudor carpenter shop. Curiously enough, the carpet looked contemporary, perhaps a Moorfields design.

'Perhaps you would care to put the animal in your bedroom, Miss Brook?' the butler inquired. It was clear to her the cat was not terribly welcome, but would be tolerated.

'And which suite is Miss Brook assigned?' the earl asked with his most lofty tone, designed to depress pretensions.

'The Holbein Chamber, milord,' the butler replied, then gave the guests an affronted look when they both quietly chuckled.

'Oh, dear,' whispered Felicia as her cases were carried to the grand stairs, 'I have a feeling this is going to be what your aunt calls an Experience.'

Chapter Seven

'I believe I shall go up with you,' the earl said to Felicia's surprise. Behind her Primrose breathed a sigh – of relief, no doubt – seeing that she had been listening to all that Lady Emma had said about the gloomy aspects of Strawberry Hill. Primrose's normally rosy countenance had turned a rather pasty color when they had entered the unusual house. The first thing she'd seen was several suits of armor and strange shadows cast by the colored glass in some upper windows.

'You wish to view the Holbein Chamber?' Felicia questioned.

'Since my aunt mentioned it, I am most curious to see what it looks like,' Chessyre admitted.

If the butler thought it peculiar that her escort chose to go with her, he gave no indication. Perhaps he was accustomed to odd behavior displayed by the guests of this house.

The hall along which they traversed was certainly gloomy in aspect, quite enough to give Primrose the shivers. The vaulted ceiling had extravagant strapwork. There was fancy decoration around the arched doorways and funereal black furniture stationed along the edge of the hall like so many soldiers on guard. Antiquities cluttered the tops of tables situated here and there as well as occupying space beneath them.

'What, Primrose, do you expect a ghost to pop from an alcove at every turn?' the earl teased.

'Iffen you think to scare me, milord, you be doing a fine job of it,' the maid muttered. She kept close to Felicia's side, darting glances left and right.

The Holbein chamber was indeed quite as shadowy and Gothic as the most devoted of clerics might wish.

'My, how, er, impressive,' Felicia said upon inspecting what was actually two rooms. She had a sitting room that featured an enormous chimneypiece designed to awe a timid soul, plus a small bedchamber.

'The ceiling is from the design of the queen's dressing room at Windsor Castle,' the butler offered, probably accustomed to giving details of the decor to visitors.

'The chimneypiece?' Lord Chessyre demanded to know, standing with his arms behind him, staring up at the dark carved piece with a frowning countenance.

'Chiefly taken from the tomb of Archbishop Warham at Canterbury, milord. The ebony furniture is thought to be of the Tudor period,' he concluded. Before leaving them, he suggested they might wish to join Mrs Damer in the Great Parlor in thirty minutes' time.

Felicia stared at the bed that held pride of place in the adjacent area. White satin lining peeped from beneath the purple covers with matching purple draperies on the tester frame, and above it all purple and white plumes atop the tester nodded in some ghostly breeze.

'I am expected to have a restful night's sleep in that bed?' she asked, more dismayed than before. Every door, even the dressing closet door, had a Gothic arch, some decorated with fanciful trim such as might be seen in a cathedral.

'No ghost would dare bother you in such a room or such a bed,' Lord Chessyre said with a chuckle. 'I imagine you are quite safe from harm here.'

'Are you reminding me that I need have caution elsewhere?' she murmured so Primrose, fussing about in the adjacent room, would not hear the warning.

'I would feel easier could I find an excuse to spend more time here,' he admitted.

'I believe you worry for nothing, my lord. I shall be fine,' Felicia said with more optimism than she felt.

'There is the matter of a fraudulent will you seem to forget. If Basil had something to do with it, you may be certain he will not hesitate to protect his interests, no matter what he has to do to accomplish those ends.'

'You seem determined to make sure I do not sleep for weeks, my lord,' Felicia snapped with asperity, not wishing to dwell on her miserly cousin.

'Never. And if you do have difficulty sleeping, ask Primrose to fix you a tisane. She most likely knows of one that is effective.' He glanced to where the maid stood, arms full of clothing she intended to put away once he was gone. Primrose made a very effective dragon.

'Pat your hair in place or whatever you do, and let us join Mrs Damer in the Great Parlor. From its name I gather it is of a grand size. I cannot wait to see what its ceiling is like.'

Felicia removed her pelisse and bonnet, retained her gloves and reticule, then turned to the door.

Lord Chessyre guided her from the sitting room into the hall. 'Do you suppose its design is also from Windsor Castle? Walpole had no scruples about borrowing, did he?'

'Not just in his designs for Strawberry,' she said. 'I dipped briefly into *The Castle of Otranto* and suspect he did a bit of borrowing there as well.'

'Bits of *Romeo and Juliet*, *Hamlet*, perhaps *Julius Caesar*, to be sure. I see Lady Macbeth in Hippolita when she wanders about with the taper.'

'I have not reached that part as yet; please do not spoil it for me,' Felicia begged as they marched down the stairs to find a footman waiting at the bottom. He led them to what obviously was the Great Parlor, where Mrs Damer and Stephen sat chatting.

'The first of our cast. How lovely to see you again,' Stephen exclaimed, coming forward to greet Felicia with that wonderful courtesy that was a part of his nature.

'The cast?' Felicia echoed, most confused. 'I understood that I was coming here to work on costumes – which I must say will be unusual, for they are from the sixteenth century if we remain faithful to the period of the book.'

'Did I forget to tell you of my utterly brilliant idea?' Stephen asked, looking comically dismayed.

'You did,' Felicia answered dryly.

'I want you to take the part of Matilda. It is a simple enough bit, and you will be a perfect foil for the girl who plays Isabella.'

'I? Act in a play? Before people? I couldn't,' Felicia declared emphatically.

'Nonsense, Miss Brook,' Mrs Damer inserted with a placid smile. 'Stephen is right. You are Matilda to perfection. We shall help you learn your lines.'

'As to that, I thought I could impose on William to assist Miss Brook. He was ever wonderful at helping me to learn lines.' Stephen turned to his esteemed relative and added, 'In fact, I hoped to persuade you to take the part of Frederic, the Marquis of Vincenza, Isabella's father.'

'I don't feel particularly fatherly, old chap,' the earl quipped.

Felicia eyed him askance, but before anyone could remark on his feeling toward Matilda, a stir at the door brought in a most beautiful young woman accompanied by a distinguished-looking older gentleman.

Stephen rushed forward to greet them; Mrs Damer languidly strolled behind.

'Lady Louisa Arden and Sir Peter Quillan, welcome to Strawberry Hill,' Mrs Damer said as Stephen took Lady Louisa's hand and seemed reluctant to let it go. 'Lord Chessyre and Miss Brook.'

Stephen drew Lady Louisa forward to stand by Felicia and Lord Chessyre. 'Lady Louisa is to play the part of Isabella, and Sir Peter will be Manfred. Did I mention that I am to play the role of Theodore?' He looked about him with a most innocent expression.

Lord Chessyre murmured softly to Felicia, 'I see the appeal. Theodore falls madly in love with the beautiful Isabella. I shouldn't think it will take much acting on his part.'

Felicia felt that stabbing sensation in her chest again. How foolish of her to mind in the least if the earl thought Lady Louisa was beautiful. She was, make no mistake about it; she was without parallel in elegance. Dark hair winged to either side from a perfect brow, while serene brown eyes looked out at the world from an exquisite oval face. Her lips were a lovely coral pink, a natural hue, and her skin was flaw-less, not a spot or freckle in sight.

'I fancy our esteemed hostess, Mrs Damer, will do Hippolita for us. I quite look forward to you in that role, Mrs Damer,' Sir Peter concluded gallantly. 'Who is to play the friar, Jerome?' he inquired of Stephen, looking about the enormous room as though to find a miss-ing person.

'I have yet to find the right sort of man for the role. He must have a hint of girth – I envision jowls, you know. I'd like a fellow who can give his words the right touch of avarice at the proper moment.'

Felicia looked at the earl. 'It almost sounds like Basil, does it not?'

Fortunately, Stephen didn't hear her, for he led Lady Louisa across the room to show her the picture Walpole claimed had inspired the spectral figure who stepped from the painting into the gallery of Manfred's castle.

'Is it true that Walpole found his inspiration for the novel in this house?' Felicia inquired, thinking that it certainly seemed a likely possibility.

'Indeed, he did. Said it was almost as though the words were spoken to him from out of the blue. Amazing chap, Walpole,' Sir Peter said jovially. 'Stephen said you are also going to do the costumes. I've participated in these little theatricals before. Make certain you check the attics first of all. There are trunks overflowing with clothing up there. You may easily find all you will need.' He beamed a smile at her before strolling off to consult with Mrs Damer about the scenery.

'How lovely!' Felicia gave a relieved sigh. She'd not looked forward to having to measure the earl or the other men. While the friar Jerome probably wore a long tunic with a cowl, the other men likely donned fashionable clothes of the day. She'd ask Stephen what he wanted.

The group finally settled onto sofas set near the gigantic fireplace with incredibly intricate tracery on the narrow mantelpiece. Mrs Damer had arranged the two sofas so they faced each other, which made for pleasant conversation with such a group. Looking about her,

Felicia decided that a few of the paintings were sufficiently large to cover an entire wall in some London homes. The ceiling and floor were plain.

'You guessed wrong – there is no strapwork on this ceiling, Windsorian or otherwise,' Felicia whispered as they were rustling into their places.

'Likely the only plain ceiling in a major room in the entire house,' he responded with equal quiet.

'Lord Chessyre,' Lady Louisa said, 'I was unaware that you enjoyed doing amateur theatricals.'

'You might know Stephen talked me into doing it. But I do not care. I believe a mind ought to be challenged on occasion.'

He smiled at her with such charm that Felicia wanted to weep. How could a girl compete with such a beauty – supposing a girl wanted to compete, that is. Felicia had at last admitted to herself that she no longer disliked the earl. She was not yet prepared to admit she had fallen in love with him, which was probably just as well considering how Lady Louisa was flashing those fetchingly demure flirtatious smiles at him. He appeared to enjoy them far too much to be pleasing.

'I have almost finished the script,' Stephen said. 'Felicia – I may call you Felicia, may I not? Felicia will start work on the costumes tomorrow, if that is agreeable?' he said, turning to Mrs Damer.

'I think that if it will not offend anyone, we shall be on an informal basis while working on the play,' she replied in turn. 'I shall be Anne to you all. Then it is Felicia, William, Louisa, and Sir Peter. Since he is our elder, we must show respect,' she teased. 'Of course we have all called Stephen by his Christian name forever. And I can only trust that whomever he finds to do Jerome will be as agreeable. Where will you look for our Jerome?' she asked.

'I intend to hunt around the next day or so. Someone is bound to present himself, one way or another.'

This brought a laugh, and the conversation dissolved into a general one following that droll remark.

'Stephen does well at this sort of thing, does he not?'

Felicia turned slightly so as to partially face the earl. 'I suppose there are those people who have that gift. I fear I am too reserved. I cannot imagine how I am to play the part of Matilda and act normally.'

'Well, you must talk to Stephen,' Lady Louisa said gaily. 'Stephen can teach you anything you wish to know about acting, I feel sure.' She rose from where she had been seated to join them on their sofa, squeezing in next to the earl, who didn't seem to mind in the least.

'Tell me, sir, how is it that we see so little of you around London? Surely every hostess in town must have you on her social list?' Her question was coyly put, but so sweetly done that one'd have to be a crab to object.

Felicia wondered if her claws showed.

'I have but recently come to town and have managed to keep rather busy,' the earl replied graciously.

Anne Damer rose to ring for refreshments. 'Stephen will have the parts ready for you tomorrow. He has promised me. And William, I will begin work on your head then as well. You may study your lines while you sit for me.'

'How clever, accomplishing two things at once!' Lady Louisa cried with a little bounce.

The butler entered the room with a massive tray holding tea and an assortment of biscuits, none of which appeared the least Gothic in looks.

It was difficult not to like Lady Louisa Arden. She had a sweet nature, a ready smile, and was the most beautiful creature Felicia had ever beheld. The more she studied Louisa, the more she reached the conclusion that the young woman was without character flaw. Agreeable, friendly, and not the least top-lofty – how could one hate the girl? Even if one tried.

'Perhaps the ladies would like to rest this afternoon?' Anne Damer suggested. 'Lord Chessyre, would you come with me? I would like to consult with you on the marble. The rest of you see Stephen regarding any questions you may have.'

For a languid lady Anne Damer could move quickly when she

chose. Before anyone could realize what she was about, the group had finished their tea and was dispersed in all directions.

Felicia shortly found herself walking at Louisa's side up the grand staircase.

'Marvelous old place, is it not?' Lady Louisa enthused. 'Such atmosphere, such charm. Although I am exceedingly grateful that Mrs Damer rid the house of Mr Walpole's spiders, even if they did lend additional ambiance to the place. I believe spiders are too much, although their webs may be pretty.'

'True, true. Spiders are not necessary with all the, er, character abounding in every corner of the house.' They had reached the landing, and a well-polished suit of armor loomed over their heads, axe in hand. Felicia gave it an apprehensive look, hoping that the axe was well fixed in place.

'Have you known Lord Chessyre very long?' Louisa inquired, most direct in her quest for information.

'Not actually. It was a chance encounter, you see. I was traveling with my aunt and uncle when their coach overturned quite near Lord Chessyre' s country home. He was a most gracious host in our time of need.'

'I trust the injuries were not serious.'

Felicia paused outside the door to the Holbein Chamber. 'Unfortunately, they were. Both of them died.'

'I'm so sorry. And they were?'

'Lord and Lady Brook of Brook Hall.'

'I met a Lord Brook the other evening. Your cousin?' Lady Louisa astutely guessed.

'Indeed,' murmured Felicia, not wanting to discuss that relative. She didn't even want to know where the elegant Lady Louisa had met the odious Basil.

'It must be difficult for you. You lived with them?'

For a stranger, Lady Louisa was being unusually inquisitive. Felicia merely nodded. There was no reason she need reveal the precise situation in which she presently found herself.

'I think Lord Chessyre . . . William, that is . . . is uncommonly handsome.' Louisa sighed dramatically. 'Those blond curls and those melting gray eyes are divine. He is a fine figure of a man, as my father would say. There are so many of the other kind around, and unfortunately I seem to draw every sort there is. Being an heiress is a distinct nuisance at times. I always wonder if a gentleman likes me for me or for my inheritance.'

Felicia couldn't help but smile at the girl. Her frankness was endearing, if perhaps unwise. 'His lordship appears to have no dilemma in the finance department.'

'My dear,' Louisa exclaimed, 'at least twenty thousand a year at the very minimum. He will be a marvelous catch for some girl.'

'I imagine he will,' Felicia said, her charity with Louisa suddenly gone. 'I believe I will rest, as Mrs Damer suggested. And . . . I must finish reading *Otranto*.'

'You've not read it all yet? Well, I shan't spoil it for you, but rest easy that you capture Theodore's heart in the end.'

Felicia smiled and let herself into her rooms. Merlin greeted her with a dignified meow, then curled around her feet until she picked him up for a cuddle.

So what was going on in Lady Louisa's beautiful head? Was she staking a claim on Lord Chessyre and tossing Felicia at Stephen? Well, those gentlemen might have something to say about that. Not that either one wouldn't leap at the chance to care for the exquisite girl, nor might Stephen look twice at Felicia when he seemed to have eyes for none but Louisa. The worst of it all was that Felicia liked her.

And then Felicia plunked herself on the hard ebony chair by the atrocious archbishop's tombstone-cum-fireplace. What was she thinking of, to even consider herself as opposition – to anything!

'Merlin, I believe I am more in need of common sense than magic, but at the moment, I'd not reject any help offered.'

The cat merely purred and wiggled more comfortably into Felicia's lap.

'He's a clever one, he is,' Primrose declared as she entered from the dressing closet. 'Already made friends with the cook. Fetched himself a nice bit of fish and a morsel of beef. I caught him afore he put them on your bed, I did. He's agreed to eat on a piece of newspaper in the dressing room.'

'You converse with the cat?'

'A'course,' Primrose replied. 'Doesn't everyone?'

Felicia merely looked at her maid and then immersed herself in the fantastic tale in which she was to act. Beyond that she didn't wish to think. *Act? Impossible.*

The following morning found Felicia prowling the attics of Strawberry Hill, intent upon finding clothing that would prove usable. When she had read the short narrative of greed and lust, the theme of which appeared to be the sins of the fathers shall be visited upon the children unto the third and fourth generations, she thought the costumes ought to be kept simple.

Manfred should wear dark, violent colors like deep blood-red, indicative of his character. Hippolita would do well in possibly a cream or white to reflect her goodness. Louisa as Isabella would be symbolic in a light green for eternal hope. As to herself, she supposed a modest blue for faithfulness and duty would do well enough. The character of Theodore would be difficult, for he changed from peasant to prince.

'Ah, there you are,' Stephen said, poking his head around a partition. 'How are you doing?'

Felicia related her theories on suitable colors for each of the characters. 'Except Jerome – and I see him in a sort of stone gray woolen robe, the sort of thing to fade into the background at will.'

'Clever girl,' Stephen cried. 'I always knew that Chessyre had excellent taste, but I didn't fully realize what an intelligent chap he is – to find a girl like you just when I have need of you.' He leaned over to plant a smacking kiss on Felicia's cheek.

'Excuse me,' Lord Chessyre said from the opening. 'I thought to offer a hand with the costumes. Perhaps I am intruding?'

'Not at all,' Stephen said jovially. 'Felicia is doing splendidly. I must return to my room. I cannot flatter myself that I will interpret the tale as would please Walpole, but I shall try my best. Carry on.'

He gave them a cheerful grin, then hurried off to the stairs.

'That was not at all what it seemed,' Felicia began to explain.

'Things seldom are with Stephen,' the earl said stiffly.

'He was pleased,' Felicia persisted, intent upon clearing the air, 'that you had found me for him just when he had need of me – or my abilities, as it were.'

The tension appeared to leave the earl. He sat down on one of the many trunks and smiled at her. 'So how far have you gone with your search?'

'Do you know that wretch never told me if he wanted authentic period costumes or merely Gothic draperies.' She exchanged a rueful look with the earl, then burst into laughter. He did as well.

It was far more comfortable once the potential misconception had been cleared between them. At least she thought it was cleared until he remarked, 'Did you know that Stephen, in addition to being my heir, has a considerable income of his own?'

'How nice for him,' she said cautiously.

'And the girl he marries,' the earl replied, looking at Felicia thoughtfully.

'Well, I doubt I shall be considered for that role. I recall a line in a novel your aunt gave me that puts it very well. I believe it goes something like this, "It is a truth universally acknowledged that a single man in possession of a good fortune must be in want of a wife." It does not stand to reason that the man with a fortune will wed a lady with none.'

'Lady Louisa is a wealthy young woman from a family who can claim an ancestor who greeted William the Conqueror when he came ashore.'

'Lovely,' Felicia said, her lips stiff with sudden tension. 'And?'

'She is beautiful, socially prominent, accomplished in all the skills thought needed by Society, has a fine lineage, and has money. Many men would find that an irresistible combination.' The earl gave Felicia a probing look.

'Yes, well, I fancy they would. She is also a nice girl. I wish her the very best. At the very least, what she desires.'

'Even if it deals a death blow to what you want?'

'How did we chance upon such a topic, my lord? You know nothing of what I want, nor shall you ever.' Felicia flashed a scowl at him. 'A man of your position cannot begin to suppose what I must want – a roof over my head, food in my stomach, a bed to sleep in – that is what I want and need at the moment. As to the future – well, that will come whether I want it or not. I am learning not to dwell on the matter; it is of little use.'

Felicia turned her back to him and deliberately began to dig into the closest trunk. She pulled out a splendid doublet in a rich burgundy with padding in the front as was customary in sixteenth-century Italy. 'I wonder, with a bit of alteration this might do for you,' she mused, forcing all other thoughts from her head.

Dipping into the trunk again, she found a simple gown with a square neck, high waist, and slashed sleeves. It was in a heavenly shade of Nile green. 'Perfect for Isabella, I believe.'

'Felicia?'

She turned to find Lord Chessyre standing at her side, staring at her. 'Do not be too unassuming, my girl. I believe all will turn out well for you, far better than you now believe.'

Felicia stared at him, wondering if he was about to kiss her again. 'I scarce know what to say to that. Perhaps I may improve my role as companion once I am done with creating costumes and this bit of acting?' His gaze was intense, and she backed away, edging around the trunk. She knelt by the trunk, her mind whirling with possibilities, none of them practical in the least.

'Now, we need a dagger for Manfred. Do you think Anne Damer would have one below?' he inquired prosaically. 'What?' Felicia said, still in her haze.

'A dagger, dear girl.' He was amused, she could tell.

Felicia glared at the expression on that handsome face. 'I feel certain that Anne Damer would offer you anything you desire, including a dagger.'

He coughed, then bent over the trunk. 'Hose in various sizes, a cape. This trunk must have been used for some other period piece our hostess had performed here in the past.'

Taking her cue from him, Felicia murmured agreement. Between them they sorted out a selection of garments that could be adapted for use in the production of *The Castle of Otranto*.

'How did your first sitting go with Mrs Damer?' Felicia asked stiffly.

The earl held up a gold-plated chain and pendant with paste stones set into the design and studied it while he absently replied, 'Fine, about what I expected. She is all business when at work. No conversation. Aunt Emma will be most relieved.'

'Do you think we have enough costumes to go on with?' Felicia inquired, not wishing to comment on Lady Emma.

'For a start. I wonder who Stephen will find to fill the part of Jerome? Odd you should think of Basil just as I did.'

'Lady Louisa told me that she met him recently. She did not say where. 'Tis fortunate that she is undoubtedly well guarded, for I can think of nothing my odious cousin would like more than to marry an heiress.'

'He and a good many other chaps who have found interesting uses for money.'

'But few who love it as does Basil. Let us hope that Stephen stumbles on a worthy character for the poor friar who believes he has lost everything.'

'Do you feel that way?' Lord Chessyre asked while helping her carry a bundle of garments to the lower floor. She had decided to take them along rather than risk sending a servant to fetch them and having the wrong things brought.

'It is true I have lost what inheritance I expected to receive, but I still have the essential me, if you follow my thinking. Is that so very Gothic of me, my lord?'

'No, I believe the essential you to be quite fine.'

Felicia heard a nuance in his voice that she would dearly have liked to explore, but was too much the coward to try. Time would tell.

'Ah, the costumes arrive,' Mrs Damer cried from the doorway to the library. 'Come in, do, and we shall inspect them to see if your selections fit the characters. I trust William was of service to you, Felicia?'

'Indeed, ma'am,' Felicia replied, 'he was all that one might wish.'

Chapter Eight

'What have you here?' Mrs Damer said, examining the collection of richly colored garments with a critical eye. 'These must be something left from Mr Walpole, for I do not recall having seen them before.'

She held up the burgundy doublet to assess its potential, then looked at Lord Chessyre. 'I simply cannot call you William again. Nor do you look to be a William, although that is your given name.' She turned to look across the room.

Felicia glanced that way as well, discovering that Lady Emma and Lord Pelham were seated near the fireplace. His lordship appeared to be thawing his bones by the heat. Apparently, the two had arrived while Felicia was in the attic. Felicia placed the rest of the garments on a convenient chair and crossed to curtsy to the pair.

'Goodness, dear girl, you have a cobweb in your hair.' Lady Emma popped up to brush the offending web from Felicia's curls. The lady inspected Felicia's person and asked softly, 'All is well?'

'Indeed,' Felicia whispered, then more loudly said, 'Thank you, Lady Emma. I was prowling about in the attics, hunting for costumes.' She made no mention of her conversation with Lord Chessyre.

'Felicia is going to be in the play, Aunt Emma,' Stephen said from the doorway. 'Chessyre, as well.'

'That is something we must change. You see, he is simply not a William, and I have decreed we shall go by our first names,' Anne

101

Damer declared in decisive tones. 'Was he ever called by any other name?'

'He was Will when a lad,' Lady Emma said with a fond smile at her nephew. 'He still is to many of us.'

Lady Louisa came to stand by Stephen at that moment, causing a most speculative look to settle on Lady Emma's face. 'I believe we have met, have we not?' she asked the lovely young woman, who stood close to Stephen as though on the most friendly of terms.

'Indeed, Lady Emma,' Lady Louisa said, crossing to dip a proper curtsy. 'My mother is an acquaintance of yours, I believe. Lady Arden?'

'True, that she is.' Lady Emma returned her gaze to Mrs Damer, who paced back and forth at the other end of the large room.

The vividly garbed Mrs Damer, whose gold and lime draperies floated about her as she moved, waved aside all these polite civilities. 'To return to the matter at hand, Will suits you far better, Lord Chessyre. Recall that William Shakespeare was called Will by some. I believe Will shall do very well. We shall call you Will. 'Tis far more dashing.'

'Indeed? I was unaware that I required *dashing* in my character.' He exchanged an amused glance with his aunt.

'You do not require it, sir. You *are* dashing,' Mrs Damer pronounced, her draperies settling around her when she came to a halt near a window. 'A gentleman of your romantic looks cannot have a prosaic name. It came to me while I worked this morning. I said to myself, "This is not a William; he is far too charming and courtly." And so you are.' There was not a tiny bit of flirtation in her voice or manner when she spoke. She was truly an original. With the sun blessing her lime-and-gold crepe gown and the froth of a gold cap on her ashen hair, she looked like an oversized daffodil.

'Will is better than Chessyre,' Stephen said with a grin. 'What say you, Felicia?'

'I say that Lord Chessyre ought to decide what he is to be called by us while here at Strawberry Hill. Not every gentlemen wishes to be dashing, you know.' Felicia gave his lordship a demure look that ill concealed the spark of mischief bubbling up within her.

'I must say, I would like to be thought dashing. Besides, a few friends call me Will now.' He slanted a look at Felicia she thought prudent to ignore.

'Capital, capital,' Lord Pelham declared, turning to Lady Emma to make a quiet aside.

Whatever his remark, Lady Emma smiled and shook her head at him.

Mrs Damer handed the doublet to Felicia, saying, 'Best try fitting these, then we may see what needs doing. Lord Pelham, if you would come with me? We will get on with your sitting.'

Lady Emma rose as well, but did not go along with the pair as they left the room. She had caught the barely perceptible shake of her nephew's head and went to his side instead, her eyes questioning.

'Do you know that Mrs Damer was all work this morning?' he informed her. 'I do not think she spoke above three lines to me all the while I was sitting for her – and that was to tell me to sit still, turn my head, and dismissing me with a muttered, "That is all for now." ' He gave his aunt a pat on her shoulder. 'Extremely dull, Aunt Emma.'

Felicia intercepted the look he gave his aunt and smiled. 'Perhaps you can have a look-in later on to see how it goes?'

'An excellent notion, dear girl. And what did you do when so summarily dismissed?' she inquired of William. 'You did not return home.'

'That must likely have been when he came to see how the costumes went,' Felicia said. 'He had to have been desperate for conversation to trail us to the attics.'

'You and another were searching for costumes?' Lady Emma glanced at Stephen, who nodded.

'I was there for a bit, then went down to work on the script. I have it almost done. Louisa has a most beautiful handwriting, and she has offered to assist with making the copies we need.'

'If it is handwriting you require, I believe I might be of assistance to you,' her ladyship said in an offhand manner, not fooling two of the group in the least.

'Splendid,' Stephen said absently, his mind already on the completion of the script.

'Would you try on this green gown, Lady Louisa?' Felicia asked politely. She found it difficult to be quite so informal as Mrs Damer wished. After all, she hadn't met the girl before, nor had they mingled in the same Society.

'Indeed, I will. Is there anything else I might do before I pick up my pen?' Lady Louisa inquired in her sweet manner. Her glossy, long hair was coiled in an intricate design on top of her head, giving Felicia the notion that Lady Louisa would look utterly smashing in the quaintly styled green gown.

'Ask Stephen what he thinks Theodore ought to wear,' Lord Chessyre demanded with a laugh. 'Stephen, do you realize you never once gave Felicia a hint of what you wanted in costumes? Poor girl. Not fair, Cousin.'

'You did well enough, I must say. I think something buff and suitable for a peasant in the first act, then toward the end I can change into something noble-looking – like silver and black – and fit for a prince.'

'Quite dramatic,' Felicia murmured softly to no one in particular.

'And what of Jerome?' Lord Chessyre queried. 'When shall we meet the fellow?'

'Do not worry, I shall find him – today if all goes well.' Stephen wandered from the room, Lady Louisa following along, listening to Stephen's discourse on the remainder of the script and what he needed to do.

'What patience that young lady must have,' Lady Emma murmured.

'Never puts a foot wrong,' her nephew replied in equally soft tones. 'Not only that, but she is beautiful, sweet-natured, and has a fortune to boot.'

Felicia added, 'Do not forget that chap who greeted William the Conqueror when he came ashore. That bit might be nearly as esteemed as her fortune.'

Free of Stephen and Lady Louisa, Felicia turned to Lord

Chessyre, wondering if she would ever dare to call him Will, and said, 'And what if all does not go well in finding someone to play Jerome?'

'Disaster is a familiar condition to Stephen, or did I forget to tell you that?'

'Goodness knows I am sufficiently familiar with that condition, so whatever might happen will not shake me to the core.' Felicia held up the simple blue gown with slashed sleeves that came to her wrist and a square neck that looked as though it would be far too low to be pleasing. Could she actually wear the thing?

'Lovely color, Felicia, dear,' Lady Emma commented. She tilted her head, causing the feathers on her hat to quiver, appearing likely to take wing at any moment. In her pelisse the color of a robin's egg she resembled a bird.

Felicia nodded her thanks for the kind words, then turned to his lordship again, a thought troubling her. 'If I may be so bold, just who is to be the audience for this drama?'

'Oh, were you not told?' Lord Chessyre said, looking as innocent as a lad who has just taken the last of Cook's jam tarts. 'She sends out invitations to her many friends and acquaintances. They all come.'

At first Felicia was horrified, then slowly became reconciled. 'I shan't know a soul, most likely. It could be worse, I suppose.'

'Just hope that she doesn't take a notion to send His Royal Highness an invitation. Prinny might just accept.'

Felicia clutched her costume to her chest. 'She wouldn't actually do that, would she?' she asked warily.

Suddenly, there was a loud crash in the entry hall, and they all hurried to see what had happened. It sounded, Felicia thought, like the clanging of a few dozen pans and pots.

On the landing, where the suit of armor that had given Felicia pause had been, sat Stephen amid the ruins. Arms, legs, the body, and helmet were scattered all about him, and two steps above, Lady Louisa sat in helpless laughter.

'Dash it all, Louisa, it is not funny,' Stephen complained. He looked rather dazed, somewhat bewildered, and not a little annoyed as her giggles continued.

'I did mention disaster, I believe,' Lord Chessyre said in an aside before striding up the steps to assist Stephen.

'Were you trying to put it on?' Felicia inquired. 'Or did you think to use it for the mysterious armor the servants think they see in *Otranto?*'

Stephen nudged aside a steel arm, the gloved hand of which pointed eerily up to the ceiling, and stared thoughtfully off into the distance. He allowed his cousin to assist him to his feet, then turned to the group assembled at the bottom of the stairs.

'I think there will have to be some omissions. We can contrive the haunted helmet from pasteboard, and plumes are easy enough to obtain, but we will not be able to get everything the audience sees.'

'You mean like the figure that steps from the portrait?' Louisa asked, ceasing her laughter and looking merely mischievous.

'That and the ghosts,' Stephen said.

'I do not think I shall like this play of yours,' Aunt Emma complained.

'But I have figured out how to simulate thunder.' He clanked a leg against the body of armor to get a nice ringing sound that didn't sound remotely like thunder. 'Well, perhaps I best think of something else,' he decided while Louisa giggled again. He glared at her, then began gathering the pieces of the suit or armor, assisted by a footman who was all too familiar with the gentleman's odd ways to look the least surprised at what had occurred.

'I believe we shall go back to the library and work there. Not the slightest bit irregular.' He took Louisa by the hand, and they retreated down the steps and along the hall to the very Gothic book room. She carried the green gown with her, likely thinking she could try it on later. Their animated chatter floated back to the others. It seemed he was willing to forgive her the laughter when he needed a scribe.

'Nothing Windsorian in the library, either,' Lord Chessyre said to Felicia. 'I believe that ceiling is painted.'

'Indeed? Let us hope there is a desk and two chairs. Such prosaic furniture for a library might not have occurred to the gentleman who built this place. I am coming to believe he was a little mad,' Felicia said while slowly walking back to the drawing room, where the costumes awaited her needle and thread.

At the door to the drawing room Lady Emma paused, lightly touching her nephew on the arm.

'I should like to look in on Lord Pelham. Regardless of what you say, I do not trust that woman,' Lady Emma declared quietly.

'If it will put your mind at ease, I will show you the way, and you can see for yourself.' William gave Felicia a look that was one of a patient man, much tried.

Felicia set to work, sorting out the long hose and assorted tops for the few men. Chessyre as Frederic she envisioned as being garbed most somberly, considering all the character had endured. The burgundy doublet looked as though it should fit well. She had pulled out a pair of black hose when his lordship and Lady Emma sailed into the room, softly arguing all the while.

Her ladyship looked as though she truly desired to scream, but was far too much the lady to indulge in such an emotional outburst.

'It is just as I imagined, and *you* were certain it would be boring. Ha! Scheming, conniving woman!' Lady Emma sniffed with disdain in a highly injured air as she settled on a chair near the fire.

'I feel sure there must be some logical explanation,' Lord Chessyre said to his aunt. Turning to Felicia, he said, 'Disaster strikes again. I opened the door to Mrs Damer's studio, and we discovered Mrs Damer with her arms about Lord Pelham. It was most disconcerting, to say the least.' He bestowed a worried look on his aunt, who gave the appearance of debating on the advisability of having a fit of the vapors.

'And what did she say?' Felicia asked, wondering how they were to soothe Lady Emma's sensibilities.

'As to that, we were so quiet I doubt she knew we were there.'

Lady Emma said sadly, '*Quite* shocking. *Just* what I suspected would occur.' She glared at her nephew, then turned to Felicia. 'It would be best if you could come home with me, but I suppose you have committed yourself to those costumes and will not leave.' She managed to look both wounded and woeful at once.

'Indeed, my lady. I promised I would help, and help I will.' Moreover Felicia didn't think that she would be of much support to Lady Emma in her present mood anyway.

'I shall,' Lady Emma said, rising dramatically to her feet, 'seek the library and assist in writing out the scripts. I will not leave this house until Lord Pelham is free of that woman. And' – she gave her nephew a pointed look – 'I shall demand an explanation of Mrs Damer's behavior from him.'

'Actually, that might not be wise, Aunt,' her beleaguered nephew replied. 'I suspect it would be better were you to take him back to the house and feed the man. The food here cannot begin to compare to what you serve.'

'Is that so?' Lady Emma paused by the doorway, looking much struck by her nephew's words. 'Perhaps I ought to send a message to Pierre? Something special?' She gave the earl a coy look.

'I intended to leave shortly anyway,' Lord Chessyre said with a resigned sigh.

'Good. I am sure you will know just what to order.' She walked down the hall until she found the library some distance away. Her fluting tones drifted back to where Felicia stood near Lord Chessyre.

'If I might fit this on you before you go, sir? Then I can begin work on alterations if need be,' Felicia said, wondering what was on the earl's mind that he should look so disgruntled.

She helped him take off his coat, then eased him into the doublet. 'It's rather large for you,' she murmured, checking the side seams, then the back. She marked several places with pins, then measured with her hands, placing them in front and behind his chest – a most intimate arrangement she tried to overlook.

'That is how it likely happened, I think,' he said with the air of one who has solved a puzzle.

Startled, Felicia peered around to look at his face. 'What is?'

'That scene we interrupted in the studio. I wager that Mrs Damer was merely arranging some draperies on Pelham, and we chanced in at the wrong moment.'

'I do hope so. Lady Emma has her hopes pinned on Lord Pelham, as you well know.' Felicia completed her efforts at fitting the doublet and stepped away from the enticing William Chessyre.

'Indeed.' He shrugged off the doublet, replacing it with his own coat of finest Bath cloth.

'For twenty-three years she has waited and hoped for this day, the day when Lord Pelham would settle down, not to roam anymore.' Felicia accepted the doublet, smoothing it over her arms as she thought about Lady Emma and her hopes.

'Would you like to place a small bet on his keeping his word?' Chessyre asked in a silky voice.

'Not when you speak in that tone. You sound too certain that he will roam once again,' Felicia said with a half smile.

'A chap *could* take a spouse with him if so inclined – to Italy or Spain, even Switzerland. I think he may be looking for company. A fellow gets lonely, you know.' He had that lad-in-the-jam-tart look again, and Felicia backed away from his tempting presence.

Felicia knew all about being lonely, but did not feel inclined to share her feelings with Lord Chessyre. She had observed the narrow look he'd given Stephen when he had been so familiar with Lady Louisa. She didn't think it stemmed from worry about impropriety. Had he not remarked earlier that Lady Louisa was perfection itself? Never puts a foot wrong; beautiful, sweet-tempered, and having a fortune was what he'd said. How could a girl compete with someone like that? Not that Felicia wished to compete, mind you. It was a theoretical question, not one to which she actually sought an answer.

'I intend to check with my solicitor to see if he has learned anything more about the will,' Lord Chessyre said before heading for the front of the house.

'Do not forget to inform Pierre about Lord Pelham, whatever you do,' Felicia couldn't resist saying. 'If anything would keep him to home, it would be the food.'

'And I am expected to sacrifice!' Chessyre tossed Felicia a martyred look, then took himself off.

The remainder of the day went amazingly well, considering. Lady

Emma did not rail at Lord Pelham when he left the studio and Mrs Damer behind.

'You poor man, you must be starved. Why do we not go to Chessyre House and see what Pierre has to offer?' she coaxed.

With Lord Pelham coaxing wasn't necessary in the least. He had his coat on and was ushering Lady Emma from the house in jig time. Felicia heard him say something about dratted females who were far too bossy and smiled. Now, if they could only persuade Lord Pelham that there were interesting things to do in England, all might be well for dear Lady Emma.

Lord Chessyre was not in a good mood when he entered his solicitor's office. 'I hope matters are satisfactory with you?'

That gentleman was happy to see him and greeted him most warmly. After the preliminary greetings were over, Mr Harding said, 'I have some good news to report. I spoke with one of the judges who oversees the wills, and the chap who tended the particular will you question has died.' At William's quick frown, he shook a hand in the air in negation. 'That is not bad; it is good. It means we shall have the right to have some other judge examine the will in his place. There will be less likelihood of bribery when Lord Brook does not know what is afoot and has no opportunity to tempt the fellow. Lord Brook is in London at present; you know this, of course?' he queried with a casualness that belied his interest.

'Indeed, I know the fellow is in Town,' William replied with a touch of irony in his voice. 'Lady Louisa Arden reported meeting him at some social gathering. Apparently, in a good many instances, money and a title are all that is required to obtain entrée to elegant functions. Character is not a requisite.' William exchanged a meaningful look with the man who was not only his solicitor but a friend as well. They had attended Oxford together and enjoyed many an escapade before Harding had settled to his law and William to administering his estates and caring for his eccentric aunt.

'My good man, were character a requisite in Society, the world would be a vastly different place in which to live. I fancy a good many situations would be a bit different.'

Since Mr Harding was the youngest son of a viscount and the most upstanding of that family, William could well understand his direction of thought.

'True, true,' William said consideringly.

'How does Miss Brook go along? Is she still with your aunt?'

William explained the circumstances involved in her removal to Strawberry Hill and what had occurred following. 'Acting in a play, by Jove? This, I must see for myself. When is it to take place?'

'I believe it has been set for two weeks' time – the week before Christmas. We all know the story, but we must learn the no doubt ridiculous lines that Stephen will foist on us.'

'And Miss Brook is to be your daughter's friend? Must make you feel like Methuselah.'

'Theatrical makeup and a bit of acting makes the difference. I must confess I have no fatherly feelings toward the young lady. Quite the opposite, I believe.' He sent a glance at his friend that said more than he realized.

'What about Lady Louisa Arden? How is she involved?'

'Plays Isabella, the girl I almost marry, but who really loves Theodore, who's naturally played by Stephen.'

'Ah, so that is the direction of matters? Should I do a bit of investigating? Stephen is a wealthy young man – not that I have heard rumors regarding the coffers of the Arden family.'

'I would appreciate it if you would, Harding. What a pleasure it is to work with a chap who is so alert on all counts.'

They parted on the best of terms, each most pleased with matters as they stood.

Up in her room Felicia surveyed the doublet she had taken in and wished, not for the first time, that she had not agreed to this silly scheme. A play in two weeks' time, to spout stupid lines before a clutch of strangers. Only, were the lines to be so stupid? In the book both Matilda and Isabella were interested in the same man. While Lady Louisa spent much time with Stephen, Felicia had not missed her speculative looks at Lord Chessyre. And there was the matter of his high praise of Lady Louisa. She possessed all desired qualities, not to mention an ancestor who'd greeted William when he first trod England's soil. Felicia well knew the value of proper lineage. Her own was not to be dismissed, having ancestors most respectable.

To make matters even worse, Lady Louisa was a dear girl, just as amiable as one could wish. Felicia could not even know the comfort of disliking her.

Gathering up her sewing, she placed what she had completed in one pile, then studied what was left.

At a gentle rap on her door, Felicia bade the person enter. Lady Louisa, who had so recently been in Felicia's thoughts, entered the room, wearing the green gown.

'It fits quite well. My maid did a few minor adjustments to make it most suitable. Will it do?' she queried anxiously, touching the slashed opening of one sleeve with a hesitant finger.

'You look like a wisp of spring,' Felicia said truthfully. Lady Louisa could capture the heart of almost any man she wished, looking as wonderful as a fine spring day. Not only the green flattered her, but the deep square of the neckline was perfect for her figure, Felicia concluded a bit enviously.

'How do the costumes progress?' Lady Louisa strolled over to the bed, where various outfits had been arranged. She lightly touched the burgundy doublet, then stroked the fine dark red wool that was Manfred's garment, before lingering on a peasant's smock of rough-spun linen. 'Stephen's, I suppose?'

'Yes,' Felicia responded, then picked up a doublet she had fashioned of silver tissue over black wool. 'This would never stand the scrutiny of an accomplished needlewoman, but I believe it will please Stephen. He seeks the effect more than the actual thing.'

'Yes, indeed,' Lady Louisa said with a touch of wistfulness. But as she was looking at the burgundy doublet, Felicia was not certain which gentleman had captured her thoughts – or her heart.

'I thought to put together a rough gray robe for the friar, Jerome, but I have left it unhemmed. As it is long, it could always be belted, should the gentleman be too short.'

'Did Stephen not send word to you? He has found the perfect Jerome.'

'How fortunate for us,' Felicia said warily. 'Who might that gentleman be? Is he tall or short?'

'You know him very well. I thought him perfect for the part, for he is able to simulate that look of grief as well as one of avarice. It is your cousin, Lord Brook.'

Stunned, Felicia sank down on one of the hard Tudor chairs that lined the Holbein Chamber.

'I did not believe fate could be so cruel,' she whispered.

'You are not pleased? Lord Brook seemed delighted at the prospect of seeing you again and acting in the play. I am sorry if I suggested wrongly.'

The girl appeared so contrite that Felicia pulled herself together and smiled, albeit a trifle wanly, and said, 'No, no, it was merely the surprise of it all. I shall shorten the robe, for Basil has no height.'

Why? Felicia demanded silently. *Why* had Basil insinuated himself into the play at Strawberry Hill? Indeed, how had he learned of it?

'I happened to mention the play to friends while at a gathering where Lord Brook was present. He chanced to hear me, and when he learned you were also present at the Hill, he seemed so anxious to see you, be a part of this experience that I thought him perfect for the part of Jerome. I trust I did not do wrong?'

Felicia rose and strode to the window, where she looked down on the gardens, taking note of the masses of plants, all the while wondering what this turn of events would bring.

Glancing at Lady Louisa, Felicia voiced her next thought. 'I must see Lord Chessyre – immediately.'

Chapter Nine

'**W**hat do you think now, sir?' Felicia demanded quietly when she was later able to draw the earl aside from the others who thronged the room that had been set aside for the theatrical production.

William glanced at the others who milled about, discussing their parts with each other. Basil, Lord Brook, stood a trifle apart, looking uneasy, yet oddly smug.

'I believe I said that Stephen is inclined to disaster from time to time, did I not?' Lord Chessyre murmured.

'I did not believe that included Basil, who, of course, is a true disaster of the first water. What are we to do?' Felicia turned slightly so she might keep her odious cousin in view. 'It is quite insupportable that we be required to be civil to him.'

'When I think of what I suspect he and his mother have done to you, I should like to shake him until his teeth rattle,' Chessyre said quietly, then added, 'No, that is not quite true. I should like to transport that chap to a far region where he would have to fend for himself without a farthing with which to bless his name – as they wished upon you, Miss Brook.'

'Were you able to learn anything of interest when you were out this afternoon?' she asked, being careful not only to keep her voice down, but also to raise her script to conceal her mouth as well.

'Indeed. Come let us stroll to the far side of the room so I may acquaint you with my modest news.' He held his script before him, as did Felicia, to maintain the illusion that they discussed the play.

She readily walked with him, managing to keep an oblique watch on Basil.

'Harding, my solicitor, tells me that the judge who ruled on the will is dead.' At Felicia's gasp, he patted her arm, then continued, 'That is not bad news, but good. It means that another judge will receive the appeal to reexamine the will, possibly to rule on its validity. Since your cousin can scarcely know that we are about to request such an event, he will not have time in which to bribe the judge. As well, if he is here, he will be too busy to check with the obnoxious Mr Smithers regarding any activity on the will. Do you not agree?'

'I find it shocking that judges can be bribed to cheat poor girls from their inheritance,' Felicia whispered, her voice harsh and angry. Then softly she added, 'I must say I find it most peculiar that so many involved in this are dead. My uncle and aunt, two witnesses, and now the judge. Can they *all* be coincidences?'

'Anything is possible.' They paused by a tall window that over-looked the gardens. There were no blooms, of course, but the patterns of greenery presented a pleasing picture. They turned to look back to where Basil stood on the fringe of the group.

'I agree that it is likely a good idea that we are able to keep an eye on Basil. I wonder how he feels playing the part of Stephen's father?' Felicia queried.

'I know not that. I suspect we will have to guard Lady Louisa against his encroaching ways, however. He must not be allowed access to the heiress.'

From the opposite end of the room, Stephen called out to the assembled cast, 'Perhaps we might have a simple reading of the play, if you please, ladies and gentlemen?'

'Harding is to pursue the matter and will report back to me as soon as anything specific develops,' Lord Chessyre went on, adhering to the matter of the will before they had to join the others. 'We shall soon know who the other witness is. Or was, as the case may be.'

'I am greatly in your debt, my lord. It is difficult, perhaps impos-sible, for one without funds to accomplish anything of this nature. I thank you.' Felicia flashed him a look of warm gratitude.

'It is only so that you receive help. I would wish someone to help my sister were she in difficulty.' He bowed, then moved away.

Felicia raised her brows, thinking that while the earl might generously assist her in delving into her lost inheritance, he was tenderly keeping watch on Lady Louisa. Felicia watched as he strolled across the room to bend an ear to her chatter. It was only natural he be drawn to her; she was wealthy, beautiful – as he had so pointedly remarked – and sweet-natured.

Felicia drifted off to join Mrs Damer, again wishing she could dislike Lady Louisa. But how could she not like the girl? As Lord Chessyre said, Louisa never put a foot wrong.

Their hostess had changed from her gold-and-lime draperies to a simple gown of antique white that ill became her. Felicia thought that if *she* had inherited Strawberry Hill and all the money needed to run the place, she might have managed to dress a trifle more becomingly.

'Will, you are free for some time,' Mrs Damer cried after paging through the script. 'Why do you not try on your costume? The rest of us will muddle along. Do not be gone too long.' To Felicia she added softly, 'I am dying to see what our earl looks like in that doublet and hose. He has splendid legs.'

Stephen sorted out his actors. 'Now remember, Manfred is trying to rush the marriage between his son, the sickly youth Conrad, and the fair Isabella. I have decided not to show the death of Conrad. It would mean another character and another costume, only to dispose of him within the first few minutes of the play. We shall begin the play with the servants rushing in to inform Manfred that his beloved son has been killed by a giant helmet that has fallen from the sky. Conrad has been crushed to death.

'To small pieces, actually,' said Basil.

Felicia started; she hadn't realized her cousin had sidled up to her. 'You sound positively ghoulish, Basil.'

'It is in the book, cousin Felicia,' he replied with the faintest sneer in his voice.

The first reading went better than Felicia had dreamt it might.

116

Anne Damer surpassed expectations as Hippolita, while Lady Louisa was utterly splendid as Isabella. In fact, when Isabella first caught sight of Stephen playing the part of the stranger, the peasant, who didn't sound in the least like a peasant, Felicia was struck by the emotion Louisa conveyed though her actions. She was truly splendid, for she captured well the young princess who is immediately drawn to this unsuitable young man.

It was with the thought of surpassing that bit of acting that Felicia pretended to be most taken with the peasant as well. After all, later on they plotted an elopement, Theodore determined to whisk her away from her father so they might marry and continue the line.

Sir Peter Quillan had arrived just before the reading, and it wasn't until Felicia faced him in the scene where he demands that Theodore, in the guise of a peasant, be killed that she knew he was there. He looked the part of the half-deranged Manfred today, hair all awry.

It was not difficult for Felicia to be struck with Theodore's princely mien and to faint when her own father orders the death of one to whom she is very drawn.

Stephen had persuaded several servants at Strawberry Hill to take their counterpart's places in the play. They did a credible job of revealing terror when they came to wail and lament about the various mysterious and eerie happenings. The portrait that steps from the wall was greeted with proper horror, while the giant sections of armor brought forth remarkable acting abilities.

Felicia decided that living with Anne Damer likely exposed the servants to a great many opportunities for roles in various productions. They were probably far more accustomed to treading the boards than the assembled cast. She murmured as much to Lord Chessyre when she found him stepping between her and Sir Peter.

Anne Damer had been correct. Lord Chessyre looked smashing in hose and doublet. 'Somehow you do not look the part of Isabella's father, the man my father schemes for me to wed,' she said as a discussion broke forth on the other side of the room regarding the men who supposedly accompanied Frederic when he arrived in pomp and ceremony, flags waving and trumpets blaring.

He surveyed himself, chuckling at the sight. 'Only a little different from today's garb. However, I am pleased I do not appear at all fatherly to you.'

'I say, old chap,' Sir Peter declared, 'Miss Brook does well as Matilda. One would swear she truly fancies your cousin.'

'I missed that bit while I was being helped into this costume. You have taken to your role, Felicia?'

At his tone, Felicia stiffened, replying, 'Indeed, for your cousin does exceedingly well as Theodore and is rather beguiling.' If Lord Chessyre was to fancy Lady Louisa, there was nothing to keep Felicia from pretending to admire Stephen, especially when his lordship looked down his nose at her at the very idea.

The argument about how they would handle the illusion of a vast army of men decided, the reading continued.

'A bad husband is better than no husband at all,' Jane Woodworth, a newly arrived member of Stephen's cast playing the maid, Bianca, declared to her mistress, Matilda.

'Do you agree with that philosophy?' Lord Chessyre inquired of Felicia later.

'Mr Walpole wrote that nonsense. No, I do not agree with it, in spite of what I said before about the difficulties of being single. I had not considered my cousin when I said that. I should not like to be wed to one such as he,' Felicia stated with a look at her cousin, who was ogling the bouncing beauty of Jane Woodworth.

'I wonder, does she have a fortune?' the earl mused softly.

'Jane Woodworth?' Felicia queried in reply. 'I scarce have met the girl. I was told Stephen found her at a party given by Lady Tower and thought she was Bianca to the life.'

'I did say Stephen was prone to disaster,' the earl admitted again.

'Think,' Felicia insisted. 'Should Basil be attracted to the fair "Bianca," it would keep him less aware of anything else around here.'

She left the earl at that point, as Stephen wanted to read over the part when she first meets him. Her annoyance with the earl possibly gave her rendition more zest than it otherwise might have had. She slipped up to the black tower to free Theodore. Captivated by the prince, she begged him to accept armor and a sword, for he needed to protect himself. He fell at her feet, kissing her hand passionately, vowing he would be her knight. 'I shall help you escape the castle!' she declared, casting a longing look at her knight. The way Stephen had written the scene was quite moving.

Stephen seemed pleased with their performance and begged Felicia to remember how she'd done that piece. She glanced at the earl and was confused to find him staring at her with a hostile gaze. Did he possibly think her serious about his young relative and heir? Well, most likely an impoverished young woman, no matter she was an 'honorable,' would not be to his liking as a wife for his cousin. Felicia decided a mere flirtation with Stephen would do no harm. It was not as though the earl was interested in her.

Then they read the scene where it was revealed that Isabella is smitten with Theodore and Matilda wonders if she must yield her love for the handsome stranger to the young woman she has come to admire and love as a sister. It was a scene that required a bit of practice, for Felicia would find it difficult in view of her attraction to Lord Chessyre. Could she become accomplished enough an actress to acquire the art of pretense?

Following this reading, Felicia found a chair upon which to rest in a quiet part of the room. She'd taken note that Basil was on the opposite side, smiling foolishly at the ample charms of Jane Woodworth. Giving a sigh of relief, Felicia pretended to study her lines.

'You seek peace, I see,' Lady Louisa said upon joining her, settling onto a nearby chair.

'Indeed, I do. I am not accustomed to such noise, so many people mulling around like this. I lived very quietly in the country before I came to London with Lady Emma.'

'You did very well in that scene with Stephen just now,' Louisa observed.

'And you were splendid with Miss Woodworth,' Felicia said warmly. 'Does she not make a perfect Bianca? just the right amount of sauciness.' Felicia cast an indulgent gaze on the buxom young woman who tempted Basil.

'You like Stephen?' Lady Louisa persisted.

'He is charming, as are all the gentlemen here, even Sir Peter. Of course, I cannot comment on my cousin – familiarity, and all that.' Felicia didn't wish to come out and directly warn Lady Louisa against Basil. In her limited experience women sometimes did stupid things, like welcome the advances of the very man they'd been cautioned against. She'd seen that at Brook Hill when a neighbor had been told a certain gentleman was up to no good. She'd married the fellow, who had turned out to be as bad as claimed. Basil would be far worse.

Apparently Lady Louisa had no interest in Basil because she murmured, 'Stephen and Lord Chessyre – Mrs Damer insists we call him Will – are nice people, are they not? I mean – helpful and kind, funny and pleasing in their ways.'

'I'll grant you Stephen might be amusing. I have failed to see that side of Lord Chessyre,' Felicia said, thinking of how he had imagined the accident outside Chessyre Court to be planned so that she could meet him. 'However, I will admit that Lord Chessyre is helpful. And pleasing in manners . . . most of the time.' Louisa's curiosity about Lord Chessyre betrayed more than casual interest in the earl.

It appeared that Lady Louisa would have continued her questioning had not Stephen decided to read the last scenes of the play just then. He called the two girls to the front of the group.

Sir Peter as Manfred picked up the dagger that Anne Damer had supplied and began the scene where Manfred, thinking it was Isabella meeting the handsome, young Theodore, plunges the dagger into the breast of his own daughter by mistake. Stephen as the horrified lover was wondrously distraught. Felicia as the brave and resigned Matilda felt she acquitted herself reasonably well. Sir Peter was a bit stiff as Manfred when he attempts to kill himself after killing his daughter, but in time would, Felicia trusted, do very well indeed.

Although they were but reading the parts, the grief Stephen revealed on the death of the woman Theodore loved so passionately could not help but affect them all. He planted kisses on her hands, just as the demented Theodore had done, begging her to return to him, to be his love forever.

To be loved like that, Felicia thought as she felt his kisses while she pretended to be dead, must be true love, indeed.

Basil read the words uttered by Friar Jerome with convincing reality until it came to revealing the fact of the fraudulent will and that Theodore was the true prince, the son of Alfonso, who had been *cheated* out of his rightful place and inheritance. Felicia vowed Basil turned a paler hue.

When the reading of the play concluded, the cast wandered off to partake of the tea promised by Mrs Damer.

'Well, that was a fascinating afternoon,' the earl said to Felicia.

'Indeed,' she murmured, still stirred by the emotions that had fluttered through her at Stephen's impassioned kisses. She was thankful that Basil had walked off at the side of audacious Jane Woodworth. 'Did you notice Basil's reaction to the part of the story where it is revealed that Theodore has been deprived of his rightful place in Society, not to mention cheated of his inheritance?'

'Turned as pale as a cooked codfish. I cannot guess whether that will work to our favor or not.'

Felicia gasped. 'Could he go haring off to Mr Smithers to reassure himself on the matter of the will, *his* will that guarantees that he receive every farthing, every bit of the Brook estate?' she demanded.

'It is a possibility we must consider,' the earl replied grimly.

'He not only has my late father's money and property, he also has what was his own father's. I know that as penurious as my late aunt was, that estate could not have been much decimated by my poor uncle. There were times when I thought she would insist upon the rest of us living on bread and water. She did not believe in that for herself; she and Basil always lived well, dined well. What a pity she was too cheeseparing to spend a night in a modest inn. It cost her rather dear.'

'I have observed that you are not as thin as you were when the accident occurred. You look much better now.'

Felicia wondered if that meant she had looked a fright when he had first seen her, and she decided that must be the case. Perhaps that is what prompted him to take pity on her? Not much liking her conclusions, she took a step from Lord Chessyre, only to be halted by his hand on her arm.

With some apprehension, she gazed up at his face.

'I expect I have somehow managed to put my foot in it and annoy you. I shall never find a wife; I cannot do the pretty,' he said with a smile.

'It is not *always* necessary to do the pretty, as you put it.' Felicia took another step away from him, only to have him step toward her.

'I was thinking that perhaps were Miss Woodworth to learn that Lord Brook is possessed of a goodly fortune, she might look favorably on him.'

'Happy thought, indeed,' Felicia said, a considering frown crossing her face. 'And who better to appraise her of that information than Lord Brook's cousin?' she added with a rueful smile.

'I suspected you might reach that conclusion. Shall we join the others at tea?' he asked, nudging her toward the hall. 'I will engage your cousin in conversation while you indulge in a little chat with Miss Woodworth.'

Felicia accepted his escort, placing a trembling hand on his proffered arm. 'We can but try,' she murmured as the noise of many voices raised at once reached them at the door to the dining room.

Rather than too obviously seek their quarry immediately, Lord Chessyre led her to the table where a young maid poured steaming cups of tea for each. Felicia selected several dainty sandwiches, then with a telling look at the earl, wandered off to locate Miss Woodworth.

'Miss Woodworth,' she quietly exclaimed when she found, to her intense relief, that young lady quite alone, 'how well you did for a first reading. I feel certain that Stephen was most pleased with it.'

'Thank you. I have done a few other plays at home – in the country, you see. I admire Mr Chessyre exceedingly, for I have heard he does well at his dramas. I cannot begin to tell you how thrilled I was when he asked if I would play Bianca. I see her as a challenge, a well-born woman who is more than attendant to the lovely Matilda. Bianca is a very Italian lady-in-waiting to a princess. The book refers to both

Isabella and Matilda as princesses.'

'I am impressed,' Felicia said with sincerity. 'You have far more experience than I do – or most of the others, I would fancy. He must have seen that in you at first sight.' She nibbled at her watercress sandwich, then said, 'What think you of Lord Brook?'

'He is well enough, I suppose.' Miss Woodworth cast a look in his direction and studied him.

'My cousin is also exceedingly wealthy, with two estates that produce a good income and many excellent investments. He needs a wife to help him with his household.' Felicia examined her words. She hadn't lied. She simply had not told the entire truth about Basil. Then she consoled herself that before anything serious developed, she would warn Miss Woodworth about his true character.

'How very interesting. The man who is with him looks at you quite often. Lord Chessyre, I think he is. Do you know him well?' Miss Woodworth sipped her tea, continuing her speculative study of the pair of men across the room.

'He has been most kind to me,' Felicia responded, thinking her reply made her sound like Merlin the cat who had been rescued in much the same manner.

'I see,' Miss Woodworth replied quite as though she did actually understand the situation. Which, at this point, was more than Felicia did.

'My cousin thinks to have a wife, but I suspect most of the girls he has met are too prim and proper. I saw you teasing him and thought perhaps he had met his match. He seemed very taken with you,' Felicia concluded with a demure smile.

'Really?' came a murmured reply before Miss Woodworth excused herself and drifted across the room in the general direction of Lord Brook.

Congratulating herself on what she had accomplished, Felicia wandered back to the table, helped herself to a few more sandwiches – plotting was hungry work – and sought a corner in which she could eat in peace.

'Dare I say well done?' the earl inquired as he joined her.

Felicia grinned, holding her sandwich up as to take a bite, then admitted, 'I daresay you might, were I the sort to crow. However, I well know that one ought not boast so early in the game.'

'It would seem she took the bait?' he questioned, darting a look at the pair now in conversation.

'It remains to be seen how it develops. Whatever did you say to Basil regarding Miss Woodworth?' Felicia wondered.

'I merely commented on what an attractive girl she is. Oh, and I also hinted that she is of the highest *ton*, and the clothes she is wearing look to come from the finest mantua-maker.' At the glance from Felicia he added, 'Lady Tower invites only the very best people to her parties.'

'How fortunate for us that she does,' Felicia concluded. Undoubtedly, Lady Louisa would have headed the guest list.

She watched as Basil escorted Miss Woodworth from the room, disappearing in the direction of the billiard room at the far end of the hall. Lord Chessyre left Felicia to speak to Lady Louisa, leaving Felicia feeling very alone.

Dinner was not the trial Felicia expected. Lady Louisa sat next to Stephen opposite Felicia, while Lord Chessyre had been placed next to their hostess. He might not have his hose and doublet on, but Anne Damer still seemed to find him smashing.

Basil fawned over Jane Woodworth, or was it merely her exceedingly low-cut gown he admired? He would have been pleased to know what Primrose had learned from Miss Woodworth's maid. The buxom young lady was worth a considerable sum of money upon her marriage – a legacy from her grandmother, if the maid had the tale correct. Felicia hoped that Jane Woodworth could do better than Basil. Unless she, like her character Bianca, felt a bad husband was better than no husband at all.

Sir Peter, as one of the cast, had been invited, as had Lady Emma and Lord Pelham. In her floating silvery mauve gown Lady Emma seemed fragile, the sort of woman who needed someone to look after her. Felicia hoped that Pelham would see her in that light.

Following a dinner that, while good, couldn't compare to the exquisite meals Pierre concocted, the group retired to the drawing room. From there a number of guests elected to wander through the various rooms of interest. Felicia found herself in the round drawing room with Lady Emma.

'My, how striking,' Felicia said for lack of a better word.

Lady Emma looked around and, seeing the others trailed behind, she whispered urgently, 'How does it go, dear girl? Your cousin – here – how does it affect you?'

'Your nephew and I have nudged him toward Miss Jane Woodworth, the heiress. Beyond that, I cannot say. Your nephew seems much taken with Lady Louisa. I see her mother attends this evening. I had wondered if the heiress would be here alone.' Felicia looked behind them to see Lord Chessyre tower over Lady Louisa. He gazed down at that young woman with what appeared to be genuine fondness. Lady Arden walked with Sir Peter, gesturing at something she noticed.

'Lady Arden is most astute. I suspect she believes that it is wise to allow her daughter a chance to lure the man she desires without someone constantly at her shoulder.' Lady Emma seemed vastly pleased at the way matters were going.

'Of course,' Felicia said bleakly. 'Perhaps Basil and Miss Woodworth will make a match of it in that case.'

'Lady Louisa is a charming young lady,' Lady Emma said with a hint of complacency in her voice.

'She has impeccable manners, perfect *ton*,' Felicia said with a pang, knowing that could scarcely be said about her. She'd wager that Lady Louisa never permitted a gentleman to kiss her!

'Indeed. Although, Felicia, dare I wonder how life might be with perfection?' Lady Emma frowned, then added, 'It could weary one in time, I believe.'

'I am sure that the earl knows what is best, my lady. He would never discredit you or his title by an improper alliance.' Felicia could hear the voices closer now, Lady Louisa politely commenting on some artifact and Lord Chessyre's low voice explaining what she viewed.

Felicia wondered how she would manage to endure the following days, seeing those two together, listening to them converse in such an unexceptional manner. As Lady Emma said, they were perfection.

When the others entered the round drawing room, exclaiming on the lovely ceiling with its decorative plaster work and the walls hung with crimson Norwich silk, Felicia felt her heart sink. What a time to be compelled to admit – to herself alone – that she most assuredly was in love with Lord Chessyre. What she had first thought to be gratitude, then suspected might be attraction, had bloomed into far more than that. She loved him.

And it appeared he was only doing her a favor, helping a maid in distress, as it were. He obviously cared for Lady Louisa – the beautiful, wealthy, well-born, and incredibly sweet Lady Louisa.

All that was left for Felicia was crumbs. Must she give up? Must she concede that perfection was for him? She glanced at the pair engrossed in a fine landscape and decided that her father didn't raise a girl who would quit without a fight.

Playbill

The Castle of Otranto

Cast of Characters

Manfred, Prince of Otranto	Sir Peter Quillan
Matilda, his daughter,	
the princess	Felicia Brook
Bianca, Matilda's lady-in-	
waiting	Jane Woodworth
Hippolita, Manfred's wife	Anne Damer
Frederic, Marquis of Vincenza	William, Lord Chessyre
Isabella, Frederic's daughter	Lady Louisa Arden
Theodore, the prince in disguise	Stephen Chessyre
Friar Jerome	Basil, Lord Brook

Chapter Ten

'**W**hat are you about, Chessyre?' Stephen quizzed as they sat in William's library. 'Do you have a particular interest in Lady Louisa?'

'I have a concern for her, to be sure,' William replied cautiously.

'Is she not the most beautiful creature in the world? I have never encountered anyone with prettier manners in my life,' Stephen declared, his exuberance almost catching.

'Indeed, she seems a nice girl,' William replied, watching his cousin with a keen gaze and listening with sharply attuned ears.

'Are you tepid because you think to discourage me in my pursuit of her? For I mean to have her as my own.' Stephen rose from his fireside chair to confront William, his face angry. 'Or do you want her for yourself?'

'You cannot have a person for your own, Stephen. She is not a pet. However, if you wish to marry the girl, you have my blessing.' William stood opposite his cousin, his hands lightly clasped behind his back, waiting for a reaction.

'I hear an unspoken *but* in that blessing,' Stephen muttered, kicking a log in the fireplace with a well-aimed boot.'

'*But* you will have to brave Lord Arden, not to mention all the countless peers who also desire this matchless beauty as a wife. Good grief, Stephen, the girl has a fortune, not to mention all those other attributes.'

'Will the others love her as I do?' Stephen demanded. 'The

moment I saw her I knew she was for me. And I believe she returns my affection.'

'You must be aware that your love for her will have no effect on her father. Settlements, Stephen,' William reminded. 'Lord Arden will be far more concerned with the condition of your estate, the amount of your bank balance, your habits – no gaming, no mistresses.'

'How could I look at another woman when there is Louisa?' Stephen said, sinking back on his chair, a bemused, rather silly expression on his face.

What William muttered to himself was just as well not heard by his younger cousin.

Then Stephen roused himself to stare at William. 'I shan't try to puff my being your heir, you know. I imagine that will end all too soon if what I suspect is true.'

'If you are fishing, try another pond,' William said, unwilling to put his feelings into words at this point. 'I suggest that if you want some sort of title, you improve your estates and make a contribution of some kind to the Prince Regent. He appreciates support,' William concluded with more than a little irony. 'Try a viscountcy. I under- stand that particular title is not in vogue at the moment, so it ought to be easy to obtain with a word in the right ear, a donation in the right pocket.'

'Bribery,' Stephen said with disgust.

'Government has always had bribery, and I suspect it always will, people being what they are. I fancy you will discover that even the matchless Lady Louisa Arden is not perfect. Would perfection not become tedious after a time?' William asked, knowing he was right.

'Well, as to that,' Stephen said slowly, 'I suppose you are correct. Possibly she has a flaw somewhere. I should like to spend a lifetime hunting for it.'

William threw up his hands. 'I can see you are determined. All I have to say to you is. . . .'

'What?' Stephen demanded, rising to confront his cousin with clenched fists.

'The best of luck, old fellow. I hope the girl appreciates you as we do.' William smiled benignly.

A gentle rap on the library door preceded the entry of Lady Emma. She drifted across the room to stand between her nephews, looking to one, then the other. 'I am pleased for you, dear boy,' she finally said to Stephen. 'Although I had thought that dearest Will would desire Lady Louisa.'

'I rather think he has ideas along that line that do not include Louisa,' Stephen said with a grin.

'Truly? I wonder who it might be? That charming Miss Woodworth? I saw you speaking with her last evening. She is, er, quite talented, I believe.'

'I rather think Lord Brook is about to annex her,' William said, looking wise. 'I have observed her, and I believe Brook might be acquiring more than he anticipates.'

'So then?' Lady Emma inquired with a bewildered expression. 'Who?'

'As I just told Stephen, if you are fishing, try another pond. I am about to depart for Strawberry Hill. You as well, Stephen? As I recall, you scheduled another rehearsal this afternoon.'

'I intend to come with one of you,' Lady Emma insisted. 'Lord Pelham has a sitting, and I have no intention of leaving him in that woman's clutches unprotected.'

William watched his aunt float from the library in what were, for her, determined steps. 'She had best drive out with you. I have no desire to be quizzed the entire trip.'

At Strawberry Hill Felicia welcomed Lady Louisa into the Holbein Chamber with mixed pleasure. 'Good morning, my lady. Will you not sit down? I was just reading over my part in the play.'

Merlin came to investigate the guest, rubbing up against Felicia in the hope his kind mistress would take pity on him and cuddle him in her arms. She did, and the cat purred loudly with satisfaction.

'I hoped we might study our lines together,' Lady Louisa said, holding up her copy of the script.'

'Excellent idea,' Felicia said, trying not to like the amiable young woman and failing.'

They settled down to business immediately, saying and repeating lines, offering cues, discussing the characters and motives with intelligence that would possibly have surprised the gentlemen involved with the play.

Another rap on the door an hour later brought in Miss Woodworth, also bearing her copy of the script.

'I do not have so many lines to learn, but you do. I thought I might help.' She gave Felicia a tentative smile, then looked to Lady Louisa. Gone was the flirt of the evening before, and instead she appeared a pleasant and discreetly garbed young woman.

'Very good notion,' Felicia said, jumping up to pull forward another ebony chair. 'We are here,' and she pointed to the place in the script where she and Lady Louisa had paused, unable to agree on how a line ought to be spoken.

'Listen to this,' Lady Louisa begged. 'Heavens, what do I hear! You, my lord! You! My father-in-law! the father of Conrad! the husband of the virtuous and tender Hippolita!'

Felicia held up a hand. 'I believe she should sound more horrified. After all, Manfred is a married man, and he just suggested that Isabella marry him since Conrad is dead. He's determined to continue his line, and since his only son is gone, he must have a new wife. Hippolita can bear him no more children. Somehow he intends to put her aside. For a Catholic girl of that time, it would be an unthinkable situation.'

'It seems to me that Lady Louisa does well at the lines, although perhaps she might recoil in honor, show her abhorrence of what this man proposes,' Jane Woodworth said diplomatically.

'I do not intend to make this a farce,' Lady Louisa objected.

'No, no,' Felicia assured her. 'The idea is to make it seem so real that the audience can feel her fear, her repugnance at what is proposed.'

Primrose stuck her head around the corner from the dressing room. 'The others are gathering belowstairs for a puncheon. Might you want to join them?'

Felicia gave her maid a grateful look. Lady Louisa might have the right of the interpretation, but she was a trifle strong in her assertions.

The three young women walked down to the bottom of the stairs, reaching the entry just as Lord Chessyre was let into the house by the butler.

Lady Louisa hurried forward, coming to a halt before the earl and beaming an enchanting smile at him. 'I hoped I might speak with you, my lord.'

Felicia watched, hoping her face revealed nothing of her inner dismay at this forwardness on the part of Lady Louisa. Or was it merely the desire of a girl to seek the company of the man she hoped to make hers?

'Good afternoon, ladies,' Chessyre said pleasantly, then offered his arm to Lady Louisa, who promptly marched him off in the direction of the dining room. The sight of his dear head bent over Louisa proved hard to bear.

'Good afternoon, indeed,' Felicia whispered, then turned a stricken gaze on Miss Woodworth. 'Shall we have something to eat? I declare, I am famished.'

If Miss Woodworth took note that Felicia pushed the few dabs of food around her plate again and again with no effort made to consume more than a bite or two, she made no comment.

'Felicia,' Stephen demanded, breezing into the room, 'where is Lady Louisa?'

'There, sir, with your cousin.' Felicia watched as Stephen joined the pair who had been in deep discussion on the far side of the room. If there were any loverlike nuances between Chessyre and Louisa, Stephen did not appear to notice them. He greeted his cousin with affection and Louisa with admiration and respect.

Lord, what fools we mortals be, Felicia thought, deciding that Shakespeare knew of what he wrote.

'Why so pensive, Felicia?' Miss Woodworth inquired.

'Jane, have you ever seen *A Midsummer Night's Dream*? The poet obviously thinks love is a form of madness, driving lovers to behave in foolish ways. He had them all so confused. I declare, I quite sympa-thize with them.'

'You are confused?' Jane asked while looking curiously at the others.

'I believe it is merely this tale we are to act that affects me.' Fearing she had revealed more than intended, Felicia rose from her dining chair, turning away from the sight of Stephen, Lady Louisa, and Lord Chessyre in amiable conversation. 'Come, let us go to some other room. See, Lady Emma is here.'

Jane observed the direction of that darted look, then walked with her new friends from the room. The three women sauntered along the hall until they found the room that had interested them before, the round drawing room.

'Ah, Miss Woodworth,' Basil exclaimed as they entered the room. 'I have been searching for you. Would you take pity on a poor chap and listen to my lines?' He cocked his head, smiling at Jane with what he obviously hoped was charm.

Apparently it did not repel Jane as it did Felicia.

'Willingly. My lines are simple to learn, so I am comfortable with them. I shall gladly help you, sir.'

Once they were out of sight and hearing, Felicia turned to Lady Emma and said quietly, 'Oh, *how* can she bear that odious toad for one minute?'

'I cannot imagine, dear girl. I suppose each person has his or her own ideas of what is desirable.'

'Surely she cannot accept what her character in the play declares, that a bad husband is better than no husband at all!'

'As to that, dearest, there are women who do feel that way, you know.' Lady Emma patted Felicia on the arm, then set about explor-ing the room's many interesting bits and pieces that Walpole had collected over the years.

When Lord Pelham joined them, Felicia decided to help Lady Emma's little affair by leaving them alone.

Offering a murmured excuse she doubted they even noticed, and she walked in the opposite direction, feeling rather lost and lonely in this vast and eerie house with its many Gothic arches and elaborate carvings that imparted a church-like atmosphere. At times one felt as though one ought to whisper. A strong wind howling about the chimney or clicking branches to fearfully haunt one's step would be quite in keeping. Perhaps floating draperies or a portrait that sighs would add a distinctive touch to the place. It certainly was effective in the story – frightened everyone half out of their wits.

'Felicia?'

She jumped at least an inch and felt as though she had gone a foot in the air. Spinning about, she found the earl watching her, with a quizzical expression.

'I am sorry if I alarmed you. This place does tend to make one think of specters and supernatural happenings. Have you learned your part? Louisa says you do very well at the drama.'

Felicia noted his informality and took refuge in civility. Folding her hands before her, she politely said, 'Lord Chessyre, you startled me. I fear Lady Louisa is being kind.' Felicia paused for a few moments, waiting for him to say something. When he didn't, she continued. 'Did you wish me to do something for you . . . or Lady Louisa?' Felicia decided that she would not give the slightest hint of her partiality for Lord Chessyre – not if it killed her.

He seemed to stiffen at her words – or was it her manner that so affected him? At any rate, they were as strangers again, just as they had been at Chessyre Court.

'I had hoped for some intelligent conversation from her. Once Stephen came, well, talk turned to the play, of course.'

'The play,' Felicia echoed. How she wished she had not agreed to act in the dratted thing. She hated having to pretend to adore Stephen when her heart was given to another. 'Of course. What would you prefer to discuss, my lord,' she said with all courtesy.

'I wish I knew what went on in your mind,' he murmured.

'Thank goodness you do not,' she said with quiet fervency.

'How do the costumes go?' he inquired with a politeness equal to her own.

'Well, I believe. Stephen's peasant's smock looks authentic, his princely garb perhaps not quite, but well enough to fool someone sitting some distance away. Just how far away do people sit?' she thought to ask.

'Far enough so you shall not notice them once the play begins. Have you seen the scenery? A friend of Stephen's is rather clever at painting blurry effects that give a sense of the scene. Come, I shall show you.'

Catching his sudden enthusiasm, Felicia hurried at his side until they reached the room where Anne Damer worked on her sculpture. Since she was out of the room, they entered to survey the canvases hung on one of the walls.

'My, that certainly looks like a Gothic castle, complete with dungeon. I fully expect to hear a moan or a clank at any moment,' Felicia cried. The scene looked ordinary, yet there seemed to be a sense of menace about it. She turned her attention to the next canvas, a rendition of Hippolita's bedroom, where Manfred confronts her regarding Isabella. Matilda's room, where the princess converses with Theodore in the prisoner's room below, was a shadowed, romantic place. It did not seem the atmosphere in which Bianca could spout her nonsense about a husband.

Felicia voiced her doubts.

'That is just it,' Lord Chessyre said calmly, 'the very contrast between the beauty of the room, the loveliness of the girl, and the judgment of Bianca regarding husbands makes it seem all the more outrageous to consider a pretty girl being forced to marry an old man.'

'Played by you. You are not old in the least; how will you look older – white powder in your hair? You are to be much struck by the charms of Matilda, actually figuring that marriage to her will aid you in succession to the principality.'

'But,' the earl reminded, 'I am seized with a passion for Matilda, remember?'

'You have a strange way of showing it, bowing politely and looking at her with admiration,' Felicia said with amusement.

'Hm, maybe I have not had enough practice as of late. Perhaps you will oblige, Felicia?'

They were alone, and before she could think of how to avoid what she desired, Lord Chessyre had captured her in his arms and placed an incredibly sweet kiss on her lips.

Felicia kept her eyes closed, wanting to savor the touch of his lips against hers, the warmth of his arms about her.

'I had best repeat the effort,' he whispered. 'I seem to have put you into a trance. 'Tis the atmosphere in here.'

He definitely improved with repetition.

However, this time she promptly flashed her eyes open, pushing him to free herself. He did not let go.

'Look at me, Felicia,' he softly demanded.

Unable to resist those seductively spoken words, she obeyed. His eyes were such a beautiful gray, fathoms deep, and, when not angry, warm and inviting. He seemed satisfied at whatever he saw, for he nodded, looking pleased. Was it at her foolishness? She'd vowed to avoid him, and here she was in his arms.

When he released her, he turned to another canvas hung on the wall, the courtyard of the final scene. Lush flowers bloomed, cascading from urns in niches and over railings. A hazy sky seemed to shimmer over the Florentine landscape.

'Here is where he really is clever,' Lord Chessyre began, quite as though that earth-shaking kiss had never taken place. 'When a light is directed on the canvas from behind, it will appear as though the ghost of Alfonso is present.'

'I trust it will amuse people and be worth all our efforts,' Felicia said, perhaps a trifle sharply, for he gave her a sudden intense look.

'Do I detect unhappiness?'

'No, no,' she said hastily, maybe too hastily, for it seemed not to satisfy him.

He glanced at the clock on the fireplace mantel and muttered a few words Felicia could not catch.

'A problem?' she wondered. Perhaps he thought to return to Lady Louisa. It was not wise to leave her with his handsome cousin for long.

'I promised Stephen I would find you for the rehearsal. He is likely ready to throttle me for my failure to return promptly.' He thrust one hand in his hair, then gave her a rueful smile. 'We had best go.'

It was an odd admission, but one that found its way to Felicia's heart with unerring speed. Lord Chessyre had rather spend time with her than with the others. How very nice. But, she sighed inwardly, of course it didn't mean anything. The perfectly beautiful, well-mannered, and sweet-natured Lady Louisa would capture the man she wanted with not the slightest difficulty.

Never mind that Felicia wanted the same man.

The days that followed brought little change in the situation. Lady Louisa captured Lord Chessyre as soon as he arrived, hanging on his arm and laughing up into his face with amazing charm. How could any man be expected to resist that amiable creature? Naturally, he couldn't withstand her prettily worded demands that he help her.

Even Felicia was not proof against her charm. Mrs Damer must work at his likeness by memory.

Poor Stephen. It was becoming obvious to Felicia – perhaps her own heightened awareness helped – that he was more than a little attracted to Louisa. The ardent looks, the unfeigned adoration of his kisses – even if on her hands – were evidence of his attachment.

At dinner Felicia managed to avoid much conversation. Mrs Damer brought in musicians every evening to entertain them with selections from Vivaldi, Handel, Bach, and Corelli. It offered an excellent reason for Felicia to remain silent. Since she truly enjoyed the music, there was no hypocrisy in her behavior.

Lady Louisa sat between Lord Chessyre and Stephen, seeming to sweetly play one against the other. The gentlemen appeared not to object in the slightest. They accepted what crumbs of her attention they merited and smiled all the while.

Felicia studied the trio several evenings after the visit to the studio. Really, if she had an ounce of brains she would learn how Louisa managed by observing her.

Her mother ought to be most proud of her daughter. Lord Chessyre was considered to be a prime catch of the Season, while

Stephen had considerable wealth and appeared to be angling for a title. Surely he wouldn't *really* invite the Prince Regent to attend the play. He couldn't. He wouldn't. He had.

'I shall swoon, I know I shall,' Felicia moaned to Jane Woodworth when she heard the news.

'It is an intimidating thought, I agree. Perhaps he will not be able to attend?' Jane said with hope.

'Happy thought!' Felicia replied, but continued, 'however, I fear we are doomed. An acceptance has come – which has put Stephen in alt, let me tell you. Lady Emma has ordered a new gown for the occasion, and Basil announced he is thinking of allowing Willa to come to London for the evening.'

'Willa? That is his sister? She prefers to live quietly in the country, I understand?' Jane inquired.

Felicia considered how best to answer this rather tricky question. 'Basil had arranged a most advantageous marriage for Willa, and she flatly refused to wed the man. Furious with her, Basil suggested that perhaps a quiet time of reflection would improve her temper.'

'Poor girl,' Jane said, brows drawn together in consideration of what she had learned about the gentleman in whose company she spent the better part of every day. 'Yet I expect he did what he considered necessary for her future comfort. Marriage is seldom for romance. More often than not it is for economic security.'

'Yes, well, we had better learn our parts letter perfect. I understand that later we are to do what Stephen calls a dress rehearsal.'

'I hope that Lord Brook returns in time. He went to consult with his solicitor.'

The very words chilled Felicia's heart. She glanced at Lord Chessyre, attempting to signal him in some manner. Perhaps he grasped her concern, for he nodded.

It was perhaps some ten minutes later that the earl sought Felicia where she stood off-stage, as it were, being the raised platform at one end of the Great Parlor.

'Did I interpret that frantic look as a sign you wished to speak with me?'

'Miss Woodworth informed me that Basil has spent the morning visiting his solicitor. Is that not interesting, my lord?' She tried to keep quavering fear from her voice, but failed.

'Hm.' Lord Chessyre glanced about him, then indicated by a tilt of his head that they should move away from the group who were practicing their lines.

'You believe he might cause trouble?' he inquired. 'Do you not, sir?' she queried in return.

'I am not sure.' The earl frowned, seeming to study the pattern cast by the sun shining through a magnificent piece of stained glass. Bloodred patches were surrounded by deep blue, vivid green, and gold. 'Be careful. That is all I may suggest for the moment. Until we know or suspect what he has learned, we can take no action.'

His words were small comfort to a worried girl.

Seeming to realize how distressed Felicia was, he touched her lightly on her shoulder as though offering the comfort she wished, and said, 'Take heart, another two evenings and we shall be done with this nonsense.'

'I would that all of it were nonsense,' Felicia shot back with a glance at where Lady Louisa and Stephen stood rehearsing the scene where they meet in the vaults. He was gazing at her as if she were the vision of a saint, while Louisa adored Stephen as though he were her defender and champion, to save her from all harm.

'They do their parts well, do they not?' the earl observed dryly.

'They do, indeed; far better than me, I fear.' She could not put her heart into being Matilda, the girl who loves Theodore, ultimately dying because of it. Poor Isabella, to be a princess deemed second best, having to endure the knowledge that as long as she lived it would be Matilda who came first in the handsome Theodore's thoughts.

'You are pensive.'

'Perhaps it is the mood of the place. I feel haunted by I know not what.'

At last Stephen decreed that they would start the play, wearing full costume, and continue to the end, as though with an audience.

There were mishaps, servants appearing before they ought, Sir

Peter not sounding as crafty as he might in the scene where he tries to convince Isabella she must marry him. But before long the mood of the plot seemed to catch everyone, and an intense quiet settled over the room as the drama reached its conclusion.

Felicia as Matilda entered the stage to meet Theodore, intent upon arranging an elopement so they could marry in spite of her father's machinations. The lovers met, clasped hands, and exchanged soft greetings. Then Sir Peter stealthily crept up on the pair, believing that Isabella was the one trysting with the man she loves. He raised his dagger and plunged it down.

Felicia screamed as incredible pain shot through her shoulder. She fell forward against Stephen, who helped her to the floor, gently easing her down.

All havoc broke lose as blood began to seep through the costume.

'What have I done?' Sir Peter cried, unconsciously using the words Manfred uses when he discovers he has stabbed his own daughter instead of Isabella.

'Light, bring us more light!' Stephen demanded.

Lady Emma rushed forward with a branch of candles, crying with horror when she saw the bloodied costume. 'How did this happen? Surely, you did not use a real dagger!'

Stephen swiftly formed a pad of gauze to press against the wound, while Lady Emma placed a comforting arm around a nearly unconscious Felicia.

Sir Peter looked at the weapon in his hand and frowned. 'This is not the dagger Mrs Damer gave me to use – the stage dagger that collapses into itself. This is a real dagger.'

Lord Chessyre inserted himself into the group, taking command of the situation at once. 'She must have a doctor. Stephen, send for one immediately.'

William gathered Felicia into his arms and strode from the platform, and through the halls, crying for warm water, soap, bandages, and ointment as he went. He charged up the stairs to the Holbein Chamber. Kicking the partly open door, he hurried into the room and went through to the bedroom to place Felicia on the bed.

Primrose was at his side immediately. Rather than ask what had happened, she promptly tore the gown away from the injury, revealing the stab wound, which while not deep, must have been extremely painful.

The blood-soaked gauze pad was tossed aside, then Primrose carefully cleaned the wound, taking a bandage to place over the injury from the tray hurriedly brought to the room.

When done, she studied her unconscious mistress, turning to Lord Chessyre to demand, 'What happened, milord?'

'It was an accident. Sir Peter used the wrong dagger. Lucky for Felicia she was more turned than usual, or the dagger would have plunged into her heart.' He shook his head, looking about as though searching for an answer. 'I cannot believe this happened!'

'It was an *accident*?' Primrose cried in disbelief.

Chapter Eleven

It was an hour before the doctor arrived. He bustled into the room, casting a disapproving look at Lord Chessyre, who had refused to leave Felicia's side. He retained a hold on Felicia's hand far more fervent than Stephen had in the death scene.

'You, sir, must leave at once,' Dr Johnstone declared, a faint burr enriching his speech.

The earl rose, glared at the doctor, but obeyed, knowing as well as anyone that his presence was improper. He had left Felicia's side to remain in the sitting room long enough for the blue gown to be stripped from her. Since then she had been covered to her neck, with her petticoats and stays concealed quite admirably.

Lady Louisa and Lady Emma were ordered from the room as well, with Primrose left to assist the Scotsman.

'I think she is not so bad, sir,' the maid offered. 'The dagger 'pears to have made a slash that bled a good deal but not gone deep. She fainted after the stabbing. Didn't come to even when his lordship put her into bed. She roused when her ladyship and I eased her gown off. S'pect she'll wake again soon enough'

The young doctor, just come from Edinburgh, where he had completed a few years' practice, examined the wound and cleansed it with something that looked suspiciously like spirits to Primrose. Then he patted the skin into place, poured a powder over all, and placed a bandage over the area, binding it in place with strips of cloth.

'It is a simple cut, a clean one with no jagged edges,' he explained to the maid. 'Give her some liquids and see that she rests.'

Primrose pulled back the covers, placing one of Felicia's arms atop them, thinking the doctor would undoubtedly cup or bleed her mistress.

'If the wound does not become infected, she will be as good as new in no time, albeit with a scar. Most likely she can hide it with some frippery lace.' He rose from the bedside to look at the face of the woman he'd treated. 'Pity, for she is so young, and pretty at that.'

'You ain't going to bleed her?' the maid said in surprise when she saw him putting his things in his bag.

'No, not unless your mistress shows signs of complications and fever. Give her broth and tea, light food, and this laudanum if she has pain – a teaspoon, no more. I shall return tomorrow to see how she does.' He left a small dark bottle on the bedside table.

Primrose hovered over her mistress as the doctor departed, her face reflecting her mixed feelings about this young fellow and his treatment. Smoothing the covers, she waited for Felicia to awaken.

The doctor was greeted with anxious cries when he left the Holbein Chamber.

'Sir, tell us how she does,' begged Lady Emma, her hands clasped before her, her eyes worried.

'Like many who are slightly wounded, she bled profusely. Given her youth and obvious good health, she will be up and around in no time.' He made his way down the hall, to be intercepted by Lord Chessyre.

'She will need to stay in bed for some days, will she not?' The earl's face was pale with apprehension.

'I think not. Allow her up when she wishes.' At the gasps of dismay from those gathered about him, the doctor smiled and added, 'The thinking now is that perhaps we have kept our patients abed too long. With proper care, she may do as she feels best. Just see to it that she does not strain her shoulder and disturb the healing process.'

He marched down the steps and was out of the house before the three on the landing could react with other than astonishment at his words.

'Nonsense, she will stay in bed until completely healed,' Lord

Chessyre insisted.

'Poor dear. She will miss being in the play.' Lady Emma shredded a handkerchief, looking nearly as pale as Felicia had in the great Holbein bed.

'I think we ought to listen to the doctor,' Lady Louisa objected. 'Newly come from Edinburgh, he would know the very latest of thinking.'

When Lord Chessyre would argue with this heresy, Lady Emma interrupted, 'But dearest boy, why not permit Felicia to decide for herself?'

'What would the patient know about it?' he asked in frustration.

'How is she?' demanded Sir Peter as he came from the Great Parlor to receive news. If the others were pale, the knight looked positively haggard. 'She must recover. Tell me the news is good.' He stood amid the splendor of the Gothic arches and windows of the entry, the suits of armor appearing like soldiers ready to cart him away to prison.

Miss Woodworth and Basil, followed by Lord Pelham, Mrs Damer, and a morose Stephen joined him, all appearing deeply concerned.

All looked to the earl, who had assumed control over the situation. He explained what Dr Johnstone had decreed and listened to the objections with a shrug.

William tried to study Basil Brook without being too obvious, wondering about the baron. Did he *pretend* his horror of the accident? He had been in the scene, certainly had ample time in which to make the exchange. *Someone* had to have made the substitution of the fake dagger with a real and deadly one. It would have been easy to conceal the deadly dagger in the folds of that shapeless gray robe he wore in the play. Sir Peter had no motive, but Basil did, bless his greedy soul.

'Well, I suppose this puts an end to our Gothic drama,' Mrs Damer said with resignation. 'I had so looked forward to this tribute to Horace Walpole.'

'Wait,' Lady Louisa cried. 'Please wait until we see how Felicia does. In two days' time she might be able to manage to do the play with only a few changes so she does not tire easily. I know she would be the last to cause a cancellation when she knows so much may depend on it.' Blushing slightly, Louisa cast a demure glance at Stephen.

'Ah, yes,' William said, his tone derisive, 'our fat prince comes, and Stephen wants that viscountcy. I had forgotten.'

'Lady Louisa is right,' Jane said stoutly. 'Permit Felicia to make her own decision.'

And so it was left at that, with the earl grumbling all the while. Had he dared, he would have demanded to stay the night. However, he knew what talk that would stir, so he regretfully left with his aunt and Lord Pelham, maintaining a moody silence on the drive home.

Once at Chessyre House, Lady Emma hurried away to change her gown while the servants arranged for a supper.

The men entered the drawing room, standing before the fireplace in silence for some moments before the earl ventured to speak.

'It was no accident. The theatrical dagger had been switched for a real one as alike as possible.'

'I agree,' Lord Pelham concurred. 'Who did it?'

'Unless I very much miss my guess, Lord Brook is the one responsible.'

Lord Pelham raised his brows, but said nothing for a minute or two, merely thinking. 'I do not know the particulars as to why you feel her cousin is guilty, but if he is, how do you prove it?'

William braced his arm on the chimneypiece and stared down into the flames. 'That's just it. I have no proof. None. And she had just thanked me for helping her. My *help* bloody near got her killed.'

'You were helping Miss Brook?' Lord Pelham inquired, standing with his hands behind him, toasting his back to the fire. Thus he was the first to see Lady Emma as she hurried into the room.

She obviously had heard what was being discussed and said, 'Felicia was cheated out of her inheritance by Basil's mother, with the acquiescence of her uncle, the late Lord Brook.' Her voice quivered with indignation. 'Can you fathom a doting father not leaving his precious daughter so much as a farthing?'

'Indeed, not. So, what can be done about it?' He looked to the earl, who had so ably taken control after the supposed accident.

'I have Harding looking into the matter. He has arranged a new reading and examination of the will. Harding explained the will brought to court was quite legal, but he feels it is fraudulent. There was no signature, only an X mark and the Brook seal well indented into the red wax.'

'No signature? How can that be legal?' Lord Pelham exclaimed.

Alford announced that a meal was prepared for them and waiting in the dining room.

'Let us discuss this over our food,' Lady Emma urged, who had heard the details before and thought to tempt Lord Pelham with some excellent fare.

William explained between bites of sole and buttered potatoes how the will had been set up, that such a procedure, while unusual, was yet legal. 'Harding says it is time that this type of will be declared an inducement to fraud and abolished. Anyone who had access to the Brook seal could have melted a blob of wax on that page, so to imprint the seal, and any fool can make an X.'

'Can Harding *prove* the will fraudulent, however?' Pelham demanded. 'If the mother is dead – and she must have been the one to instigate the forged will – how do you punish the heir?'

'That is another matter. Harding says he thinks he knows of a way. After this attempt on Felicia's life, I am more determined than ever to see that she receives her proper inheritance. The most dreadful thing that could happen to Brook is to lose the money. I believe that would hit him harder than being transported.'

'Seems to me that if Lady Brook ordered the forged will, she would have been a deal more clever to give the girl a modest sum. Far less likely to raise questions that way,' Lord Pelham remarked between forkfuls of excellent pigeon pie.

'The present Lord Brook has boundless greed. I did a bit of mousing around to learn that Rothschild is investing large sums on his behalf to make as much profit as he can – regardless of where the investment lies. Brook has bought shares in a slave trader.'

Lady Emma gasped. 'I daresay there are those who accept slavery, but I cannot. What a dreadful man. Dearest boy, you must do something about Basil!'

'I fully intend to, dear Aunt. The matter is, how to do it!' Lord
Chessyre leaned back on his dining chair. With an elbow on the chair
arm, his hand rubbing his chin, he mulled over the problem.

'I will never forgive myself for scarring such a beautiful young
woman,' Sir Peter declared after a hasty and often interrupted meal.
No one had been hungry, merely nibbling on the proffered food. He
shared a look with Mrs Damer, who placed a comforting hand over
his.

'Have you no notion as to how another dagger came to be substituted for the fake one I obtained from the theater?'

'None at all. I went to where I'd kept the dratted thing, did not
bother to examine it, just picked it up and went on the stage.' Sir
Peter rose to restlessly pace back and forth before the dining room
fireplace.

'Anyone could have access to it, from the servants to all of us in the
cast,' she observed. She leaned back in her chair, running her gaze
from Lady Louisa – who had refused to leave until Felicia was
conscious once again, to Jane Woodworth – who felt the same, then
on to Lord Brook – who insisted he would escort Miss Woodworth to
her home when she wished to leave. Stephen sat in stunned silence at
the end of the table, moodily staring off into space while fiddling with
his wineglass.

'I would swear there is no one around who would wish the charming Miss Brook ill. Is that not correct, Lord Brook?' Mrs Damer
languidly inquired of the baron.

'Indeed, ma'am. Indeed,' he said after clearing his throat. 'Not a
soul.'

Felicia woke to pain. Her left shoulder felt as though it were on fire;
an ache shot through her chest if she so much as moved an inch.

'Primrose, I am trussed like a Christmas goose. Help me untangle
myself from these covers,' Felicia murmured.

'Indeed, you will not move, ma'am. You were wounded – do you not remember?' The maid hovered by the bed, testing the pale face for a fever and thankfully finding none.

Another twinge of pain shot through Felicia as she picked at the bandage covering her shoulder. With that her memory returned, and with it the recollection of being held close by Lord Chessyre before she lost consciousness.

'I'm thirsty, Primrose. Help me to sit up against my pillows.' At the expression of dismay on her maid's face, Felicia smiled wanly. 'I shall not break, and I will be careful not to aggravate the wound. I shall have pain whether I am flat or against the pillows. My throat is as dry as the proverbial desert.'

'Barley water, ma'am. 'Tis what that Scotsman said for ye to have.' Primrose, clearly against her inclinations, assisted Felicia to a comfortable position – not quite sitting up, but at least able to sip her drink without spilling it across the sheets. She stuffed another pillow behind her mistress, then poured a glass of barley water for Felicia to drink.

With a grimace Felicia downed the contents, then handed the glass to Primrose.

'It aches something fearful at the moment,' Felicia said after considering the injury for a time while resting against the mound of pillows. 'But I believe I shall mend.'

'Just so no infection sets in, the doctor said,' the maid cautioned, giving the mound of pillows a dubious look.

A gentle tap on the door sent Primrose scurrying to answer it. Lady Louisa entered, tiptoeing into the sitting room while casting an anxious look at the great bed, where nothing more than a mound of pillows and a purple coverlet might be seen.

Felicia turned her head, gasping only slightly at the pain. 'Please, come in. I fear the hours will pass slowly while I recover.'

'Oh, I am so glad to hear your voice and that you sound so well.' Louisa hurried into the bedroom, seating herself on the chair left in place by the doctor.

'The rest of me is fine, but all my sensibilities are centered in my shoulder. Tell me, what happened?'

'Someone substituted a real dagger for the pretend one that Mrs Damer obtained from the theater. No one has a clue as to who might have done this dreadful thing.'

'Where is everyone now?' Felicia inquired.

'Lady Emma, Lord Chessyre, and Lord Pelham have gone, not without a good bit of persuasion. They will return in the morning. Stephen is desolate. Poor man, I believe he feels responsible for dragging you into this affair.'

Felicia cautiously shook her head. 'Never. The one who put out the real dagger is the culprit. Be thankful that you did not play Matilda. What a horrid part.'

'That Scot doctor said you might get out of bed whenever you please. I cannot believe it is so. My mother would have me in bed for a month should I have a like wound.'

'Whenever I please?' Felicia asked with a look at Primrose. 'How interesting. What about the play?'

'Stephen wants to cancel it, but in view of what Johnstone said, I suggested that we wait for your word on the matter.' Louisa gave Felicia a worried look, then said, 'The play was to be in two days' time.'

'Why do we not see how I feel come morning? It is only a small gash, is it not? The dagger was a little one.'

'Lord Chessyre said that had you not turned just as you did, that the dagger could have plunged into your heart.'

'I did not have to know that at this moment,' Felicia murmured.

'I am sorry,' Lady Louisa cried. 'Oh, I pray that you will feel more the thing tomorrow.'

Felicia said nothing on that score, thinking that perhaps Lady Louisa was as much concerned for Stephen and his desire for the title as she was for Felicia's restored health. It was the first flaw found in the young lady, and though it could not please, Felicia took strange comfort that the girl was not perfect after all. At that point she asked Louisa to greet the others and tell them she was doing well.

'Particularly tell my cousin. I feel certain that Basil will be most concerned for my state of health.' The irony in Felicia's tone was lost on Louisa.

She rose from the chair with a relieved smile. 'Of course. I shall assure them all that you are very brave and improving by the minute.'

When Primrose returned after seeing Lady Louisa to the door, Felicia said, 'Under no circumstances is my cousin to be allowed in my sitting room. And any food that is brought here must be tested by' – she searched for someone faithful and saw Merlin – 'the cat.'

'Trouble afoot, ma'am? I shall guard you as best I can.' Primrose set about removing the petticoats and the stays, then assisting her mistress into a nightrobe of fine embroidered muslin. Then she carefully tucked the nut brown curls into a ruffled nightcap.

'Such a lot has happened since we left Brook Hall, has it not, Primrose?' Felicia inquired wistfully.

The maid nodded, adding, 'It will turn out fine, miss. I feel it in my bones.'

'I hope your bones feel better than I do.'

Felicia accepted the spoon of laudanum to help her sleep, sipped at her barley water, then relaxed against the pillows.

'Good Primrose. The best thing I have done is to bring you with me.' Felicia bestowed a grateful smile on her maid.

'I been paid well, miss. Not but what I'd tend you all the same. Lord Chessyre, he gave me a year's pay to look after you.' The maid folded her hands before her, giving Felicia a proud look. 'I'll see to it that you mend quick, and I won't let no one else tend you, neither.'

'A year's pay? Another debt I owe him. Will there be no end to it?' Then the drug took effect, and she drifted off to dream of the handsome lord carrying her in his arms as they walked through fields of daffodils laughing all the while.

The scent of flowers reached her when she awoke in the morning. Shaking off the effects of her drug-induced sleep, she turned her head to see a veritable conservatory of blooms that covered every available space in her room.

Primrose bustled in with another bowl of flowers, not showing effects of her broken sleep in the least. That she had been up many times in the night to check on Felicia she considered a part of her job. A good mistress was not easy to find, and Miss Felicia was one of the better ones.

'Good heavens,' Felicia exclaimed as she pushed her way up on the pillows, careful not to disturb her shoulder. It hurt some, but not like last evening.

'I do believe his lordship has bought out every flower seller in all of London, ma'am,' Primrose declared proudly. 'There be carnations and roses, and asters, and flowers I ain't never seen afore.'

'Perhaps some could go into the sitting room. I intend to move there as soon as I may.' Felicia moved her feet to the edge of the bed, wanting nothing more than to rise. She had decided that merely being in bed made one feel ill.

'Out of bed? I don't think so. Besides, there be flowers in there already,' the maid informed her.

'Then I shall do so by myself,' Felicia declared. Using her feet, she shoved the covers aside, then edged one foot over the side of the bed. 'It is the outside of enough that I should remain in bed. The doctor said I might rise,' she reminded.

'Oh, miss,' Primrose cried, her plain face revealing her horror. 'Wait! Sit still; I will help you in a trice.'

Primrose set the flowers on the floor, then rushed to assure herself that Felicia did not exert herself in the slightest while sliding off the bed onto admittedly shaky feet. Of course the maid had to notice that Felicia trembled just a little.

'It is merely the effect of that laudanum I took. Perhaps I might take not more than a half teaspoon this morning. The pain is less, but I would sit up.'

She availed herself of the necessary in the adjacent room, then, suitably robed and slippered, she sat on one of the ebony chairs in the sitting room. And sighed.

'I had forgotten how very uncomfortable these chairs are. Mr Walpole may have desired a Gothic atmosphere in his home. He certainly did not consider comfort.' Felicia allowed Primrose to tuck a pillow behind her, then sat back to admire the multitude of floral offerings that decorated the room. There was scarcely room for a tray of food.

'Shall I talk with that toffee-nosed butler and see what might be done for you, ma'am?' Primrose said, only her eyes betraying her glee at baiting the gentleman. She tucked a blanket about Felicia, then stood back for orders.

'Yes, do. Oh, and Primrose, please fetch me a plate of eggs and toast. I am quite famished for eggs and toast. Two buttered eggs and two slices of toast with strawberry jam as well.'

The maid cast her mistress a look most comical. Pride in Felicia's excellent recovery warred with the desire to be dragon and lord it over all those who wanted to see the poor dear girl. 'I will be back in a few minutes, miss.'

No sooner had Primrose gone, but there was a rap on the door, followed by Lady Louisa's head peeking around.

'I could not credit your maid when she said you were up. What a heroine you are!' Lady Louisa exclaimed. Then she looked around the room, taking note of the many flowers overflowing every table and even the mantel. 'My goodness,' she said, quite awed. 'I expect some-one admires you greatly. Dare I guess?'

'Primrose informed me that Lord Chessyre raided every flower seller in Town to find this lot,' Felicia said with a ghost of a smile. She leaned back against the pillow, wishing for her old overstuffed chair at Brook Hall. Chintz-covered and rather worn, it had been her comfort through every childhood ailment.

The door had been left ajar, and within minutes Lady Emma peered around the corner, to exclaim, 'Will, dearest boy, she is sitting on a chair!'

'Good morning, my lady. I am as you see,' Felicia said in a subdued voice. Perhaps Primrose had been right. Maybe it would have been better had Felicia not tried to prove she was quite able to be up and about.

The door was flung open, and Felicia blushed to see Lord Chessyre standing in the hall, staring at her as though she were a box of sweets in the sweetshop.

'A footstool, I think,' he muttered. 'And a better chair. That cannot be comfortable. Another table is needed.' He summoned a footman, barking orders left and right, making Felicia want to laugh.

'I have tables enough, sir. They seem to be hidden by flowers.' She managed a smile, for she suspected to laugh would hurt a bit.

'You can smile? Good grief, woman, I am amazed you will even speak to me this morning. This is all my fault. I ordered you to come to London, to allow me to help you. And you come to this!' The poor man looked beside himself.

'It is not so very bad, I think. I shan't wish to wear low-necked gowns, I suppose. Primrose said there will be a little scar – a very little one.' She wished they would all go away, except for the one she longed to look at, and that wasn't possible – propriety and all that. She sighed and wished she hadn't, for the movement pulled at the wound.

'You are in pain. Is there nothing you may have? Laudanum? Something? Perhaps willow bark?' The earl ran a hand through his neatly arranged hair, looking frustrated. 'I cannot like to see you in pain, Miss Brook.'

Primrose elbowed her way past the three standing by the door, carrying the breakfast tray loaded with the buttered eggs and toast with jam, plus a pot of tea, all with the prettiest of china.

'A table,' she muttered, looking about her with vexation.

'Here,' the earl said, brushing aside the two women to clear a small table, placing the bowl of flowers on the floor for the moment. He took the tray from Primrose to set it just so, then stood, anxiously watching Felicia as she picked up a fork to eat.

'I shall be quite all right, eventually. I intend to eat this bit of food, then return to my bed for a nap,' Felicia explained.

'Good,' his lordship said softly. 'Very good. Excellent. I shall see you in a while.' With that, he turned and left the room.

'Poor Will has been like one demented all morning. He was that worried about you, dear Felicia. I declare, you have become like one of the family in these past months,' Lady Emma said, drifting over to settle on one of the ebony chairs. Lady Louisa followed suit, perching on the edge of her chair as though ready to flee.

Since Felicia did not feel the least like a sister to Lord Chessyre, she made no comment to this, other than one of those noncommittal murmurs one makes when one cannot think of what to say. Instead, she polished off the buttered eggs and toast, and two cups of tea Primrose poured for her.

'By the bye,' Primrose said softly, 'I watched the eggs and toast fixed myself. They be fine.'

Felicia knew what the maid meant. Basil hadn't been near her food, nor had anyone else.

Primrose took the tray – every bit of food gone, the teapot drained dry – and left the room.

'I believe I shall make my way back to bed,' Felicia said, hoping her legs would not betray her.

'I am amazed that you are so strong, so well in such a brief time,' Lady Louisa began. 'I shouldn't wonder that you would be able to act in the play tomorrow evening – with great care taken to see you rest whenever possible.'

My, Felicia thought, Louisa truly wanted Stephen to have that title. Perhaps she felt that her father would be more receptive to the amateur theatrical producer and actor were he to possess a title in addition to a good estate and properly invested funds.

Lord Chessyre stepped into the room at that moment. 'Lady Louisa, you cannot be thinking Miss Brook would be able to manage such a tiring evening by then.'

Catching sight of the desperate longing in Louisa's eyes, Felicia made up her mind then and there. 'But she is right. I shall be perfectly able to perform tomorrow evening. Only . . . Theodore will have to pick up the armor for himself!'

They laughed as she had intended.

'Felicia means to take a nap now,' Lady Emma reminded them all. 'I suggest we return later.'

Lord Chessyre said nothing, but bent over to pick up the blanket and tossed it aside, then scoop Felicia into his arms. Within minutes she was safely tucked into her bed, and he wore a most satisfied expression on his handsome face.

'That is where I want to see you – resting. A bit of laudanum, some sleep, and you will be much more the thing.'

'I could not have put it better myself,' Dr Johnstone declared from the entrance to the bedroom. 'Good day to you, sir,' the doctor said, a hint of dismissal in his manner.

'I shall return later, in time to help you to the better chair.'

'I see you have a champion. Every lady should be so fortunate,' the doctor said, settling down to check his patient.

Chapter Twelve

'A champion,' Dr Johnstone had declared, Felicia thought muzzily upon waking a few hours later. Well, as to that, she suspected it was as Lady Emma had said – the earl thought of Felicia as a sort of sister, a relative for whom he must be responsible. And, he admitted that he felt guilty for her accident. She knew he had nothing to do with the dagger. He meant he felt at fault that she had been in London and involved with the play. But . . . Basil would have found some way to eliminate her, and whatever other method he used might not have been so easily deflected.

She wished they had never begun the investigation into the will; then Mr Smithers would not have warned Basil he had something to fear. And Felicia would not have a scar to endure.

It wasn't as though she wore such terribly low-cut gowns. She would be scarred and imperfect, and a man might not care for such a wife unless he loved Felicia to distraction, and that was unlikely. One rarely saw such a love.

Feeling confident that she could negotiate the distance to the small water closet, Felicia slipped from her bed and cautiously made her way to the tiny room. From there she checked her image in the looking glass to see precisely where the scar would be. *Vain creature!* She ought to be thankful she was not dead! But it was comforting to see that it was off to one side near her shoulder bone.

After adjusting her robe and firmly tying the sash, she walked to her sitting room.

'Miss!' Primrose cried in horror. 'I thought you be asleep. We were trying most hard to not disturb you.'

The earl turned to study Felicia, who was certain she must be blushing clear to her toes. 'I am feeling much more the thing. What are you doing?' She hoped by diverting attention from herself that he would cease staring at her and Primrose would natter on as she sometimes did.

When the maid stepped away, a rather queer chair stood revealed. The upper part of the chair leaned backward, yet the seat was level, and there was a most peculiar extension coming out from the seat to the floor, a bit like an attached footrest. Griffins decorated the front corners of the chair, and a fanciful arm went off to the right side with a small slant-top table at the end of that.

'May I inquire what this extraordinary thing might be?' Felicia asked Lord Chessyre, for she suspected Primrose hadn't a clue.

'I found it off in a corner of Walpole's library. It is a reclining chair. One sits in it and is able to lean back, put up one's feet, even read or write if one pleases. Pocock designed it, and it's a clever bit of furniture. I intend to order one something like it for myself – without the griffins.'

Felicia gave the unusual chair a dubious look, but feeling a trifle weak, she decided it best to try the thing before she collapsed. The laudanum had been too much. She'd not take it anymore, for it made her feel dizzy even if it dulled the pain.

'Amazing, it actually is quite comfortable,' she said quietly after the earl had assisted her onto the chair. 'Although I do agree about the griffins. I imagine they look well in Mr Walpole's library, however. You know,' she added, 'we really ought to discuss him properly by his correct title, Lord Orford.'

'Indeed,' Chessyre replied, 'but the earldom came to him shortly before his death, and people tend to think of him as Walpole, the creator of this house and the writer of his *Letters* and *The Castle of Otranto*.' Once she was comfortably settled, he took a step back toward the open door, then paused. 'How do you feel?'

'A little better, I believe. The fire in my shoulder has subsided to a dull ache.'

He shook his head, giving her a troubled look. 'I feel responsible.'

Felicia broke in on what she feared would be a brotherly apology. 'Nonsense. You could never know that Basil would behave in such a dastardly manner.' She relaxed against the chair and wished she might ease his mind.

His gaze sharpened, but he said nothing, then disappeared around the corner.

Felicia felt bereft. Wherever she looked there were flowers, even more than before. She'd rather have been enjoying his lordship's company, as improper as it might be. No doubt he felt as though his duty had been done with the masses of flowers and finding the chair for her. And of course it would be, she reminded herself. She was the one who had tumbled into love with the man who merely sought to help her. It was not his fault in the least that she was little better than a fool.

'Your cousin sent a bouquet of posies, that one over there,' Primrose said, pointing to a dainty collection of purple asters and greenery. 'And the others have brought flowers as well. Place looks like a blooming flower shop.'

Felicia chuckled, and the maid gave her a quizzical look, not having seen anything amusing in her words.

The remainder of the day passed quietly. Jane Woodworth kindly read poetry to Felicia for a while, then related bits and pieces of gossip.

'How lovely it smells in here, like a garden in summer,' Lady Louisa exclaimed as she entered the room, where Felicia queened it from the reclining chair. She perched on one of the ebony chairs to study Felicia with anxious eyes.

'It is an improvement over musty antiquities,' Felicia admitted with a smile.

'Indeed,' Louisa murmured, casting her gaze restlessly from one bouquet to another. She shifted on the hard surface of the ebony chair, twisting her hands in her lap. 'You look exceedingly well,' she said at long last, as though determined to be cheerful.

'I feel a little better,' Felicia said, repeating her earlier assessment while wondering what was at the root of this visit.

'How do you imagine you might feel by tomorrow?' Louisa inquired, a trifle apprehensive.

'Do you mean, will I be able to appear in Stephen's play?' Felicia queried dryly.

'It is terribly important. Just think, the Prince Regent himself has promised to attend.' Louisa leaned forward, extending a hand in an imploring gesture.

'And all his friends and attendants, no doubt,' Jane Woodworth added from the other side of the reclining chair.

'Are you trying to frighten me into not appearing?' Felicia asked with a half laugh. She shifted and winced at the pull at her shoulder. At their alarm, Felicia assured them, 'It is not so bad, just a momentary twinge. I am certain I shall be able to be in the play. Perhaps a footman might convey me downstairs this evening, and we can assess how I may do?'

'Wonderful!' Lady Louisa exclaimed, jumping to her feet. 'I shall go at once to inform Stephen, that is, Mr Chessyre.' She blushed a delightful pink, then fled from the room, her footsteps heard running lightly down the hall.

'It would seem that her ladyship has found true love,' Jane Woodworth said kindly. 'Mr Stephen Chessyre will make her an agreeable husband.'

'Perhaps. However, I suspect love is not what it always seems to be.' For instance, her own love for Lord Chessyre was certainly one-sided. He thought of her as a responsibility, a task to be handled with cleverness and a certain amount of skill. His worry, the concern he displayed was merely for one who had been hurt and might have been killed had it not been for a chance turning.

'What is this I hear?' The object of her thoughts appeared in the doorway to stare at her, hands on hips and looking as though a thundercloud had taken residence on his brow. 'Lady Louisa claims you are to act tomorrow night. I forbid it. You must have more rest. If you move or are jostled unduly, you could reopen the wound. Infection is an ever-present danger.'

'As I told you before, I do feel better. I thought I might go down-stairs this evening. We shall see how I do then.' Felicia returned his glare. Odious creature, to think he might order her around. He was not her keeper, even if she loved the dratted man. And, she admitted, her love warred with the desire to thwart him. The latter won.

'If you do not have a care for yourself, someone must.'

Which remark stabbed Felicia to the quick. There was no one else to care for her. She was alone in the world and had best come to accept her penniless, solitary state. It was unlikely a judge would rule in favor of a woman, even if the Earl of Chessyre instigated the inquiry.

'That is scarcely necessary, my lord. I have tended my affairs for some years now. I trust it will do no harm for me to join the others this evening.' Felicia instilled frost in her voice with the hope of sounding firm in her resolve. 'I can sit there as well as here.'

'And that is your final word? You insist on this foolish behavior?' He glanced about the room, then brought his gaze back to her. He looked utterly furious.

Pleased, for some reason, Felicia allowed a half smile to cross her lips. 'I do, indeed, sir.'

He glanced at the clock on the mantelpiece. 'I shall be here in two hours to take you down. I want that chair moved for you, so that you may sit in comfort. It is comfortable, is it not?'

Remorseful that she had been so cool in the face of what seemed to be sincere concern, Felicia relented. 'It is vastly comfortable, and I would be much obliged if you were to see to my removal.'

He looked about the room again, then back to where she reclined on the chair.

Felicia suspected her robe was awry and she must look a fright. Primrose had been busy overseeing a nuncheon for her and had not had a moment to comb her hair or help change her robe. 'I intend to change before I go down,' she warned.

Jane Woodworth rose, coming to stand by Felicia's chair. 'I shall look after her, my lord. I believe she is anxious to help your nephew, and that is a most noble reason for exerting herself.'

'Stephen!' the earl declared, then turned on his heel and left the room.

'How odd,' Jane murmured.

'He does like to have his way,' Felicia replied by way of explanation. However, she wondered why he seemed so annoyed with his cousin. Surely he did not begrudge a title for Stephen?

'Rest, do. Your maid promised to bring you tea. I believe Dr Johnstone will be here before long as well. I will read some more from this charming book of poems until he comes.'

Felicia listened with half an ear as Jane began.

'My heart leaps up when I behold a rainbow in the sky.' Jane commenced on the Wordsworth poem, reading in a soothing tone that did nothing to calm Felicia in the least.

The doctor approved her removal, cautioning against straining her shoulder, then proceeded downstairs.

'I protest, Doctor,' Lord Chessyre said with all the pomposity he displayed when annoyed.

'And what have you to say in the matter?' the doctor queried gently. 'She is young and healthy and will heal fast. Her shoulder is improving by the hour. She will be fine. I shan't need to return unless something happens to reopen her wound. Call me if you need me.'

The earl watched the doctor depart, a harassed expression on his face. Then he walked down the hall, quite defeated in his attempt to guard Felicia.

'Stephen,' William said as he entered the library in a determined stride, 'I must speak with you.'

Stephen looked to Lady Louisa, who nodded and rose, slipping from the room with silent steps.

'I must know something,' William began, unsure how to proceed. 'How do you feel toward Miss Brook?' he asked, placing his hands behind him and strolling over to stand by one of the windows.

'Grateful that she will perform tomorrow evening,' Stephen said promptly. 'She is an uncommonly good and brave woman, a rare one, indeed.' He lounged back on his chair at the desk, giving William a searching look.

'You feel nothing but gratitude to her, nothing stronger?' William persisted, wanting to know, but fearing to learn what he did not wish to hear.

'She would make a dashed good sister . . . or possibly a cousin?' Stephen said with a sly question in his voice.

'Is that so? Sister?' William said, ignoring the bit about her being a cousin. That notion still battled within him, and he was not sure which side was winning at the moment. Never had he known such a stubborn, pigheaded woman. Gentle and understanding she might be, but a more tenacious creature he couldn't imagine.

'Lady Louisa,' William said, 'seems to return your interest. You think this all worth the effort to fetch yourself a title?'

'I'd not have given it a thought had you not mentioned the possibility,' Stephen argued. 'You forget it is our hostess, Mrs Damer, who enjoys these amateur theatricals. It was a misfortune that Felicia was hurt. An accident, nothing more. Surely you do not really suspect one of us to have tried to wound, or worse yet, kill her?'

'I said before that it was no accident, and I stick to that assumption. I cannot prove my theory, but Basil—'

'The cousin with all the money and rest of the inheritance,' Stephen reflected with a nod.

'The will and testament left everything to him. As Pelham remarked last evening, it would have been more clever had Lady Brook – for I am convinced she was the instigator of the plot – arranged for a modest sum to be left Felicia. How do we prove the will is false?'

'In whose handwriting is the will?' Stephen asked, leaning forward as he puzzled the conundrum.

'Handwriting,' William echoed. 'Of course, we must obtain a sample of Mr Smithers's handwriting, which will help establish that Felicia's father had nothing whatsoever to do with that will. Another point not in Basil's favor is that *he* turned out to be the third witness. Harding dug out that fact. As he had an ultimate interest in the will, his witness is invalid, unless I miss my guess. Harding required three disinterested witnesses when I made out my will and testament. I'd forgotten that for the moment. Thank you, Stephen, for reminding me.' William, feeling better than he had in days, turned to leave, pausing at the door to add, 'Need I say carry on?'

Stephen grinned and replied, 'Let Louisa know that you are on your way somewhere.'

William did as asked, then left the house. Really, they had used Mrs Damer's hospitality abominably, moving furniture, coming and going as though they owned the place. Yet she seemed to enjoy all the hustle and bustle. She entered into the play with enthusiasm and had seemed genuinely distressed when Felicia was injured. One of these days he might actually have her finish that bust of him.

When William found Harding in his office, the first words he uttered were, 'So the present Lord Brook was a witness to that odious will! What effect will that have on the judge's ruling? Likely they thought he was far enough removed so that he would be acceptable. Since he stood to ultimately inherit, they didn't have to dispose of him.' William exchanged a knowing look with his solicitor.

'As to that, I have checked records of those two deaths, and the heart attack appears real enough, but there was a question regarding the carriage in which the steward rode. It appears that the axle was damaged.' Harding looked at his patron and friend, then returned to the interesting bit of information he'd found.

'Indeed, I observed Brook's signature. The judge may use that to discredit the will. I'd have thought old Lady Brook had more sense than that. But every crook seems to slip up eventually.'

'I'd like to see a sample of Mr Smithers's handwriting if possible. I believe it would prove beyond a doubt that Felicia's father had nothing to do with that will.'

'It so happens I have it on file. He wrote me a letter some time ago, and I have kept it. It was not done by his clerk, for it was a sensitive matter, one of some delicacy. I will take it to the judge who is to examine the will.'

'Do you have any idea as to when he will make his ruling?' William inquired, hoping he didn't sound as impatient as he feared he did.

'Hard to tell what is on his desk. He will read it when he reads it, is all I can offer you.'

William sat back in the Windsor arm chair, wanting to demand, insist that this judge begin his scrutiny of the will immediately. The longer the delay, the more danger would surround Felicia.

He left the office only partially satisfied with his call. After a pause at White's to catch up on the latest *on-dits* and a stop at Chessyre House to inform Lady Emma of the latest developments, he returned to Strawberry Hill. Tooling up the graveled drive, he marveled anew at the Gothic drama of the house. Walpole said that the house had moved him to write the book, inspiring him as he wrote. Not too unlikely, in William's estimate.

It was over two hours from the time he'd left Felicia when he entered the house once again. Mrs Damer was crossing the entryway as he came in, and paused to greet him.

'Good afternoon, my lord. I trust you had a worthwhile trip into Town?' Her gown of bloodred and wine crepe seemed almost ghoulish to William, and he barely refrained from commenting on it. Perhaps it suited her mood of the day. Her manner was arch, and he hadn't observed before how she most subtly flirted with him. *Good grief!* The woman was old enough . . . well, not old enough to be his mother, but too old to interest him. She had William confused with the Prince Regent, who was known to be attracted to older women.

Then a peculiar notion struck him. Mrs Damer noticed everything. Perhaps she had observed his interest in Felicia and wanted to eliminate the girl, thinking she would run away after an accident. Anne Damer knew where the daggers were kept, had access to them. The very idea staggered him.

'Do you know if Miss Brook is awake and up?' he inquired politely, watching Anne Damer's face closely.

'Last I heard she was still napping. Lady Louisa had paused to chat, and I believe it was some time before she left the room. And you, sir, you must come with me. I would have your head for a few minutes.'

He knew what she meant, but she certainly sounded macabre for a moment. He said in a jocular reply, 'I trust you mean that figuratively?'

'What other?' Mrs Damer led the way into her studio and was all business while she studied William for a time. He could not see her skilled hands at work, but he could hear her working the clay in which she modeled a head before commencing on the final bust.

'There you are. I had a bit of trouble with your chin, sir,' she said with a coy smile. Maybe her arms about Lord Pelham was not so innocent after all.

'Excuse me, I must see how Miss Brook does,' William said, wanting to mull over his new theory on his own.

'Of course, dear little Miss Brook,' Mrs Damer said lightly. 'I imagine she will improve so as to act tomorrow evening. I know she will not wish to disappoint your cousin.'

'Indeed. Miss Brook is dependable as well as a lovely person. We were all saddened at her injury.'

'Not everyone,' Mrs Damer murmured as she drifted away from him in the direction of the library.

'What time is it, Primrose?' Felicia demanded, only for the third occasion.

'Twenty minutes later than the last time you asked me,' the maid replied with great impatience.

'My hair – does it look well in the back? And this dress, the neckline conceals the bandage?' Felicia turned her head a trifle, but was careful not to pull the muscles of her chest. The wound hurt less when she was quiet.

'You are fine as fivepence, miss. Just rest on your bed. The footmen are taking that contraption down the stairs at any moment,' she concluded, referring to the reclining chair.

'His lordship said he would remove me to the drawing room. 'Tis well past two hours,' Felicia fretted. Most likely he had found some fascinating creature with whom to while away an afternoon.

'You might have napped a bit longer, miss,' Primrose reminded.

Felicia ignored that remark, for Primrose was correct. The problem was that Felicia couldn't sleep. She had spent the hours thinking over what she must do once the play was performed and she was free to go. At the moment she had to be very careful just how she rested on the bed, not to mention she had to remember not to move her arm any more than absolutely necessary. It surprised her how many muscles were connected in some way to her shoulder.

'Primrose, let me know when his lordship comes,' Felicia said, trying not to sound impatient.

'He be here now, ma'am,' the maid whispered, then stood back as the earl walked into the room.

'This is improper, I suppose,' he drawled. 'But good Primrose will keep things fitting, I am sure.'

'It is merely to assist me to the drawing room, sir,' Felicia said with a light laugh.

The earl didn't reply to that bit of nonsense. Rather, he gathered Felicia in his arms as though she were a bouquet of rare and beautiful flowers. She could hear the thudding of his heart while he marched down the hall. When he spoke, although his voice was soft, she could almost feel the resonance in his chest with her head held snugly against him. She almost missed his words, so intent was she on her sensations.

'Do you have any suspicions regarding Anne Damer?' he repeated as he began the walk down the stairs.

'Mrs Damer?' Felicia said with a squeak in her voice. 'Of what? Assuredly not of wanting to do me in!'

'I thought not, either, until this afternoon. The lady is a flirt.'

'That bothered you?' Felicia inquired cautiously.

'A woman of her standing does not flirt with a man of my position. Unless I was mistaken in her,' he muttered under his breath.

Felicia heard the barely spoken words and pondered the puzzling notion of Mrs Damer eliminating Felicia because she was interested in Lord Chessyre. It made not the least sense.

'I believe you must be mistaken. What could her motive be?' Felicia asked, frowning at the earl as he gently deposited her on the reclining chair.

'That is a puzzle,' he agreed, but sounding reluctant in that agreement.

There was a footman stationed by the door, but far enough away so she felt comfortable in speaking quietly to his lordship. 'Thank you for carrying me downstairs.' She also blessed Primrose, who had insisted upon giving her a dab of the laudanum to cut any pain.

'Stephen was pleased you are going to be able to perform after all,' the earl said, giving Felicia a searching look. He spoke quietly, apparently as aware of the listening ears as was Felicia.

'You admit I am to perform, then? You will not try to stop me?' Felicia quizzed.

'You would risk that for Stephen?' he asked, ignoring the footman and raising his voice a little.

'Not just for Stephen, for us all, but Stephen in particular,' Felicia explained.

'You are aware of his partiality for Lady Louisa?'

'I am. She is quite enamored of him as well. It would seem they are a destined pair.' Felicia leaned back on the chair, wincing as she slightly pulled her shoulder.

'You are in pain. Is there anything I might fetch you? Laudanum? A sherry, perhaps?'

The earl thrust his hands behind him, looking frustrated, although why he should be so upset at her slightest twinge was more than she could see.

'Rubbish,' Felicia said stoutly. 'I just moved the wrong way.'

What the earl might have said to that was lost as Miss Woodworth entered the room on Basil's arm.

'I see the cast has begun to assemble,' Jane said with a glance at her escort.

'How glad we are that Felicia is on the mend,' Lady Louisa cried upon swishing into the drawing room, a picture in pale violet taffeta with triple flounces and a string of pearls at her neck.

Felicia took note of the fashionably low neckline, and her hand crept up to finger the delicate aerophane crepe that fashioned the upper portion of her bodice, then formed a ruff at her neck. Sheer, it gave the illusion of skin, yet discreetly helped hide the bandage. It could not be helped if it made her feel frumpish.

Stephen entered the room and went immediately to Lady Louisa's side. Felicia glanced at the earl and found his gaze resting on her. He looked concerned, and she smiled at him, attempting to reassure him that she was as fit as a fiddle. Which was nonsense, of course. She would far rather have been in bed, hiding beneath a mound of covers.

Lady Emma, Lord Pelham, and Mrs Damer came together, conversing amiably. Felicia wondered if Lord Chessyre observed the hostile looks his aunt bestowed on Mrs Damer when she thought no one was watching.

'I attempted to repair and clean that pretty blue gown you were to wear in the play, but it is beyond hope,' Lady Emma declared, meaning, of course, that her maid had tried to restore the gown and it was beyond redemption.

'There must be another one in the attic, Aunt,' the earl said, soothing her with his words and smile.

'I shall take a look to see what is to be found,' Mrs Damer said languidly, 'tomorrow.'

'Tomorrow we perform,' Stephen reminded them all. 'There must be time to alter if necessary.'

'No one will be fussy about a gown that is not quite perfect,' Mrs Damer objected with a wave of her hand.

'As soon as we are finished eating, I propose we do a final run-through the play,' Stephen said with a look at Felicia.

'Excellent,' she said before she cried craven and begged to return to her room. What if Basil had another trick up his sleeve?

'And I,' Sir Peter stated firmly, 'will make certain that when I pick up that dagger, it is not a real dagger.'

This brought forth a few chuckles, and they made their way to the dining room.

When Lord Chessyre would have gathered Felicia into his arms once again, she shook her head. 'I would walk, sir. I cannot be pampered. How will I go on stage? Do you intend to carry me there as well?' she queried. 'The injury is to my shoulder, not my feet.'

With such irrefutable logic, his lordship was compelled to agree. Instead, he offered his arm and guided Felicia down the steps to the dining room as though they walked on eggshells.

She survived dinner nicely, then faced the ordeal of the practice with more fortitude than she'd have believed.

Stephen, as Theodore, picked up his own armor when it came to the scene where she freed him from the black tower. Finally, having rested as much as possible beforehand, she spoke the lines that Sir Peter, as Manfred, misunderstood.

He lunged forward, avoiding touching her completely. To an audience it would have looked as though he had plunged the dagger as he had the previous time.

The tension that had been building evaporated at once, with all breathing sighs of relief. The scene and play rapidly came to a conclusion following what all agreed was the high point of the drama.

Felicia was not allowed to join the cast for any celebration. Lord Chessyre gathered her in his arms and told her to say good night to all.

'I am fine, really I am,' she said while fighting not to wilt against him.

'Stubborn creature,' he scolded, but with what Felicia thought might be affection in his voice. She wished it were. Well, one could become fond of a stray. She had become quite attached to Merlin. Only . . . it was not quite the same thing, was it?

Chapter Thirteen

'One more day and we can be gone from here,' Primrose said with an anxious look around the Holbein Chamber.

'But it is so, ah, historical with all those antiquities sitting about the place and the chimneypiece taken from the tomb of Archbishop Warham at Canterbury. Especially that chimney-piece.' Felicia looked at the elaborately carved fireplace surround and shuddered. She felt things of the grave were best suited to a cathedral, not a bedroom! 'I admit that it is a bit like sleeping in a museum – or a church.'

'Spooky, is what I'd say,' Primrose said with another look at the fireplace.

The wound throbbed this morning. Felicia suspected that she had turned in the night in spite of the pillows Primrose had propped about her to keep her from moving. She hoped she had not torn the cut open. It was difficult to be so still while in bed.

'Pains you, does it?' her maid asked perceptively. 'I had best have a look at it.' It took but minutes to remove Felicia's nightrail, then the bandage.

Felicia watched Primrose's face, concerned at the maid's expression. If Primrose looked worried, the condition of the wound could not be good.

The maid went off, to return in moments with a small bottle of ointment. She poured a bit over the wound, then took a scrap of clean cloth and spread it around. 'That Scot doctor, he told me not to put my hands on that cut. Said I'm to put this ointment on once a day. Fussy man, worse than an old tabby.'

'Surely not,' Felicia said, then jumped when the ointment stung. 'I wonder what is in it, for it is not very soothing.'

'T'will be.' The maid ignored Felicia's reaction and placed a clean bandage over the wound with tender care. 'Now you be set to face all those friends of yours who have been asking about you this past hour.'

'Past hour! How late is it?' Felicia glanced at the clock to see she had slept the morning half away. 'You put something in that tisane last evening,' she accused.

'Sleep is the best healer, doctor said. You needed sleep, so I saw you slept.' Primrose assisted Felicia from her bed, then added, 'That peer of yours has been out to the flower sellers again. More posies than I can count.'

'Oh, dear,' Felicia murmured, feeling dreadful instead of pleased. It was one more indication of the guilt he felt for her injury. 'I fear he is not *my* peer, Primrose. He merely feels responsible for my accident.'

'Which weren't no accident, beggin' your pardon, miss.'

'That is another matter entirely.' Refusing to discuss the problem with the maid, Felicia managed to dress, eat her breakfast, and settle in the reclining chair for what was likely to be a dull day. Never mind that she felt as though she were in a garden in the middle of summer, instead of the dead of winter and approaching Christmas.

A tap on the door brought Lady Louisa. She hovered anxiously inside the door, studying Felicia as though she were some rare exhibit.

'I feel quite well this morning,' Felicia volunteered.

The resultant sigh of relief would have been amusing had Felicia actually felt that good. Always in the back of her mind was the knowledge that she must leave Chessyre House and find another position. Surely Lady Emma would give her a reference. She must.

'Well, for someone who claims to be better, you have a decided droop about you. I shall cheer you up,' Lady Louisa declared.

Jane Woodworth peered around the corner of the door, then entered at Felicia's smile. Lady Louisa beamed at her as well, saying, 'Oh, good, now there are two of us to cheer her up.'

'Do you need cheering after your splendid performance last evening? I vow you put the rest of us in the shade when you died so beautifully. I quite had tears in my eyes, and I know it is but a play,' Jane declared, a gentle smile lighting her eyes. Her buxom beauty was discreetly attired in a soft blue wool.

'Why, thank you, Jane. How kind you are to say my poor efforts are acceptable,' Felicia said, feeling warmth toward the other girl.

'At any rate there was no problem of a mistaken dagger last evening. How strange the theatrical dagger should have been switched,' Jane said, settling on one of the ebony chairs, a pleasant look on her face. 'One of the little mysteries of life, I suppose.'

'Are you in great pain this morning?' Lady Louisa inquired anxiously. 'I fear you would not tell us if you were.'

'I do well enough.' Felicia gave her new acquaintances a grateful look. Once she left here, then Chessyre House, she doubted if she'd see them again. She was not likely to cross their paths as a companion to some elderly lady.

'Lord Chessyre is most concerned,' Jane inserted, casting a look about the room at the lovely bouquets of flowers. She raised her brows a trifle, then smiled. 'I fancy he has more than a little interest in a certain young lady?'

'It is your fancy, nothing more.' Felicia wished she might confide the circumstances of her association with the earl so the women might comprehend just how futile her future with him was, but decided to remain silent. He had cautioned her against divulging her concerns. She might as well follow his suggestion, for she had none of her own at the moment.

'Good morning, ladies,' said a voice from the open door. 'We are come to take Miss Brook down to the library.' The earl gestured to the two stalwart footmen who stood respectfully to one side while the earl swept Felicia into his arms, taking great care not to further injure her shoulder.

'We make a parade,' she whispered with a soft chuckle as he marched down the stairs to the ground floor. Behind them came the two footmen bearing the strange reclining chair and after them followed Lady Louisa and Jane, chattering about the coming evening. Felicia relished the texture of his coat against her cheek, his scent.

'Indeed, and a fine one. I have a bit of news for you. The will has been accepted for investigation by the judge we hoped to obtain. Harding tried, as subtly as he could, to let him know it was a matter of some urgency, as you were under some hardship as a result of the fraudulent will.'

'I cannot believe that would make a scrap of difference to a judge. Does he not simply look at the will and declare it valid or invalid by reason of evidence?' Felicia asked as they entered the library. She was glad she had kept her voice to a mere thread of sound upon discovering that the room seemed full of people.

'Excellent thinking, for 'tis true enough. But, this particular judge was cheated by a relative some years ago, and Harding thinks he has never forgotten that. As well, 'tis rumored he has no fondness for Smithers. It ought to work in our favor.' He came to a halt, holding her close to his chest while the footmen settled the chair not far from the window. Then he gently set her down, watching her face with a worried expression.

'Such nebulous hopes,' she replied, while arranging her skirts, once placed in the chair. It had been so wonderful to be cradled in the earl's arms for that brief time. 'And do not frown so, for I am fine.' 'Fine' covered such an abundance of conditions. And if she stretched the truth a little, what difference did it make?

Jane glided over to stand by Basil, offering conversation on the play that evening. Lady Louisa seemed content enough to listen to Stephen expound on who all was likely to attend.

'You seem displeased,' Lord Chessyre said, bending over so his words were heard by no one else.

'You must know I worry about having His Royal Highness here this evening. What if something goes wrong?'

'I will be there for you,' the earl replied firmly.

'As Frederic, you are seldom near me on stage,' she reminded. 'Only at the point where I agree to marry you.' She frowned. 'How

172

foolish that Stephen included those lines about the passion you feel for Matilda.'

'You think it foolish that I have a passion for you?' the earl inquired, an odd expression on his face.

'It is a very short time for Frederic to conceive a passion for his enemy's daughter. And he certainly yields her to Theodore with little fuss, nor does he seem very grief-stricken when she dies.'

'I would be desolate were you to die, Felicia. And now to business,' he said quietly, drawing up a chair to her side, and appearing to settle for a comfortable coze. 'We have checked the dagger and all the props for this evening's performance. I can conceive of no manner in which you might be harmed.'

'Good.' There was still one way in which she could sustain injury, but Felicia did not mention it. Should someone jostle her, the cut could be opened and the bleeding resume. She had no wish to destroy the carefully made plans and end what might be an advancement for Stephen. She looked in his direction. 'Your cousin seems happy, at any rate.'

'Lord and Lady Arden will be here this evening. I believe he has high hopes in that direction.'

'She is a sweet girl and appears genuinely fond of him,' Felicia said with a smile of affection for the lady.

'As does Miss Woodworth of your cousin. We seem to have a merging of cousins here, do we not?' There was a note of irony in his voice she could not mistake.

And, thought Felicia, that was likely as close as they might become, given the circumstances.

'As the maid, Bianca, she gives a creditable performance.' Again, he seemed to be striving for polite conversation.

Felicia glanced at the man who persisted in remaining at her side. 'As does Lady Louisa. I trust her parents will not be dismayed at her portrayal of the lovely Isabella.'

'Isabella, thought to be the loveliest in the land?' the earl queried. 'I believe most parents would appreciate that view of their eldest and most eligible daughter.'

Felicia told herself she was being fanciful in thinking there was a touch of wistfulness in the earl's voice and manner. Did he prefer the beautiful Louisa for himself? And generously step aside for his cousin? How noble of him, if true.

'I wish this evening were over,' Lord Chessyre murmured so quietly that Felicia was certain she was the only one in the room to have heard him. 'I suppose I am a fool, but I am still uncomfortable about that final scene.'

'What a consolation, my lord!' Felicia cried softly in mock alarm. Actually, there was little mockery in her feelings that she so painfully tried to hide.

Following a nuncheon that few were able to do more than nibble, all retired to rooms to rest, study lines, and check their costumes.

'By the bye,' Mrs Damer said at the bottom of the stairs as Lord Chessyre was about to carry Felicia to her room. 'I have a costume for you. It seems the same size as the blue, and I believe will look well on you. I meant to send it up earlier but forgot.'

A maid appeared with a white gown that had turned to old ivory over the years. It looked well enough, and if not, what did it matter?

'She forgot?' the earl said as he placed Felicia on her bed. Primrose stood ready to assist her mistress, and the two footmen settled the reclining chair in the Holbein Chamber again. The earl ignored them, fastening his gaze on Felicia. 'If that dress is not suitable, have Primrose notify me at once. I will send to a costume shop for a replacement. I will not have you look less than splendid.'

'How kind you are, sir. Do not tell me you care not for Stephen's acquisition of a title. You are very good.'

He raised his brows, giving her a wry look before leaving her rooms.

'I 'spect you had best try this dress on in case it needs fixing, miss,' Primrose said while holding the garment up for inspection.

The ivory satin was a complete surprise. It fit well, became her far more than the blue, and best of all, the design ensured that her wound and bandage could be concealed.

'I shall find a bit of blue ribbon for your hair to go with the blue flowers embroidered down the front,' Primrose said. She walked toward the door, mumbling about taking in the waist and looking over the seams for repairs. 'You look a treat, miss, and that's the truth,' she assured before leaving Felicia to her rest.

The cast was universally nervous when they gathered behind the curtain, although they tried not to show it. Miss Woodworth fiddled with the lovely embroidered cream apron she wore over her red gown. Lady Louisa was a vision in her elaborate green gown, which swished eloquently when she marched into the room.

Basil hurried in to speak with Miss Woodworth while Stephen reminded Louisa of changes he had made at the last minute. Sir Peter and Lord Chessyre conferred on the far side of the stage. Felicia sat on the chair where Lord Chessyre had placed her, admonishing her to rest as much as possible.

'Rest,' she muttered to the faithful Primrose as she watched the man she loved stride away from her as though glad to be gone. 'As if I could when there are a million butterflies in my stomach.'

'Do you wish me to stay with you?' Primrose asked. 'Or can I stand with the other servants in the back of the room? I'd not want to miss the fun.'

'Fun, is it?' Felicia asked, more to herself. 'Go, go, watch from wherever you please.' It was just as well to be by herself in her present mood. Small talk required too much of one. She looked at the earl, so engrossed in his speech with Sir Peter, and wondered what topic could be so fascinating.

William glanced across the room to where Felicia now sat alone. 'You agree with me, then? Just because nothing happened last evening during our final practice does not mean tonight will be free of so-called accidents. Be on your guard, and I shall be as well. I do not trust her cousin.'

'Nor do I,' Sir Peter agreed. 'A shiftier chap I cannot recall seeing.' He also looked at Felicia, then glanced at his young friend. 'Miss Brook looks uncommonly pretty this evening. Most angelic in that ivory thing with the blue flowers on it. Nice Mrs Damer could find a gown that would conceal the bandage.'

'Indeed,' William murmured. 'She surprised me in that.'

'There are a great many people assembled out there,' Lady Louisa cried, her eyes huge with excitement. 'Mama and Papa have come as has the rest of the family. Lady Emma sits with Mama,' she said to the earl. 'Stephen says he intends to begin promptly, and His Highness has not arrived as yet. I should not wish to have the play interrupted with his entrance – all the curtsies and bowing and whispering will quite put me in a quake.'

'He comes now,' Miss Woodworth exclaimed in a loud whisper. 'Come, let us take our places.'

Felicia thought the other women looked quite beautiful in their colorful gowns. Even Mrs Damer, whose brightly rouged cheeks were even brighter this evening, looked well in her simple white gown.

The curtains were drawn back and the play began.

Stephen had divided the play into two acts, and when the first act concluded, the cast huddled together, listening to the applause with cautious expressions.

'They are being kind, but I think we do well,' Jane Woodworth said.

'Of course we do,' Felicia said stoutly. 'Although when we first had to curtsy to the prince, I thought my courage might fail me.'

'I hope he is pleased,' Lady Louisa said, worrying her lower lip.

Stephen paced back and forth before consulting with the servants who assisted with the various props.

The second act began none too soon for Felicia. Although she dreaded parting from Lord Chessyre and his dear aunt, it was practical for her to cut the connection as soon as possible. There was no way in which she could watch him marry another, as Lady Emma had implied would take place before long. Of course he must wed and continue his line – even if Stephen was a most unexceptional heir. That did not mean she had to be witness to the wooing.

The tension among the cast when the moment came that Manfred mistakes his daughter, Matilda, for the beautiful Isabella was tangible.

Sir Peter, the dagger in hand, crept around the papier-mâché rocks. Listening first to the worried words between the lovers, he moved closer. He drew the dagger upon seeing Theodore, then plunged forward.

There was a moment of fright as the fake dagger touched Felicia's ivory gown. Drawing a relieved breath, she went on with her part. She was unhurt. Nothing was amiss; the play continued to the dramatic conclusion when Theodore leaves the castle and the walls come tumbling down, with the body of the 'dead' Matilda left behind and the faithful Isabella at Theodore's side.

Felicia remained on the pallet where she'd been deposited, resting and preparing for the ordeal of meeting the prince, greeting others. Lady Louisa had insisted she must meet her large family. Miss Woodworth had given Felicia a smile of understanding so gentle and sweet that she quite longed to spend more time with her.

The moment when the castle walls fall and the vision of the sainted Alfonso appears was at hand. Felicia studied the 'rocks,' thinking how very realistic they were, then the servants appeared to push them over.

The crash proved more realistic than ever before. Several of the rocks fell close to Felicia, then one tumbled on top of her. She gasped, for if papier-mâché, it was astoundingly heavy. She dared not move. If she so much as tried to push it aside, she would injure her shoulder again for certain. Pinned beneath the rock, she could only wait and hope that the actors showed no inclination to dawdle at their lines.

Apparently the servants believed she preferred to remain on the pallet until the play concluded, for they didn't pause to so much as look in her direction. Maybe they did not even see her, for the rocks might have hidden her from their view. She couldn't call out, for it would disturb the play.

Minutes passed, and no one came. Her brow felt damp, covered with beads of perspiration. Her arms and torso ached, and she wondered if she might try edging from beneath the rock. When she attempted to move, she felt the immediate pull at the wound and stopped. Her slight movement caused another rock to teeter, then join the one atop Felicia, adding to her woe. Now there was pain, and not merely in her shoulder.

'Where is Felicia?' Lady Louisa cried as the cast exited from the stage after an enthusiastic round of applause. 'She ought to have joined us for our curtain call. I vow, the prince seemed to lead the clapping. I do believe he was pleased with our little play.'

'Felicia,' the earl said, then repeated her name more loudly. 'Felicia!'

'I am here,' she managed to reply, although it was not easy. The rocks crushed against her chest and stomach, as well as her arm.

'Dear girl! What happened?' he asked while bending to take the rocks from her slender form. He frowned as he picked up the first. When he moved the second and larger one, he called to Sir Peter.

'What is going on here?' Sir Peter demanded. 'Why is she still on that pallet?'

'I did not bother to move, for I wanted to rest and where better? I thought I could push aside any of those papier-mâché rocks that chanced near me. I had not realized that papier-mâché was so heavy!' She spoke the final words to the earl, not wanting the others to hear her accusation.

'I believe it is more than that. Someone tampered with those rocks. You must have attention.' He looked up and called out, 'Lady Louisa, see if Dr Johnstone came.' William hovered over Felicia as though wondering what to do and frustrated by his lack of knowledge.

The good doctor came before Felicia had a chance to explain that she would be able to rise if someone would assist her. Everyone gathered around her, and all spoke at once.

The doctor ordered them all but William to leave and suggested they circulate with the audience. Then he began his examination of Felicia's battered form.

'You do seem to have bad luck, ma'am,' he said with a grim smile. 'At least the slash from the dagger has not been reopened, most likely because you remained still. That could not have been easy for you.' He looked up behind Felicia and added, 'I would recommend a quiet stay in the country after this, my lord. She has been most ill-used.'

Felicia wondered how many shades of pink and red would be possible in a blush. It had been bad enough for the doctor to check her limbs, stomach, and slip the gown from her shoulders so to examine the wound, but that someone was here to observe! Worst of all, she had a sinking feeling who it was he addressed.

'I shall see she receives the best of care, doctor.'

Felicia knew that voice. She shut her eyes tightly, hoping that if she pretended to faint, he might go away.

'Somewhat battered and slightly worse for wear, but in one piece, thanks to her intelligent reaction,' Dr Johnstone declared as he rose to face Lord Chessyre.

'Thank you for your concern, Doctor. I shall see that you benefit.' The men shook hands, with the earl giving the doctor a meaningful look.

Another debt she owed the dratted man, Felicia fumed silently. Why did he not go away so she might summon Primrose and creep to her room to gather her belongings? She wanted nothing more than to flee this dreadful house of horrors.

'You may open your eyes now, Felicia. I intend to carry you to the other part of the room so you may meet His Royal Highness and pretend for a few moments that you have not been harmed in the least. I have a reason for this, so do not scold me. I know you must hurt like the devil and long for your bed.'

'What a tyrant you are, my lord,' Felicia said, wishing she had the strength to rise from the pallet and march out the front door, never to see these people again as long as she lived.

'Good girl,' he murmured, gathering her in his arms like a load of laundry, then carrying her around the curtains to face those of the audience who lingered.

Lord and Lady Arden were delightful, as were Lady Louisa's sisters and brother.

Miss Woodworth could be glimpsed on the far side of the room, deep in conversation with Basil, and did not come to see how Felicia now fared, a circumstance she found hurtful. Maybe some of her cousin's nasty ways had rubbed off on the sweet Jane? Had she perhaps concluded a bad husband was better than no husband at all, as Bianca claimed in the play? Basil would most definitely be a bad husband.

It appeared the prince had remained to chat with a number of people he knew. Mrs Damer lingered close by, looking faintly alarmed when Felicia was carried over by Lord Chessyre. Could she have instructed her servants to tamper with the papier-mâché rocks? Possibly. She looked disturbed, not concerned.

Lord Chessyre introduced Felicia, apologizing for her inability to curtsy.

'What is this?' the prince demanded. 'Is our heroine truly wounded? I vow, I thought Mr Chessyre would have used a stage dagger for the scene.' He frowned at Stephen, who hastened to deny the charge.

'Miss Brook was slightly injured when a few of those papier-mâché rocks tumbled on her. Silly girl had not moved from that pallet,' Lord Chessyre explained, making light of the injuries.

Felicia stirred in Lord Chessyre's arms. 'You may put me down, my lord.' He must have sensed she was ready to create a scene and obliged without argument.

She managed a wobbly curtsy to the prince, then she added, 'Everyone has been so kind and concerned. It was a foolish thing for me to stay on the pallet. I trust you enjoyed Stephen's play, Your Highness?'

'First-rate,' the prince replied courteously and turned away to speak with Stephen.

'Good girl. I am proud of you, Felicia,' the earl said softly into her curls.

'I would like to go to my room at this moment, sir. Would someone summon Primrose?'

'I be here, ma'am,' the maid said quietly from behind them. She put an arm about her mistress to assist her from the large room still full of people.

'Good evening,' Felicia said to the others, but not in a loud enough voice to have carried far.

The remainder of those still present were far more absorbed with His Royal Highness, and Felicia doubted if her absence would be noted for some time if at all.

'Felicia,' Lord Chessyre said insistently. He was thwarted from leaving with her by a demand from his prince that he explain something regarding the play. He might ignore others; he dare not the prince.

'Did you pack our things as I requested?' Felicia asked, pausing on the landing to catch her breath. Although bruised and battered, she would be gone shortly.

'Yes, miss,' Primrose said with more enthusiasm than she had shown for some time. 'Our cases are closed and waiting by the door. I left out a gown for you to change into as you asked. Be you sure you are fit to travel? Why was his lordship carrying you from back of the curtains just now. Did something else happen?'

'Happen?' Felicia echoed. 'Indeed, it did.' She swiftly explained while they gained the Holbein Chamber and she changed from her costume into a soft gray gown and pelisse that did nothing for her. She ignored the colorful bruises forming on her torso and arm. Tying the strings of her chip straw bonnet under her chin, she paused to rest on the reclining chair for a time before risking the stairs and who knew what outside.

'Perhaps you might ask Lady Louisa to take you in for a day or two?' Primrose ventured.

'Dearest girl, here you are!' Lady Emma exclaimed as she rounded the corner into Felicia's room. 'How provident – packed and ready to go with us. William thought you might be and urged me to fetch you and Primrose at once. Poor dear, to be so ill-treated. You will feel better once you are tucked in bed and have a bowl of Pierre's broth inside you. The play was delightful, but far too hazardous. I trust that next time she puts on a play, Mrs Damer will choose with greater care.'

Felicia found no opportunity to speak while Lady Emma rattled on, ushering her from the room and down the stairs to the front door. Mrs Damer was there, waiting. She expressed pleasure at Felicia's efforts, tucking a small packet into her gloved hands before the Chessyre group left the house. A shadowy figure joined them at the carriage. Felicia jumped as the man spoke softly to her.

'And now, Felicia, we may settle this business.'

Chapter Fourteen

It was two days following her return to Chessyre House that Felicia rose from her bed to feel free from aches. When Lord Chessyre had carried her in from the carriage that night after the play, she had been near collapse from pain and fright. Her injuries had caught up with her.

Lady Emma insisted that Felicia remain abed until she felt more the thing. And now she must face her future, for Primrose reported that it appeared Lady Emma was near to becoming Lady Pelham – at long last. At least, it was Tupper's opinion, and often an abigail knew things before her mistress did.

Tucked up on a most comfortable chair close to the fireplace in her cozy room, intent on one of Lady Emma's novels, it was difficult to think of a life beyond these walls. However, she must. And it should not be put off.

Lady Emma, as though conjured from Felicia's mind, peeped around the partly open door. She entered to join Felicia by the fireside, studying her companion for a time. Like a bird, she perched on her chair, head tilted, a wispy concoction on her head resembling a nest of feathers.

'Primrose told Tupper you consider leaving here soon,' Lady Emma said at last. 'You cannot do such a thing, dearest girl. Where would you go? No, you must remain here to assist me. I believe that Pelham will propose any day. He is most concerned about me.' Her ladyship frowned delicately, then added, 'He seems to think you will leave me for another position and believes I need a protector. A husband does very well at that sort of thing.'

'I *must* leave you eventually, Lady Emma. You have been so very kind to me, but once you marry Lord Pelham you shan't need a companion anymore; you will have him. I fear you have retained me out of your generosity of heart. I must make my own way in the world – and I intend to avoid my cousin, you may be sure.'

'Dreadful man. He had the effrontery to come here to inquire about your health. William said to listen to him, you would think he had nothing to do with those so-called accidents!' She frowned, then her face cleared. 'I have such plans, my dear. Now that you are well, I desire you come with me to the mantua-maker, the milliner, all sorts of shops and whatnot. I cannot buy my bride clothes all by myself, you know. I shall want the opinion of one I can trust.'

'I am scarcely one to have an opinion on bride clothes,' Felicia objected. 'I am a spinster.'

'But I wish you for an attendant. Had you not been here at this time, I believe Pelham would have thought dearest William needed me and not come to the sticking point – as I believe he is at last. I should not be surprised were he to ask for my hand soon, very soon, indeed.'

'It sounds exciting,' Felicia said with a chuckle.

'Oh, it is, believe me. And I have waited for so long. Twenty-three years he has roamed. I cannot bear to think of some other woman catching him after I have waited so faithfully.'

Felicia wondered if perhaps the marriage might have transpired sooner had Lady Emma not waited so faithfully and instead made it evident she was willing to travel at Lord Pelham's side. She gave voice to her thought, suitably edited.

'Heavens no, dearest girl,' Lady Emma replied earnestly. 'He went to some frightful places he longed to see where I would not have been allowed to go – like China. They do not like Englishwomen in the Chinese court – the emperor, you see. And Africa does not appeal to me, fighting off headhunters and lions and the like. He wrote me all those years, in spite of the impropriety of sending letters to a single lady,' she said with a blush. 'I lived his travels with him, and I believe he enjoyed sharing his experiences with someone, for I was an eager correspondent. I will be able to reminisce with him about those travels, so all is not lost to him.'

'I think you are a very wise lady,' Felicia observed, revising her opinion of the woman she'd considered featherheaded.

'Oh' – Lady Emma gave Felicia a guilty glance – 'I was supposed to tell you that dearest William wishes to see you in his library whenever you are up and about.' Her ladyship rose from the dainty chair where she had perched to add anxiously, 'You *will* help me with my wedding clothes, will you not, dear girl? You will not leave just yet?'

'I would be the veriest clod to refuse, and I should hope I am not sunk to that!' Felicia replied with a warm chuckle and a smile for the woman she had come to admire.

Lady Emma drifted from the room on a cloud of lavender scent while muttering something about seeing to a replacement for dearest William's chef.

Lord Chessyre would not appreciate his chef being stolen from him – even by his aunt, Felicia thought. Although judging by what Aunt Emma had said, he would likely marry before long, so that matter would be solved. With a heartfelt sigh Felicia rose from her chair, slipped on her shoes, then adjusted her rose-sprigged muslin dress before heading for the library.

There was no point in postponing her discussion with Lord Chessyre. She fancied he would explain her duties until his aunt married, then offer a letter of reference for a new post. The very idea stabbed her to the quick. For some days she had realized that she wanted nothing more than to remain in this house, not as a companion to a charming older woman but as his lordship's wife. It was not just Aunt Emma who thought of him as 'dearest William.'

After pausing on the landing, she slowly continued a step at a time while memories of being cradled in his arms, held close to his heart, returned. She would cherish forever her recollection of the texture of the smooth Bath cloth with the faint scent of costmary against her cheek as he carried her. She remembered the thud of his heartbeat, so strong and vital. Other memories, a shaft of sunlight on his golden hair, the warmth of his gray eyes when lit with pleasure, the touch of his hand when comforting her, all surged forth from the back of her mind where they had dwelt, waiting to return. Would they haunt her as memories seemed to do to spinsters when they grew old and gray?

She hesitated outside the library door, than rapped briskly. Better to be done with this interview, then proceed with the remainder of what promised to be a dull life. Upon being bid to enter, she obeyed. At his gesture, she crossed to seat herself in the chair by the fireplace.

Unlike the library at Strawberry Hill there were no elaborate Gothic arches of pierced work, no painted ceiling, nor a tomb-inspired chimneypiece. It was a sensible room, designed for books, and reflected the taste of the man who occupied it. He had risen from the Sheraton desk to join her, and she studied his dear face while attempting to compose her thoughts.

'I trust you are feeling more the thing now?' he asked politely, looking down at her with an unreadable expression.

'Yes, my lord. Primrose and Tupper conspired to keep me abed until my bruises faded and the wound was well healed.' Her gaze followed his figure as he paced back and forth between the fireplace and the tall window that looked over a small courtyard.

'Good. And you have no doubt heard that the Prince Regent has offered a viscountcy to Stephen? He donated a considerable sum of money to the prince so he could obtain a much-desired set of Meissen vases and a clock the prince had his heart set upon. Such gratitude costs His Royal Highness nothing, yet pleases the receiver.' The irony in Lord Chessyre's voice was unmistakable. He stared out of the window a moment before resuming his slow pacing.

'Then Stephen will likely be able to marry Lady Louisa. Her father will look more favorably on a title.' Felicia noted a tensing of Chessyre's shoulder before he turned to face her again.

'How do you feel about that?' he queried. 'She was friend to you at Strawberry Hill, yet she marries Stephen.'

'I think him fortunate to make such a happy alliance. They will deal admirably together. She is a very dear lady.' Felicia stared up at the earl's face, wondering how he felt about the beautiful Louisa marrying his cousin when she had shown such partiality to Lord Chessyre.

'Indeed,' he murmured.

'I hope that the marriage will not come between you and Stephen – you are so obviously fond of one another. That is,' Felicia floundered, not quite sure how to express her concerns, 'she was so very particular in her attentions to you while at Strawberry Hill.' Felicia stared at the handkerchief in her hand she'd been wise enough to carry.

He cleared his throat, bringing her gaze to where he stood not far from where she sat.

'I reckon her motive was two-fold. She asked me to tell her everything regarding Stephen and his life history. And I believe she also wanted to stir a bit of jealousy in him, let him know that he was not the only man around.'

'Sounds devious to me,' Felicia said with a tentative smile, sitting a trifle straighter.

'There are times when a bit of cunning is useful, my dear.' He took several steps, then stopped as though a thought had just struck him. 'Did you believe I was enamored of Louisa?'

'Well,' Felicia temporized, 'she is very beautiful, and has a sweet disposition, and ample wealth – the sort of woman you ought to marry, sir.'

'And so you dreamed I would marry her – the girl my cousin has his heart set on to wed? What must you think of me?' He leaned against his desk, rubbing his chin while studying Felicia with a look so piercing she thought she must feel it. At last he said, 'And I suspected you of harboring like feelings for Stephen – of desiring to marry him. You spoke so warmly of him.'

'He is charming, kind, and good – who could not like him? But love him, no,' she concluded simply. Then shyly, she continued, 'You are also charming company, and most kind and good. Does the same logic apply there?'

He observed her a few moments, then crossed to draw her to her feet. 'I do believe we have been at cross-purposes. Perhaps we can begin anew?'

'If you please,' Felicia replied faintly, wondering what was in his mind. She discovered that a moment later when he gently pulled her into his arms, mindful of her tender shoulder, and kissed her with all the warmth she recalled and something beyond warmth. It brought a desire curling up within her, a yearning she could not understand. His arms enfolded her, pressing her against him in a most delightful manner. She felt all soft and tender inside, her love mushrooming up within, wanting to spring forth.

Her hands hesitantly reached up to caress the golden hair she admired so much, then slid down to rest on those strong shoulders. When he withdrew from the heavenly kiss, Felicia felt more than bereft – she was lost, alone again.

'As a new beginning, I believe that is most tolerable,' he mused, then reluctantly set her aside when an imperative rap was heard at the door.

Felicia thought he muttered a dreadful word before requesting the person to enter.

Alford stared off into space as he announced the arrival of Lord Pelham, who urgently desired to speak with his lordship.'

'Show him in here,' the earl replied before turning to Felicia. 'We have not finished our talk, not in the least. You are not to think of removing from this house before we speak again. Agreed?'

'I agree,' Felicia answered, wondering how soon she might think clearly. She had heard Lady Emma refer to Lord Chessyre as *dearest William* for so long and so often that Felicia had begun to think of him as such as well. If she could remember not to address him in that manner, it would be a blessing. *How embarrassing!* Yet, how else could she possibly think of him? He was her dearest and always would be.

She slipped down the hall, passing Lord Pelham with no more than a murmured greeting. In her room she might relive those tender moments once again and postpone thoughts of departure, foolish girl that she was.

Pelham paused at the open door to the Chessyre town library, then entered slowly. 'I trust I have not come at an inopportune moment, Chessyre?'

'A damnable moment, but that can be remedied. What news do you bring?' William gestured to the chair Felicia had occupied not long before. 'Wine? A brandy, perhaps?'

'Claret would not be amiss. I feel a fool, Chessyre. A damn fool,' Pelham reluctantly admitted.

William handed the older gentleman a glass of claret, then with a patient air settled on the chair facing him.

'I wonder, do I request your aunt's hand in marriage from you?' Pelham said, looking as though he indeed felt a trifle silly and hated it. 'You have no objections? She has been the mainstay of your home since your parents died. She wrote me of that, and her faithful administration of your home. I might have returned sooner had I felt she needed someone to take care of her. She is a very fragile lady, you know. If you marry – which she has assured me you intend to do before long – I would not wish her to be sharing a house with you and your family.'

'I believe your proposal will be well received by my aunt, and I can say nothing more than to wish you happy. Welcome to the family.' William leaned forward to shake the other man's proffered hand.

'As to family – her companion, the delightful Felicia Brook, said that forty is not a very advanced age. I believe someone in the Brook family had a child at that age. I wonder we dare risk it,' he said with a frown.

Surprised that Pelham would venture to touch on so personal a topic, William sought to assure him. 'There are times when risks must be endured.'

'Nothing ventured, nothing gained, and all that sort of rot, I suppose,' Pelham said with a shake of his head. 'You know, when I was in the courts of China, the jungles of Africa, or the western coast of America, I always knew she was here, waiting. I hope I have not kept her waiting too long.'

'I suspect even now she awaits you in the drawing room, unless the servants failed to relay that you are come to call.' William rose, as did

Lord Pelham. They faced each other for a moment, then William grinned and said, 'The best of luck to you, sir.'

And, William thought when Pelham had gone from the room, luck to himself, for he was not sure where the delightful Felicia Brook stood in respect to marriage to him.

'A message, sir.' Alford held out the silver salver.

The familiar writing of his solicitor scrawled on the outside alerted William to the contents, and he accepted the folded missive, breaking the seal to scan its contents.

'I must leave at once. Summon a hackney for me – I'll not wait for the carriage to be brought.' Felicia Brook would have to wait until later.

Traffic was thick, as was normal in the city; throngs of people hurried to and fro like so many fish in a stream.

Once at Threadneedle Street, he paid off the jarvey, then hurried up the steps to Harding's office. Having gained the office, he gave his solicitor and friend an impatient look. 'I gather you have news for me?'

'The judge has ruled – in favor of Felicia Brook.' He ignored William's pleased comment to continue, 'There were several factors that tipped the decision in her favor. That a devoted father would not leave his only child so much as a farthing was not as weighty as the fact that it was written by Smithers – whom the judge indeed dislikes – and rather than signed by George, Lord Brook, had the Brook seal and the X mark. Then also, the three witnesses, one of whom was illegal, also helped to nullify the will and testament. It was acceptable for William Brook to inherit, but to have his son serve as a witness pushed our judge too far. While Basil was not a direct heir, he had an interest, and that is not allowed.'

'You said the will *and* testament was nullified? What does that mean to Felicia?' William inquired, rubbing his chin while thoughts danced about in his mind.

If Harding thought Lord Chessyre was being a trifle familiar regarding his aunt's companion, he gave no indication. He smiled, raised his brows, then quietly said, 'She inherits the lot, everything –

house, furniture, land, and all the money Basil has so carefully invested. There was no entailment with the title. Brook stood to inherit only what was left him. Hoping you would approve, I have sent a man down to secure the property, not trusting Basil Brook one iota.'

'Very good,' William said. 'The cad might try to abscond with a number of valuable paintings, not to mention some of the fine furniture. And when does transfer take place?' he asked.

'The process has begun. The cash is hers immediately, for the judge was truly annoyed with Smithers and cared not a whit about Basil Brook and his careful investments. The bank where Brook does business has been notified as of this morning, and the money conveyed to an account I set up for Miss Brook. It shall be in her name?'

'Indeed. If she marries, I shall have you draw up settlements on her behalf. Rest assured, I feel Miss Brook will look on your efforts with great gratitude.'

'The property is not so complicated as you might think. Nothing was signed; he merely took it over. I would say that in a week or two she might move home. My man will assist her in anything she wishes.'

William shook his solicitor's hand, mentioned the matter of a sum of money that should promptly be directed to Dr Johnstone, then settled other accounts brought to his attention before leaving the office.

It was on his way back to Chessyre House that it hit him. Felicia was independently wealthy now. She did not need him to rescue her from a life as a companion. Indeed, she could hire one for herself if she chose. And she did not need marriage.

When he had embarked on this scheme to investigate the will and testament of her father, he'd not thought ahead to what would happen should she actually inherit – nor had he expected to fall in love with the girl. But then, he'd not anticipated Felicia would acquire *both* the land and the money. *Egad!* George, Lord Brook, had been reputed to be a wise investor and conservator of his property. Basil was as shrewd as could be when it came to investing funds, hanging on to every

191

farthing not needed. The way it seemed to William was that Felicia was likely to be as wealthy as he was himself. He should have asked Harding.

He returned to the house, exiting the hackney with a heavy heart, considering what he had striven for had succeeded. There was not a thing Basil Brook could do to regain the estate, either. Once the matter of the witness who had an interest in the estate was pointed out, there wouldn't be another judge in England who would change the ruling. Felicia was now an heiress.

'Alford,' William inquired upon entering the house, 'where is Miss Brook?'

'She went with your aunt, milord. I believe a protracted visit to the mantua-maker is contemplated; a milliner and a shoemaker were mentioned as well.'

'I take it that Lord Pelham was accepted?' William asked with a perfectly straight face.

'Indeed, sir. Lady Emma remarked she wished to have a Christmas wedding.' Alford offered the silver salver with a pile of letters and invitations.

'So soon?' William murmured to himself as he strode to his library so he could think in peace. He glanced at the post. Sorting through the invitations, he came on one for the Woodworth rout. Felicia liked Miss Woodworth, although William distrusted her friendship with Basil. But then, he'd have felt that way about anyone who had deal-ings with the man. Good luck to the woman if she actually felt as did her character, Bianca. Should she feel a bad husband was better than no husband at all, she had found one in Basil Brook. Wealth was not everything.

Scrawling an acceptance for himself, Felicia, and his aunt, he placed it in the stack of post to go out. Then he applied himself to the rest of the post.

The Woodworth rout was a gala affair, with everyone who was anyone attending. Lady Louisa Arden, affianced bride of Stephen Chessyre, soon to be the Viscount Eliot, decorated one corner of the drawing room, a court of friends surrounding them. Gay laughter filtered from the group.

Felicia paused at the entrance to the lovely room. Whatever else one might say, one had to admit that Mrs Woodworth had excellent taste. Delicate cream wallpaper served as a background for chairs and sofas covered in sapphire blue, mahogany pier tables gleamed with polish, and delicate crystal chandeliers offered pleasing light for the guests. Overhead a sapphire-painted sky had cherubs peeking down on the assembly below.

William tucked her hand close to his side, then made their way through the throng to where Lady Louisa and Stephen awaited them.

'Have you told Stephen about the judge's ruling?' Felicia asked as they skirted their way around a cluster of guests. She had spent so much time with Lady Emma at the mantua-maker's, the shoemaker's, and the milliner's that she scarce had a moment to call her own. That much of what was ordered was now for herself was beside the point. There had hardly been a minute to be quiet with dearest William to talk, really talk.

'We have yet to have a serious discussion regarding your future. I cannot recall when the calendar has been so overflowing with functions. You must decide when you wish to inspect your home. I would not be surprised if Basil took a few things with him when he went. If so, they must be returned, for not one thing was willed to him.'

'Poor Willa. I wonder what he will do with her?' Felicia glanced back at her determined escort. He had attended every gathering this week, which was surprising in the light of Lady Emma's remark that he was not fond of this sort of thing. White's was more to his taste, it seemed. It was as though he still feared for her safety, which was nonsense. Nothing had happened to her since she left Strawberry Hill.

'She will marry that old man he chose for her, or die of starvation, I suppose. He once said he'd not tolerate any nonsense from her.' William drew Felicia closer to avoid contact with another group – of which Jane Woodworth was one.

'Hello, you two,' Miss Woodworth exclaimed with pleasure,

leaving her friends to join William and Felicia. 'How delightful to see you once again. I see Lady Emma is to marry Lord Pelham. How lovely for her. And for you,' she added with a mischievous look at Felicia.

'Jane,' Felicia cautioned.

The other girl merely smiled, then held up her hand to display a gold band with a modest diamond, visible through the dainty lace of her gloves. 'You must wish me happy. Basil and I are engaged. That will make us cousins, dear Felicia.'

'Happy thought, indeed,' Felicia said, feeling sorry for poor Jane. They chatted a bit longer, enough to be polite, then continued on to where Stephen and Louisa stood.

'Well, now I do not have to fear Basil will kidnap me and force me to marry him in order for him to retrieve my estates,' Felicia said as quietly as possible.

'Had you feared that?' Chessyre asked, a concerned expression on his face.

'Indeed. I know my cousin fairly well, you see. I would put nothing past him.' Felicia considered how safe she felt with dearest William at her side, how lost she would be when Lady Emma was married and gone. Felicia would go then as well. Alone.

'Uncomfortable thought when going to bed, I must say,' William offered before greeting his cousin and Louisa.

They were a gay group that evening. Lady Emma and Lord Pelham were toasted many times, and when Mr Woodworth announced Jane's betrothal to Lord Brook, polite enthusiasm carried the day for the bride-to-be. Although Basil, Lord Brook was not greatly admired, he was known to be wealthy and a shrewd investor. Money is always respected, even if not liked. Felicia wondered if opinion would alter once the court ruling was known and that Basil's estate was now far less.

'I am glad this is not a ball,' Felicia said. 'I should not wish to be compelled by good manners to dance with my cousin.'

'Remember, there is nothing he can do to you as long as I am at your side,' Lord Chessyre assured her.

And, wondered Felicia, what happened when Lord Chessyre was no longer there?

'Basil must know of the transfer of funds by now, one would think,' Felicia said. 'Unless Mr Smithers or Basil's banker has neglected to keep him informed on matters of such importance. What about the property? When will he learn the complete decision of the judge? Unless he has, and I cannot believe that. He has given no indication of his displeasure in the matter to me this evening,' Felicia concluded when Stephen and Louisa were chatting with other friends and she and dearest William were relatively alone – if one counted being surrounded by a hundred people who ignored one meant being alone.

The rout lasted until well into the small hours of the morning. When it came time to depart, Jane Woodworth embraced Felicia briefly, then said, 'Do promise to take a drive with me soon. Tomorrow? Or the next day?' She looked beyond Felicia to Lord Chessyre for his reaction.

'I think Felicia would enjoy a drive with you, am I not correct, Felicia?' he asked with a protective arm remaining about her after draping her fur-lined cloak about her shoulders.

'I should like it above all things, Jane,' Felicia said warmly. Just because Jane was to be the bride of cousin Basil did not mean she couldn't be agreeable company. And if they were to be cousins – even if by marriage – it would be nice to at least be on speaking terms.

It was agreed that Felicia would drive out with Jane on the day after tomorrow, which, considering it had gone past midnight, was not long off.

'She will need to sleep late after such a gala evening,' Felicia said to Chessyre, once in the carriage.

'And you no longer need rest in the afternoon?' he asked in a teasing way.

'I told you I was perfectly fine, and I am.'

Lady Emma and Lord Pelham awaited them when they arrived at Chessyre House, and the four sat over a light supper to discuss the evening before heading off to bed.

At the top of the stairs Lady Emma turned to Felicia and smiled.

'Christmas is not far off. I shall like you in rose chiffon as my bridal attendant. You are a dear girl.'

Felicia kissed Lady Emma on the cheek, then retired to her pretty room. Soon, very soon she must have that talk with Lord Chessyre, dearest William.

'To the future,' she said in a mock toast, then shed a few tears while she prepared for bed. If Primrose noticed a damp cheek, she said nothing.

Chapter Fifteen

The day for Felicia's drive with Jane Woodworth dawned bright and sunny for a December day. True, there was a nip in the air, but the sun dispelled the notion that one must remain indoors. Felicia wore her new sable-lined cloak, tucking her gloved hands in her equally new sable muff. She was finding her recovered wealth a definite pleasure. Once again she might enjoy the pleasure of being Miss Brook of Brook Hall with all the attendant niceties.

'I shall be back before long,' she said to Primrose, who remained behind. There was no need for a maid when it was two women in a carriage with the driver and groom along for protection and only for a short drive.

Cleo came to dance about Felicia, begging to go along, her little teeth bared in a nasty grin. Curled on the counterpane, Merlin gave the dog a superior look, as though scornful of an animal that had to be walked.

'Be an angel and take Cleo out,' Felicia requested. 'I vow Lady Emma is far too distracted to think of that dog at this moment.'

'Lord Pelham ain't fond of that animal,' Primrose observed. 'Wonder if Cleo stays or goes?'

'Chessyre will not keep her here – too many slippers chewed up, you know. I fancy Lady Emma will find a way. She usually does, I believe. Look at me – a companion and now bridal attendant!'

'But, you, miss, are a companion with a difference. You are now an heiress.' Primrose attached a leash to Cleo's collar, then headed to the stairs to fetch her coat.

'Do you know,' Felicia said thoughtfully, 'I do not believe that would make any difference to Lady Emma. She has her own set of values.'

It was just before noon when Jane came for her, welcoming Felicia into her fine closed carriage with a smile and a merry greeting. Hot bricks and warmed lap robes were pleasant to have, and Felicia complimented Jane on the carriage as well as her thoughtfulness.

'I believe we shall have a lovely outing,' Felicia said after a few moments.

'As we are to be cousins, I cannot but offer you the very best,' Jane said with enthusiasm.

Felicia wondered where Jane planned to take her. There was a picnic basket on the opposite seat. She looked at it, then at Jane with an inquiring raise of her brows.

'I thought it would be fun to pause in the country for tea. That is agreeable with you, I hope?'

The girl was so anxious that Felicia hastened to assure her, 'Of course, tea sounds delightful.' Odd, but delightful. She was even more thankful for the fur-lined cloak and her cozy muff.

It seemed they were to bypass the usual parks in the city, for they were ignored. When they headed for Twickenham, Felicia thought they might be going to Strawberry Hill. But the turning came and they passed it.

Feeling oddly uneasy for no reason at all, Felicia turned to Jane and asked, 'Where do you plan to take tea?'

'I thought Brook Hall would be nice,' Jane said, smiling pleasantly, a bland smile that gave no clue to her inner thoughts.

'Brook Hall! But that is my home,' Felicia cried, all at sea. 'It seems rather far to go for tea!' What was Jane thinking? Why was she taking Felicia to her own home for a picnic tea, of all things? They would scarcely arrive when they would have to leave again.

'Have you seen the house?' Felicia wondered aloud, full of curiosity. 'I have not been there since Basil's parents died. It was so festive at Christmas when my parents were still alive,' she remembered. 'We had garlands of greenery and kissing balls. My mother had holly and ivy in every vase and urn in the house. And it always smelled wonderful with the aroma of puddings and cakes baking in the kitchen.' But not since then, and certainly not now. So why should they go to a vacant house? Felicia wondered.

'You miss it,' Jane said, sympathy in her voice.

'When Papa died and Aunt and Uncle Brook came to live at the Hall, life became quite different,' was all Felicia would say in reply to that comment. How could she tell the girl what a gudgeon Lady Brook had been? Jane had accepted the hand of Cousin Basil – such as it was. Trouble was, Basil was going to turn out to be just like his mother, and that was indeed a pity. Poor Jane. But Brook Hall was no longer Basil's. Of course, Jane might not know about that.

The winter sunlight was thin when they turned into the drive to the Hall. Clouds had blown up from the west, and it looked to come on snow before too long.

Felicia shifted uneasily on the comfortably cushioned seat. As much as she wanted to see the house and to check if her odious cousin had made off with any of the family treasures, she would have far preferred to come here by herself – or with William.

'It will be a hasty tea, I fear. The weather is not favorable to lingering.' Felicia peered out of the carriage window as they bowled up the drive. Those clouds most assuredly looked threatening.

'Never fear, dearest Felicia. I have thought of everything.' Jane edged forward on the seat and placed a hand on the basket, ready to disembark on an instant.

The carriage drew to a halt before the familiar brick front of the house. The groom opened the carriage door, let down the steps, then assisted Felicia and Jane from the carriage with proper deference.

'You may go,' Jane said, then with her hand on Felicia's arm guided her up the steps to the front door, opening it with a key she pulled from her muff.

'Where is Risford? Why is there no one to answer the door?' Felicia wondered aloud as she strolled about the entry hall, feeling more a stranger than the owner of the house.

She chanced a glance out the door just as Jane was closing it and saw the carriage disappearing down the drive toward the main road.

'Why is the carriage leaving? There is something rather strange going on here,' she said quietly to a silent Jane. 'What?'

'I suppose you will think so. I promised Basil I would bring you here. When he has time, he will join us.' Jane drew Felicia to the small sitting room that led off the back of the entryway. It was a small, cozy room with comfortable chairs and good light from several windows. Now the room was chilly, and with draperies pulled, dim and unwelcoming.

'Where is Willa?' Felicia asked.

'Married. Basil took a firm hand with his foolish sister. She finally agreed to marry as he wished.'

Felicia decided Willa had sensibly preferred marriage to starvation, as Lord Chessyre had predicted.

'First, a fire, I think,' Jane said, placing the picnic basket on a table. 'Perhaps you will light it? You are most likely familiar with all the fireplaces in the house, seeing you lived here at Lady Brook's generosity after Basil's father inherited.'

Felicia whirled about from her place by the windows, where she had drawn one drapery aside. 'What do you mean by that? 'Tis true I was allowed to remain in my home when Papa died, but Lady Brook was not a kind person. There was not a generous bone in her body.'

'Basil has learned how your Lord Chessyre managed to find a judge to overturn the will and testament of your father. To think you would be so disobedient as to run counter to his wishes! It is unthinkable.'

'This is all a bad dream, I know it is,' Felicia muttered as she knelt to kindle the neatly laid fire. 'What have you done with all the servants?' she demanded, looking back at Jane while waiting for the blaze to take hold.

'We decided it was not necessary to keep staff here until we married. There is a couple who come now and again to tend to the house, building a fire to ward off damp, things like that,' Jane said complacently.

'I see,' Felicia said, not really seeing at all. With the flames leaping up to consume the kindling, she placed a log, then some coal on the fire before turning to her oddly menacing hostess.

'Perhaps I should take a look around before we have tea, if tea we have. There is no way we may return to the city today, not in this weather. If we must spend the night here, the beds must be readied, fires started.'

'I shall watch you, for I do not do that sort of thing myself.' Jane tucked her hands daintily into her muff, looked over the supply of candles arranged on the large central table, then went to stand by the door.

Felicia bit back a retort to the effect that it was as well that she knew about starting a fire or they could freeze their toes before morning came. Blankets could warm you just so much.

Their footsteps echoed as they crossed the hall, then mounted the stairs to the first floor. As in many country homes, the bedrooms were located on the first floor, with the living areas on the ground floor. Servants' quarters were found in a wing that went off from the rear of the house, opposite the estate office wing.

'Basil did not replace the steward or the housekeeper who died?' Felicia inquired as she paused before the first of the bedroom doors.

'We prefer to hire someone we could trust. There will be time come spring.' Jane gave her a sweet smile that made Felicia shiver.

'You will not be here in the spring, my dear,' Felicia ground out in anger. 'When the will and testament was overturned, ruled a fraud, I received title to everything – land, house, furnishings, not to mention the money. Nothing here belongs to Basil now. Unless,' she added scrupulously, 'he has a few personal effects remaining.'

'Have you made a will?' Jane asked, a sly look in her eyes.

Startled at the strange question, Felicia slowly replied, 'No, I have not had time to prepare a will.'

'According to Basil, in the event of your death, all reverts to him as the heir to the title. There is no one else.'

The words chilled Felicia's heart, but not half so much as the bland expression on Jane's face. Heaven forbid, the woman intended to murder Felicia without a qualm!

Pretending she did not realize the full impact of Jane's statement,

Felicia proceeded into the bedroom, lit the fire, then prudently placed a screen before it. She did likewise in the next bedroom. When she had the fires blazing nicely with a decent amount of coal added to keep them going for a time, she paused in the hallway, glancing about at the familiar walls. Nothing appeared to be missing here, at any rate.

'Does Basil come this evening?' she inquired boldly.

'I do not know,' Jane admitted. 'He told me he would come when he could.'

'Lovely,' Felicia said with an irony that was lost on Jane Woodworth.

'I think so. I truly do not wish to kill you. Basil said he would. Isn't that thoughtful of him?' Jane walked down the hall to the beautiful curving stairs that led to the ground floor. 'But I will if I must. Basil told me that you are not a nice person and deserve to die. I shall always do as Basil tells me, for that is being a dutiful wife. I fear I displeased him when I substituted the knife and you remained alive. I hoped the falling rocks might do the trick, but they failed, too. Next time I shall succeed.'

The woman was mad, that was all there was to it. Sane people didn't think like this, nor do crazy things like threaten murder in such calm, complacent tones.

'I should like my tea now,' Jane said at the bottom of the stairs. 'Can you boil water? I always have a maid to do it for me, so you will have to prepare it.'

'Fine time to ask me,' Felicia murmured as she headed back to the little sitting room, where the fire burned merrily away, bringing warmth to the house.

The chill was fading, and Felicia took heart that the sky had darkened, the snow looking to fall momentarily. She knew Basil well enough to be certain he would not put his horses on the road in inclement weather. He must have learned a lesson from his parents' death. There were times when one must be prudent, greed or not.

It was a simple matter to fetch water in a kettle from the kitchen pump, then place the kettle on the hook to be swung over the fire.

Felicia had done the task many a time as a child, then later for Lady Brook.

Once the water came to a boil, she warmed the teapot, adding the tea leaves found in the kitchen pantry. She decided she would eat or drink nothing that Jane did not sample first. Self-preservation was making her doubly wary.

While Felicia performed this mundane task, Jane delved into the depths of the basket, pulling forth a variety of foods – cheese, a roasted chicken, thinly sliced ham, bread, and an apple tart. They all looked perfectly delicious and quite innocent of tampering.

'As soon as tea is ready, I shall pour for you,' Felicia said, proud her voice didn't shake in the least. 'Did you happen to wonder what they will think at Chessyre House when I do not come home? Lady Emma and I were to go out this evening.'

'I left a missive to be delivered late this afternoon, informing them that you decided to stay with me for a special treat.' Jane looked excessively smug as she placed a slice of ham on a chunk of buttered bread.

Felicia faltered, teapot in hand, to wonder if ever before in history a murder was labeled a special treat. After pouring two cups of tea, she placed the pot close to her plate. She would not allow any foreign substance to be slipped into the pot. She broke off the next chunk of bread and took a bit of the ham, hoping that they were safe to eat. Poison, she had read, was not a pleasant way to die.

'Isn't this a lovely repast?' Jane said, munching on her bread and ham with an enthusiasm Felicia found incredible. *Mad.* The woman had to be mad – mad as May-butter.

'Tea?' Felicia offered as she poured a second sustaining cup for herself.

'Indeed, that is why we are here, is it not? For tea?'

'Dearest William, she simply would not do such a thing?' Lady Emma insisted. 'Felicia is so dependable; she never fails to keep her word. She promised to go with me this evening to the Pickering musicale. Since she loves good music, she is unlikely to forgo such a treat.'

'But this missive from Jane Woodworth seems so definite,' William objected, recalling his distrust of the woman.

'Please humor an old woman and go to the Woodworth house. Speak with Felicia. Satisfy my curiosity. I simply will not believe that she sent that message. Think – *why* did she not write it herself!' Lady Emma plumped herself on one of the chairs in the library to bestow a triumphant look at her nephew. 'Answer me that if you can.'

'I will go at once,' William replied, recalling his uneasiness when in the presence of Jane Woodworth the last time he had chatted with her. She had been so happy to see Felicia and him, and by then she ought to have heard from Basil of the decision regarding the will. By rights, she ought to have been furious. He had half expected to be barred from the house, or at the very least, snubbed. Instead, they had been greeted with pleasure. In retrospect, that ought to have made him suspicious. But then, he was so absorbed with Felicia that little notice had been paid to anything else.

Of course, Mrs Woodworth knew the *ton* would gossip frightfully did such an event occur, and likely cautioned her daughter against such behavior. Still, something had not rung true. He should have heeded his instincts.

A short time later, William entered the Woodworth house on Great Stanhope Street. Mrs Woodworth greeted him in the drawing room, obviously puzzled to receive a call from a gentleman at this late hour.

'I apologize for intruding on you at this time of the day, ma'am. I wonder if I might speak with Miss Brook? It is a matter of some urgency. Your butler seemed unaware that she is here,' he added by way of explanation.

'Indeed, she is not here,' Mrs Woodworth said. 'Why, she is at your house! Miss Brook invited Jane for tea following their drive in the park. Jane sent me a note. So kind of Miss Brook to keep the family ties.' The lady went to a small table near the door to the hall, picked up a crisp white paper, then returned to hand it to William. 'Perhaps the girls are in Miss Brook's room?'

'I fear not, ma'am,' William said after examining the note. The paper and handwriting were the same as that sent to Chessyre House. 'This is your daughter's handwriting?'

'Indeed, it is. The dear girl has such a distinctive slant to her letters,' the mother said proudly.

'Has Lord Brook been here today, by any chance?' William asked, his words clipped.

'No, indeed not. However, he is to take Jane out tomorrow evening to the opera, I believe. Why do you ask?'

'Ma'am, I fear there has been foul play. Neither Miss Brook nor Miss Woodworth are at Chessyre House. Since they are not here – where are they?'

Mrs Woodworth sank down on the closest chair, her hand fluttering to her throat. 'Dear heaven, where can they be?'

'I intend to find out. Does Miss Woodworth have a personal maid? Could I question her? Would you object if I did?' William asked, growing uneasy as the minutes passed.

'No, indeed.' Mrs Woodworth summoned the footman, who in turn summoned the maid, Bates.

'Could you tell us what you know of Miss Woodworth's plans for the day? How did she dress? What did she tell you?' William barked out his questions in sharp order.

The woman gave him a puzzled look, then said, 'She dressed warmly, for she said she would go for a drive with Miss Brook. She wore a blue kerseymere gown under her fur-lined pelisse and took her fur muff with her. Her bonnet was the blue velvet one. Oh, and she requested a picnic basket be packed – a rather ample one for two young ladies if I may say so. Roast chicken, cheese and ham, bread, and one of Cook's apple tarts, ma'am.'

'Why was I not informed of this unusual request, Bates?' Mrs Woodworth inquired haughtily.

'It was none of my affair if Miss Woodworth chooses to have a picnic in December, ma'am,' the maid said with a hint of insolence.

William, deciding he would get no more from the maid, asked if the coachman was available, or could he go to their stables to see what might be learned there.

'The stables might be best,' the lady suggested. 'If the coachman went with Jane, he may not be there, but someone else might know something.' She leaned back in the chair, looking as though her world had just fallen apart.

Dashing down the stairs to the narrow entry hall, William was thankful Mrs Woodworth proved to be so sensible. No vapors or hysterics at his news.

In the stables he found a more promising lead. The coach-man had not returned with the closed carriage. One groom had gone with him, no one else.

'They was told they was to stay overnight in the country,' the stable lad said. 'Right curious they was, too, but nothin' else was told 'em.'

'Coachman took a valise. Groom, too,' said the undergroom.

William mulled over what he had learned for a few minutes, asked another question or two, then left. He paused to inform Mrs Woodworth that the young ladies were likely visiting a friend in the country, for it appeared they had planned to stay overnight.

Bates, who was still being quizzed by Mrs Woodworth, offered, 'I could look to see if any of her clothes are missing, milord.'

Deciding it might be worth the time, William assented.

In short order the maid hurried back into the drawing room, a flustered expression on her face. 'Miss took a bandbox, for it is missing. As well, her warmest nightrail, a shawl, and some, er, unmentionables as well,' she concluded with a red-faced glance at William.

'Overnight, in a cooler house, but not for a long stay, I fancy,' William said to Mrs Woodworth. 'At least we can rule out a kidnapping.'

'Merciful heavens, I'd not thought of that!' Mrs Woodworth exclaimed, looking faint.

The maid assisted the mistress back to her chair, then looked to William. She motioned with her head that she wished to speak with him privately.

'I will ask around the belowstairs, ma'am,' the woman said politely, then left the room, scurrying down the stairs in a run.

William excused himself and followed her, curious as to what she might have to tell him.

At the bottom of the stairs Bates drew him into the shadows. 'Miss

Woodworth was a strange one. Had a hard time keeping a maid. She told me that she was taking a profitable drive today. Now, I ask you – what sort of drive does a young lady take that is going to be profitable? And where did they go?'

A growing sense of horror filled William. There were far too many possibilities, and few of them pleasant. He scarcely knew where to begin to look.

After a pause at Chessyre House on South Audley Street, William sought out his solicitor, who lived with his brother not far away.

'Mr Harding is about to leave for the evening, but I will tell him you are here,' the footman said politely as William made known his desire to speak with his solicitor.

'What is it, Will? You rarely seek me out at this hour of the day,' Edmond Harding joked as he entered the library, where the footman had left William to cool his heels.

'Trouble,' William replied succinctly. 'Miss Woodworth has kidnapped Felicia, and only God knows what she has done with her.' Quickly, he outlined all he had learned, concluding with the bit about the profitable trip.

'That last does not sound good,' Mr Harding said. 'You are well aware that a young woman of her beauty would be in great demand in certain quarters. If Miss Woodworth sought to eliminate Miss Brook without murder, she could hand Miss Brook over for a tidy sum, and no one would be the wiser.'

'Except Miss Brook,' William added dryly.

'As you say,' Harding agreed. He strode to his brother's desk, picked up the pen, and scribbled several notes while William waited impatiently. 'I am requesting several chaps I have used in the past to prowl about the docks and mouse about one of the cadging houses, one run by a Scotsman. He's an honest cove and knows a good deal of what goes on in that area.'

'Offer a reward for Miss Brook. Make it enough to tempt the person who might have taken her – if she indeed is in the hands of a slaver or a madam.' He shuddered at the thought of his precious Felicia in such environs.

'That's not to say she has been sold. She could be elsewhere,' Harding said in an effort to cheer William.

'Pray that is the case. If anything happens to her, I shall see to it that Basil and Jane do not live to see another day.' William excused himself, then went off to do a bit of his own sleuthing. He checked out White's, dropped in at Boodles, then had a look in the more disreputable gambling houses. Basil never gambled except on a reasonably sure thing, and that in the form of an investment. But that didn't mean one of his cronies might not be found – and convinced to talk.

When William finally let himself into Chessyre House, he drooped with fatigue. He had followed every hunch, every lead, tracked down Basil, only to discover the man had impeccable alibis for the entire day.

Lady Emma, her nighttime attire covered with a delicate lavender wrapper, waited in the doorway to his library. Behind her William could see a fire burning brightly and a tray holding drinks and sandwiches.

'You need not have stayed up for me,' he scolded gently.

'You have been gone a very long time. I came home early from the musicale, for I could not bear to listen to music when I did not know where Felicia might be. Did you learn anything at all?' She went to the pot of coffee, kept hot over a candle flame, and poured him a cup.

William accepted the cup and sank upon a chair by the fire, rubbing his tired eyes and sighing deeply. 'Nothing.'

'Oh.' Lady Emma perched on the chair opposite his, to stare into the flames.

'Harding has sent notes to a number of men who make it their business to know what's afoot in the stews of London.'

'Will dearest,' she cried, 'you cannot think Jane would have done something dreadful with Felicia!'

Curse his loose tongue. William glanced at his aunt, who looked more angry than frightened. Sturdy stuff, his aunt, not one given to vapors no matter her delicate look.

'I do not know. They have vanished from London in the Woodworth carriage with a picnic hamper of food. Neither the carriage nor coachman and groom has returned to London. This gives me hope to think they may have gone to the country, been caught in the wretched weather, and decided to stay with a friend.'

He kept from his aunt the part concerning a 'profitable' trip. She might accept his glib suggestion about a forced stay in the country, but not if he mentioned the other portion of what he had learned.

'You had best sleep on it, dearest Will. Tomorrow will be another day, and things always look better come morning.' She rose from the chair and placed an affectionate hand on his shoulder. 'I know you will find her if anyone could. Pray she is safe in a nice bed and has had a good meal. That come morning the roads will be clear and the girls may return to London. So foolish, to go for a drive in the country in December. As for a picnic, unthinkable. But, in a way, it was fortuitous, for they were prepared for any eventuality. They shan't go hungry.'

Nodding and placing his hand atop hers for a moment of comfort before she left, William sat alone in the library for a time, staring into the fire and wondering precisely where Felicia was and how she fared. He had no great confidence in the morrow. He would pray, but he recalled that God tended to help those who helped themselves. And William did not know what to do next.

Chapter Sixteen

The next day went by with no news from any of Harding's contacts. No sign of Miss Woodworth or Miss Brook had been seen anywhere in the city, according to the chaps who roamed the docks and Covent Garden area. The Woodworth carriage had not returned, nor had the watch seen any evidence of it, although that was not conclusive. For as all knew, a stolen carriage was soon dismantled, or painted and sold to a jarvey for use as a hackney.

William was exhausted, yet he drove himself to search everywhere he or his aunt might think a possibility. He never made the mistake of underestimating his good aunt. For all her featherheaded look, she had common sense beneath, and he paid attention to her suggestions.

'You were up before dawn, Will dearest,' Lady Emma complained. 'You must eat something. We will talk while you do.'

It was while they were at dinner that Harding called.

William pushed aside a partially eaten meal to hurry to the entryway, motioning for his solicitor to join him in the library. 'Come along. 'Tis a cold night, and a warm fire will feel good. Brandy?'

Edmond Harding shook his head, but did stand close to the fire. 'I've had a curious bit of news. It may be nothing, but then again, I've this feeling it might be significant.'

William paused in the act of pouring a glass of brandy, placed the decanter and glass on the table, and crossed to stand by Edmond.

'What?' he demanded. 'Tell me at once!'

'The chap I sent down to Brook Hall came into London last evening on an errand for Brook, brought some of his personal things from the house that Brook had rightly claimed for his own. My man figured as long as Basil didn't go into the country, there was nothing to worry about – he had checked to see if anything appeared to have been removed, but all seemed as it ought. Once in London, Brook kept him at his house so late complaining of one thing and another – as though my man could do anything about it – that the fellow could not return to Brook Hall last evening.'

'So?' William said, not seeing a great deal of significance in this.

'So today, Brook requested that he find some new servants for the Hall. Seems as though all the previous ones had been let go. Odd, what? You or I would have figured that Miss Brook would prefer the familiar faces she had known years ago. Not so Brook. Knowing it would take all day, my man came to report to me. I'd had Brook kept under watch; I know *he* stayed in the city. But such a request would not normally be one Brook would give a man who just happened to be at the house on a day when Brook paused there to remove a few things he claimed were his own possessions. I checked, and apparently they were. The inventory of the household goods lists nothing he designated as his.'

'Did Brook know that man worked for you?' William thought to ask.

'He was informed that the man I sent was merely a member of the clerk's office, intended to oversee the transition of the property. Brook doesn't know there isn't such a position. He truly imposed, you know. My man, had he been a clerk, would have said it wasn't his job and ignored the demand. So I'm curious as to why Brook wanted no one around Brook Hall yesterday and today?'

'I see.' William's mind had not only followed Edmond's line of reasoning, he had galloped past him. He walked to the door, informed his footman to order the traveling coach and a team of four, then turned again to Edmond Harding.

'You might very well have something. I will go at once.' William stood by the door, his thoughts elsewhere.

'With the roads as they are? It grows dark out, my friend.' Edmond gave William a worried look.

'The roads will likely be no better on the morrow, and I dare not take a chance with Felicia's life another night. I believe Brook is desperate enough to do something rather nasty, if you catch my meaning. Felicia has not made a will, and Brook may know this. As things stand, he would inherit all were she to die.'

Edmond nodded with understanding. 'I trust you will find her there when you arrive. Let me know when possible, and I will call off my men if you have found her.'

William thrust his arms into the warmest greatcoat he owned, fur-lined and ankle-length. His fur-lined gloves awaited him, as did a warm scarf and his low-crowned hat.

'You plan to drive?' Edmond inquired, suspecting full well that no one else would be allowed the reins.

'Indeed, I shall.' William walked along with Edmond to the front door, gathering what he thought he might find useful on the way. 'Aunt Emma?' he called out. 'I shall return with Felicia. Mark my words!'

'God go with you!' Her blessing followed him out the door.

Edmond stood with William as they waited for the traveling coach to come round from the stables.

'I'll never forget your help in this, Edmond,' William said, shifting impatiently from foot to foot, slapping his well-gloved hand lightly with his whip.

'I hope my hunch is correct.'

'I believe in hunches; I have the same feeling. As to the why and wherefores, I cannot imagine. Miss Woodworth and Brook are in this together, that is certain.'

'One of the sweetest old ladies I ever met turned out to have murdered her husband,' Edmond said quietly. 'Do not underestimate Miss Woodworth.'

'You have no idea how those words fill me with dread,' William replied, listening to the clatter of hooves on the cobled street as they came nearer.

'I told you for a reason. Such a woman must be met with great caution and cunning if she is indeed in league with Basil Brook.'

'I'll not barge into the house at once,' William promised.

'Finesse is called for, I believe. Remember the time we pulled the trick on old Biddleton? No one ever guessed who had done the deed.' Harding clapped William on the shoulder, then stood back as the earl swung himself up on the driver's seat of the coach. 'Good luck!'

'Foxy as they come, my friend,' William cried, then was off, skillfully tooling the cumbersome traveling carriage down the streets as though it were a sporting gig, the four matched bays under superb control.

Felicia glanced out of the window to note the snow had stopped. She wondered when Basil would show up to do his dirty work. Or would he? As crafty as he was, perhaps he intended Jane Woodworth to do the deed, then if discovered, place all the blame on her and send her off to Australia or the gallows, whichever was decreed in murder.

'The snow has ceased. Dear Basil ought to be here before long,' Jane said quietly from where she was curled up by the fireplace. 'Then you shall know your fate.'

'Would you like more tea?' Felicia inquired civilly, for although the teapot was empty, there was more tea in the pantry. Felicia racked her brain for some way to deal with Jane. It would be foolish to underestimate her.

'I believe I would,' Jane replied indolently, then yawned. 'We shall have to replace the mattress in that bed I used last night. Most lumpish, I declare. My mother never has a lumpy mattress in the house – unless 'tis an old one given to the servants.'

Felicia longed to tell the girl she would never be there to replace one thing, but decided to hold her tongue. It would not do to anger Jane, for mad people might do anything when stirred, and Jane was most assuredly mad as May-butter.

Going to the kitchen pantry, Felicia reached for the container of tea leaves. She also found a tisane that Primrose had concocted to help Aunt Brook sleep. It was but a simple matter to make up the tea along with the tisane in a pretty china pot, then separately brew herself a strong cup of black tea.

She was not certain what she could do if Jane did fall into a deep slumber – with snow all about the house and night approaching – but perhaps something would occur to her.

A pretty tray laid with the nicest cloth Felicia could find and the last of the apple tart seemed to please Jane very much. She poured out a cup of the tea–tisane mixture, then glanced at Felicia.

'You do not join me?' she asked in her oddly polite manner.

It was clear to Felicia that as a villain Jane had not had much practice. 'No. I shall sit over here, if you do not mind.'

'Please yourself.' Jane took a bite of the apple tart, then shot a sly look at Felicia. 'I do say that our cook makes an exceptional apple tart. I believe I shall lure her away from Mother.' She yawned again, but Felicia sat quietly, believing it would take some time for the tisane to have any effect, if indeed it did work on Jane.

Felicia dug about and found some knitting abandoned by her aunt, and thought to keep her hands occupied. The house was still, with only the ticking of a longcase clock, the crackling of the fire, and the click of knitting needles to be heard. They were soothing, lulling sounds, and Felicia thought she might sleep herself, did Jane not succumb soon. Instead, Felicia knitted away on a perfectly dreadful scarf. Had Jane been a true villain, she'd have removed the needles; indeed, most likely tied Felicia to a chair or something worse.

Jane liked the niceties of life, and that included being waited upon. Basil would have to provide her with ample servants. He wouldn't like that.

'I think Basil should come tomorrow,' Jane said sleepily, then gave a prodigious yawn. She downed the very last of the pot of tea, plunked the cup on its saucer, and leaned against the high-backed

Windsor armchair to close her eyes.

Felicia sat still as could be, not rustling her skirts nor making a sound save for the click of her needles. She prayed for William to come or Jane's sleep, preferably both.

Jane snored. To be sure, it was a feminine sound, not one to rattle the cupboards, but she snored nonetheless.

With great caution Felicia put aside the knitting, covered Jane with a throw that had been on the sofa so as to keep her warm and sleepy, then went to the front of the house. Taking a branch of candles with her, she searched out her pelisse and muff, found the velvet bonnet she'd worn, then banked the fire in both the bedrooms. With those rooms closed and Jane's things in her valise, Felicia brought everything to the front hall.

All she needed now was her champion. Foolish to think that dearest William would find her. Who would think to look at Brook Hall? She was not certain he even knew where the Hall was. It was an easy place to find, however.

Just then she thought she heard a noise. In the utter stillness, a door creaked. She stood and listened with care. When she saw a dark shape come from the kitchen, she looked wildly about for a weapon to bash Basil over the skull. She'd not expected him to come in the evening, believing it too snowy and cold for the likes of him. She placed the candle-holder on the floor, then grabbed a statue.

She had the heavy statue in hand, ready to swing it over Basil, when she realized that it was not her cousin after all, but a tall, handsome man whose blond hair insisted on falling over his forehead.

'William!' she whispered. 'Thank the Lord you have come.' She set the heavy statue down and flew across the room into dearest William's welcoming arms. With her face tilted to his, and his lips as hungry as hers, it was but a moment before they were joined in a most satisfying kiss.

'What the devil are you doing out here?' he demanded.

'Hush! I managed to put Jane to sleep, and I'd not want her wakened. She is not at all what we believed!'

William picked up the branch of candles, then guided his Felicia across the hall to the nearest room and carefully eased the door closed. Placing the candles on a table, he turned to wrap his arms about her once more. He was not going to allow her any distance; he needed to be certain she was safe in his arms. He also observed – in spite of his concern – that she showed no inclination to leave his side. In fact, she clung to him like a sweet limpet.

Quickly, Felicia explained what had happened and what Basil intended be her lot. William looked terribly fierce as she told the story and clasped her so tightly against him that she wondered she could even breathe. However, to feel so cherished was a great comfort, and she snuggled as close as she might inside the warmth of William's fur-lined greatcoat. The room was cold, she told herself; her desire to be close to him had nothing to do with her love for the man. Well, perhaps a little.

'What are we going to do now?' she whispered, anxious to be free of the house, yet wanting to do something to Jane and Basil. What was to prevent them from striking again?

'I need a will,' she mumbled against William's chest, recalling what Jane had told her.

William, content for the moment to merely hold Felicia close to him, his relief a tangible thing, said, 'We will take care of that matter as soon as possible.'

'Until I have made a will, Basil inherits all, since I have no other close relative. Of course he inherited his father's possessions – but wanted mine as well. Greedy man,' she concluded.

'That will shortly be solved, my sweet. We will marry, you will have a husband who also will help you administer your estate, and Basil can sail off to the Antipodes for all we care. You will be safe.'

'You are not going to marry merely to keep me from being murdered,' Felicia objected, no matter that it was her dearest wish to be William's wife.

What William might have said to that was lost as he heard a sound. Placing a finger against Felicia's lips, he edged toward the door, listening.

Shivering without the warmth found inside William's coat, Felicia listened as well. There was someone else in the house. Footsteps were heard in the hall. They paused, and Felicia wondered if someone was taking note of the pile of clothes and the valise left in the entry.

'Jane, where are you?'

'It is Basil,' Felicia whispered. 'Now what do we do?'

'Kill two birds with one stone, what else?' William said, a wicked grin spreading across his face.

'I do not wish to kill them, just send them to Australia or somewhere far away,' the gentle Felicia replied, edging closer to William and wondering how he hoped to accomplish his objective.

The footsteps continued on through to the back of the house, where Jane dozed in the sitting room.

'Wake up, you foolish woman. Where is my cousin?' Basil loudly demanded.

'She is here; where else would she go? There is no carriage,' Jane replied with the certainty of one who never walked when it was possible to drive. Her yawn must have been prodigious, for they could hear it even where they stood. 'I did not sleep at all well last night,' Jane complained. 'We shall need all new mattresses, for I suspect the rest are equally bad. My mother does not have any old mattresses in the house.'

'Bother your mother – where is my cousin?' Basil demanded.

William and Felicia listened to the sound of chairs being pushed aside, a screen overturned, doors slammed as Basil hunted for Felicia.

'He will come in here soon,' Felicia said. 'What then?'

'He must not find us. Where can we hide? Someplace he'd not be familiar with in the least.' William looked at Felicia, then gazed about the room in search of concealment.

'Come, follow me,' Felicia whispered, grabbing the branch of candles and tugging at William's hand. She led him to a bookcase, pressed a leaf in the design, then pulled him inside a small, windowless book room. The case swung shut behind them, and they were alone.

'We might be safe in here for the moment, but eventually we must be out of this hiding place,' William said, glancing at the tidy rows of very old books worth a goodly sum, unless he missed his guess. Basil would like to auction those off, no doubt. 'Does Brook know this room is here?' The candles threw a wavering light on their features.

'No,' Felicia said with a grin. 'It was the one place where my uncle could hide from my aunt. Neither Aunt nor Basil were aware of the existence of this bolt hole. Poor uncle, to be so plagued with such a woman.'

'Where is your other cousin?' William said, wrapping Felicia into his warmth when he saw her shiver.

'Willa was compelled to marry that old rich man she had first refused. I gather starving to death didn't appeal to her.' Felicia exchanged a look with William, then placed her head against his chest, absorbing comfort.

'Nice chap, your cousin. Remind me not to be kind to him. How do we get out of here, my love?' he asked, dropping a kiss on Felicia's tousled curls.

Felicia ignored the last two words, leaving William's warmth to show him another carved panel with a central rose. 'You press this, and the case swings open into what was Papa's dressing room. My uncle had these rooms while my aunt had a suite upstairs.'

'Close family,' William commented. He pulled Felicia back into his arms again and effectively revealed what he thought about closeness between a husband and wife.

Felicia happily nestled against him, wishing Basil and Jane to the ends of the earth. 'I hated leaving my home, but I was not the least sorry to be rid of my relatives.'

'You shall like your new ones, I promise. I've a sister in Scotland who takes after Aunt Emma. Enough said there.' He paused, listening to the ranting going on in the nearby rooms. 'One can hear well in here.'

'Indeed. It is a central room.' Felicia huddled against William, wondering how they would manage to escape Basil and Jane. She didn't underestimate either one of them.

Basil could be heard berating Jane for allowing Felicia to leave, then Jane pointed out that his cousin's pelisse and muff were still in the entryway.

'Drat,' Felicia whispered. 'I ought to have put them on – then I'd not be freezing.'

'If I weren't otherwise occupied, I would tend to your needs at once, my love. Where are Basil and Jane now?'

Felicia wrapped her arms about her and listened. 'I believe they are still in the entry. And now they seem to be going upstairs.'

'Out we go, my love.' He pressed the rose she'd shown him, and the bookcase swung open on silent hinges. 'Well-oiled,' he commented. 'Bring the candles.'

'Uncle made sure no one could learn his whereabouts!' she said, stifling a giggle at William's grin of understanding. 'Be serious!'

'I am, sweetheart; believe me, I am.'

They tiptoed through her uncle's Spartan bedroom, then out to the hall, where they again paused to listen.

'I think they are returning,' Felicia said, touching William for reas-surance. Bless the man, he understood her fears and quelled them with a squeeze on her shoulder – the good one.

William pulled several items from the pockets of his great-coat, then made certain the small rug by the entry to the sitting room was in such a way that he could keep his foot on it while standing behind the door.

He had no need to tell her to be quiet. When he motioned to her to take a chair by the fire, she didn't argue, but went at once.

'She is nowhere to be found,' Basil cried, clearly exasperated. 'We have searched every room in the house.'

'What about the cellars?' Jane asked.

'She didn't like going to the cellars. She'd freeze there now,' Basil said nastily while looking in a cupboard.

Felicia almost snorted with derision. Basil was the one who hated being in the cellar. He feared rats, although the cats had always kept the area clean of them.

Then the pair returned to the sitting room and spotted Felicia calmly sitting by the fire.

'Felicia, dear, where have you been?' Jane inquired in her high, sweet voice, crossing to stand by the fire.

'Here.'

'Obviously not, for we have been here and you were not,' Basil snarled as he entered the room to pause at the door as though to prevent her from slipping out once again.

'I was in the kitchen for a time,' Felicia admitted. 'Hiding?' Basil sneered.

'I have no wish to die,' Felicia said in a quiet voice, refusing to show fear before her evil cousin.

Basil was about to take a step into the room, as though to go for Felicia, when the rug was pulled out from under him and he went down, hitting his head against the door frame as he fell.

'Grab Jane,' William cried while he took up the rope he'd brought to tie Basil.

Jane, still a trifle slow from all the tisane she'd consumed, merely gave Felicia a groggy look when Felicia flipped the shawl from around Jane's shoulders to tie her snugly as a sausage in a bun.

'Whatever are you doing, Felicia, dear?' Jane asked, her tone as sweet as always.

'She is mad, you know,' Felicia whispered to William. 'Do not trust a word she says.'

'That goes double for Basil,' William replied while taking another length of rope to truss Jane neatly in a package. 'Now to take them away.'

'Where?' Felicia asked, ready to travel at once. She pushed Jane ahead of her, while William removed Basil to the entry-way. Jane stood, stupidly glaring at them, Basil most of all, while Felicia whipped on her cloak and bonnet, then grabbed her gloves and muff.

'I'll retrieve the coach, then think of where we will drop them off,' William declared. 'Thank goodness Basil did not question our tracks.'

'I am cold,' Jane announced plaintively.

Felicia didn't reply, but tucked the warm pelisse around Jane and then plopped Jane's bonnet on her head. 'There, you will be better soon,' Felicia assured without revealing a thing more. Best not to anger a mad woman.

William hurried out the door, intent upon getting the coach. They would be off within minutes, but where?

Chapter Seventeen

The sharp, salty tang of December air brought roses to Felicia's cheeks. She stood close to William on the Southampton dock, watching a particular ship as it made its way past other vessels in the harbor, intent upon gaining the open sea.

'They are truly gone,' she said at last. 'How ironic that the first ship scheduled to set sail proved to be one headed for Africa and intended to be a slaver.'

'Most appropriate,' William replied, drawing her away from the sight and toward the comfortable inn where they had stayed the night before. 'Come, we must return to the warmth of the inn before you freeze. The wind is rising, and while the captain of that ship will appreciate it, I doubt you will.'

Felicia obediently turned from the view of the harbor and walked at William's side toward the inn. 'There will likely be a monumental scandal in all this. Questions will arise when my cousin and Jane fail to return to London. Basil might not be missed, but Jane assuredly will.'

'We shall tell her parents that we discovered Jane and Basil in the process of eloping, and since they were well compromised, we saw them on their way,' he said with a slight shrug, helping Felicia up a short flight of steps. 'It will be simple enough to allow the gossips to filter the word through the *ton*.'

'You do realize this presents a slight problem for us, do you not? That is to say, what is to prevent the spread of a different scandal?'

Felicia inquired awkwardly, not wishing to bring the matter to his attention, but feeling that it must be discussed in an intelligent manner, that something had to be decided.

'Dr Johnstone suggested a quiet stay in the country,' William teased. 'Stay long enough, and no one will recall a thing.'

'True, true,' she replied, pulling away form the man who now confused her greatly. Surely those kisses, his protective manner meant something!

William stopped, turning Felicia to face him. He studied the woman he loved and knew how fully he did love her when he realized the threat of scandal did not bother him in the least. While he'd not loved Sophie enough to risk a breath of scandal, he did love Felicia enough to slay dragons for her and would as long as he lived. Oblivious of the curious looks from the few people who passed, he quietly said, 'Dearest Felicia, whose name means happiness, dare I hope you will make me the happiest of men and consent to be my wife? I offer you a cat and a house – will you take me as well?'

'Indeed, I will,' Felicia said, joy lighting her eyes as she placed her hands trustingly in his. 'I have come to love you very much, not just as my champion, but as the finest man I have ever known. But a stay in the country?' she quizzed, tilting her head, mischief sparkling her eyes.

'Long enough to use the special license I obtained for us a week ago. We shall steal a march on my aunt and return to attend the Cecilian Society's concert on Christmas Eve as a happily married couple.'

'I doubt anyone will believe this a love match.'

William urged her in the direction of the church not too far away, where he'd sent his groom not an hour before, banking on Felicia's acceptance of his offer. 'We shall have to be most unfashionable and prove to one and all it is precisely that, my love.'

In the shadows of the vaulted stone entry, William took Felicia in his arms to seal their betrothal with a kiss, then entered the church with his dearest girl on his arm.

When Felicia saw the cleric awaiting them, along with witnesses, she murmured fervently, 'Oh, I do love you, dearest Will.'

'And I you, my sweet.'